WHITE OR BLACK...
GREY

Joseph Melesh

WHITE OR BLACK... Grey

I hope you enjoy this story as much as I did creating this world.—

Copyright © 2019 By Melesh Publishing

All rights reserved. No part of this book may be reproduced in any form or by any electronic or mechanical means, including information storage and retrieval systems, without permission in writing from the publisher, except by reviewers, who may quote brief passages in a review.

This is a work of fiction, the world, places and people within these pages have been created entirely by the author's imagination or are used fictitiously. Any similarity to persons, living or dead, is coincidental and not intended by the author.

Edited by Chris Rhatigan
Cover Design by Eight Little Pages
Cover Copyright by Eight Little Pages
Author Headshot by Lindsey MacDonald
Photography Copyright by Lindsey MacDonald Photography

First Edition, 2019
ISBNs: 978-1-9994281-0-5 (trade paperback), 978-1-9994281-2-9 (ebook)
Published by Melesh Publishing
Burlington, ON, CA
Visit www.josephmelesh.com

I would like to dedicate this book to my wife and my daughter, Che and Lyta. You have put up with my long hours, my nocturnal, coffee driven craziness. Without your love support I would not have been able to finish this.

To My Readers,

Time although infinite can also be very finite. With the hustle of our daily lives. Trying to fit everything and everyone into our day can be overwhelming. The term *free-time* that glorious *me-time* is far from free and calling it that seems a disservice. As an author it is a great honor and privilege to me, that you have chosen to take the time to enter my world. This is the first in a large series of books that will follow the members of the BAU on a journey that will tax and test the depths of their souls and their commitment to each other.
Art in any form is a very personal journey, for both the artist and the audience. Thank you for allowing me to introduce you to their story.

Joseph Melesh

I don't believe in fate or destiny. I believe in various degrees of hatred, paranoia and abandonment. However much of that gets heaped on you doesn't matter—it's only a matter of how much you can take and what it does to you."

Henry Rollins

PROLOGUE

"Stop him? Shit, we didn't even know this was happening, until—"

"How could you? You're federal agents, not psychics, right?" The bureau's stress counselor says to her Tuesday afternoon appointment. "In our first session you said, 'My team has never encountered a case like this.' How could you be prepared?"

"It's our job to protect. *Fidelity, bravery, integrity.* It's right there, hanging on every wall. But with that look on *her* face, and on all our faces, when we finally realized what we were dealing with…No matter how hard I try, I can't get them out of my mind. I'm numb. Each time I come in here you ask me how I feel? Well, there, that's how I feel. I can't sleep. When I close my eyes, there they all are, every one of them. When I open my eyes, there he is."

U.S. Department of Justice
Federal Bureau of Investigation

CHAPTER ONE: Daddy's Home
1963

"…Robbie, not now, Daddy's going to be home soon. You know I have to get dinner ready. You know how he hates it when things aren't just so." Terri pauses and stares out the kitchen window. This time last year she would have been racing home from high school in time to get dinner ready. "It's not his fault, none of this is. It's just the way it is. You have to be more careful. Daddy works all day and some nights too. He's tired and, well, you know. It's not his fault."

Looking at her left arm and the faint outline of two large bruises, she says, "See they're almost gone." The tattoos of love fade but soon replaced with new ones. Terri tunes the transistor radio her boyfriend Josh gave her, then ushers her little brother out of the kitchen.

It has only been three months since the class of sixty-two graduated, yet Terri can barely remember the names of most of her classmates. So much has happened since then. Robbie is much too young to understand. *I can only be in so many places at one time*, she thinks to herself. *He is so small, so young and he just doesn't understand. If he will just play in his room, out of the way.*

"You see, Daddy wants his beer and dinner, not your favorite toy shoved in his damn face when he gets home. I'll play with you after dinner, I promise." Terri walks Robbie to his room. "You stay here, safe and out of the way." She places a tender kiss on his forehead and pats his bottom as she closes the door.

In the kitchen, steam wafts into the air as the pot finally begins to boil. *Sausages and pasta, he liked this last week. Damn, was it this much?* Terri stirs in what she hopes is the right amount of seasoning. Tiny beads of sweat form on her forehead as Terri finishes preparing dinner.

Her pulse begins to quicken—that feeling, *he's home.* Looking out the kitchen window, the dust cloud rises from the laneway and drifts toward the house. She feels the rumble his tires make as they roll over the ground. *Daddy's home.* Her wrist hits the handle of the pot as she reaches for a towel to wipe her hands. The scalding contents slosh as the pot is shaken, slopping over the sides, onto the stove, the floor, and her wrist. "Damn it, ow!" Terri screams. Frantically removing the evidence, she wipes the stove and kneels to clean the floor, unaware of Robbie as he runs to where he heard her scream.

Bang—his car door slams. Her body shudders at the sound. His footsteps get louder with each step as he walks across the gravel and to the door. *It's clean, it's clean, stand up, smile. Everything is okay. It's clean.* Thoughts race through her mind as she hears the weight of his footsteps on the porch. The rusty hinges announce his arrival as the screen door swings open.

His arms and hands are filthy, covered in dirt and grease, and the acrid stench of body odor and cigarettes follows him as he walks past Terri. The smell of beer already on his breath as he passes her, he heads straight to the refrigerator. With a fresh, cold beer in hand, he looks at the sauce on Terri's wrist and chides, "You missed a spot…"

U.S. Department of Justice
Federal Bureau of Investigation

CHAPTER TWO: Survey Grid 12.7.2
Present Day

"Are you sure that thing is working?" George asks Carlo. "When was the last time you calibrated it?"

"It's freaking fine! It's been sending out correct data all day long. That stuff is moving down there. There's no other explanation. We've gotta call this in. You've got no choice, boss."

"You're right, you're right, it just pisses me off. This will probably shut us down for days. I can hear the bastards back at the office right now, 'We have deadlines to meet.' Toss me the cell phone." George catches the phone and presses the speed dial number for their field office. The only sound coming from the receiver is the tones of the touch pad as the number dials. "Can you hear me now?" George's voice echoes through the air as he mimics that guy from the Verizon commercial. As usual, the remoteness of their location has unreliable cell coverage. "Useless piece of…"

"I don't think that guy has ever been here," Carlo says, sarcastically shaking his head. Working for a geological exploration company, George and his partner Carlo have been mapping natural gas deposits in western Montana.

"Shit cross your fingers. I'll try the sat phone," George says. Their progress halts as their attention, fixed on an image forming on the video monitor in front of them.

"What the…" Carlo stops mid-sentence as the image completes. "…get the goddamn office on the line right now! You see that? There's the edge of the thing. It's huge, at least thirty feet long by…looks like maybe ten feet wide. What the hell is that?" Carlo's face pales as the images display.

George and Carlo have worked for Deep Image for just over two years and are in the sixth month of the ten-month survey of the Montana Thrust Belt. The Thrust Belt encompasses over forty-one thousand square miles and is laden with mineral and hydrocarbon deposits. Their client, a land developer, has contracted Deep Image to locate natural gas deposits. The developer is hoping to find a deposit large enough to provide a sustainable fuel source for their latest development called Eco-Town. Their survey area covers approximately fifty-two hundred square miles.

"Just relax. How deep are those things?" George asks Carlo.

"Twenty feet, maybe deeper. Whatever that is, it's only moving in the deeper one. Another toxic sludge pool just like we had in Texas. Here we go again." Carlo sends the images to the printer. "At least in

Texas, we were close to town. This is God's country and it doesn't look like he's been here for a while."

George hands the field contact list to Carlo. Carlo scans the list. "Who is the 'go-to' in this county?" George asks Carlo. "Where are we exactly? Private or public land?"

"Doesn't say. Why?" Carlo says.

"Protocols."

"Give me a minute." Carlo opens a large binder containing the land title information and searches the information. "Doesn't matter, this property borders federal land. You get to call everyone."

"Wonderful. Carlo, you're sure we have tanks here, and not just some old mine shaft?"

"Does this look like an old mine shaft?" Carlo turns the monitor in George's direction.

George calls the company field office in Kalispell and informs their supervisor that they have found what appear to be two very large underground storage tanks in survey grid 12.7.2. "Yes, way the hell out here. I'm just about to call the forestry service and the EPA. The rest of our day looks like it's all shot to shit." As he speaks with his superiors, his attention is focused on the images being displayed on the monitor. "Yes, for sure. We'll probably have to hold their goddamn hands all day tomorrow or at least until some bureaucrat says, 'dig it up.'" George motions to Carlo as the image changes. Carlo can only shrug. "They had better bring an excavator with them and hopefully this doesn't play out like that last tank we found. We lost three days waiting for them to get their shit together.

You tell me, what are we supposed to do in the meantime? We got work to do here."

Carlo yells out, "We're deep in the freakin bush here, middle of Goddamn nowhere."

George says, "Exactly, we're at least an hour from the road. If you want us to stay on schedule they had better have their shit together. These things are fucking huge! Forty footers—and we can't tell if they're hot or even if they're leaking. They'll need a damn good excavator to dig these up, that's all I know. Fuck, I don't know, we both could already be contaminated. We got hundreds of more grids to complete and no time to do things twice if you want us to meet your deadlines." Shaking his head, George finishes his call.

U.S. Department of Justice
Federal Bureau of Investigation

CHAPTER THREE: The Discovery
Present Day

George walks to their survey truck, the TV-1450, one of several seismic vibrator trucks owned and operated by Deep Image. George recounts the details of his call to the office to Carlo. "We'll see what happens. I would have rather made the calls but the brass back in Kalispell said *they'll* take care of it. We better get things setup here for show and tell." George is referring to the questions and answer session, which will no doubt follow when the various government officials arrive.

Because they work in very remote locations, gaining access to survey locations has always been their greatest challenge. Even with the ATV, finding the safest way to bring the 1450 through the bush is difficult. Nothing is ever straight as the crow flies. Actual routes can easily be three or more times the physical distance shown on their GPS. Understanding the challenges, they faced getting the 1450 to this location, George and Carlo know that crawling an excavator large enough to remove these tanks from the ground, from the access road, will take at least half a day.

As George and Carlo pack up for the day, the sat phone rings. George's boss Len says, "I got in touch with the local forest service and managed to speak to a ranger. The guy sounds like he's eighteen. I might as well have told him you found an iPad out there. Come to think about it, that would have probably perked his interest. He has no clue what I was talking about or what you're dealing with up there."

"Pinch me, I'm all excited," George says.

"What the fuck?" Carlo says.

"The office managed to get in touch with Forest Ranger Dan, and guess what? He has no fucking clue what the hell we have found up here." George muffles his phone and updates Carlo.

"Well, that makes three of us," Carlo says dryly.

"Oh, and by the way," Len says, "the land developer's project manager expressed a great deal of interest in some of the data that you two uploaded yesterday. He explained that the data from two grids in particular show extremely large deposits and if these pockets intersect with their current location, there may be enough natural gas for five Eco-Towns."

"Great, well, we'll do what we have to do. We'll kiss his ass. We'll make it happen," George tells his boss.

"Whose ass are we kissing now? Do I want to know?" Carlo laughs as he asks George.

"Trust me, you don't want to know." George explains the details of his conversation, "They're telling me that we might have found what the client is looking for and time is ticking, do the math."

***

The access road branches off US Highway 93 and winds through the mountains and canyons west of Evergreen, Montana. Used mainly as a fire road, the route is rugged but accessible with four-wheel drive or a large truck. Clive Hemming, a junior deputy with the Montana Forest Service, based in Evergreen, is en route to meet up with George and Carlo. Working his second summer for the Forest Service, Clive attends the University of Montana, at Missoula and is a sophomore in the forest management program.

"Can't do. I'll have to meet up with you later. I got to go meet a couple of surveyors. They found, I don't know, a tank or something. It'll take a couple hours at least. You bet I've got my fishing gear with me, some crank baits and floaters. Yeah, talk to you later." Living in Evergreen his entire life, he would rather be fishing or hunting with his buddies than working. Clive finishes his call and turns onto the access road.

***

George and Carlo finally arrive back at their truck parked on the access road. The dust in the air settles as Clive introduces himself to George and Carlo. "Thank you for getting out here so fast and we're really sorry for messing up your day," George says.

"No problem don't worry about it. The office said you found an old tank? Like a gun tank from the war? Where is it?"

George shakes his head he explains who they are and what they were doing when they made their discovery. "What we do isn't rocket science, but our truck is pretty high tech. What we have is ground-penetrating radar on steroids." George hands Clive a printout of the site that shows in detail the outline of two very large, rectangular objects buried in the ground. "The truck is an articulated four-wheel drive twenty-ton chassis, with a seven-ton vibrator plate suspended in the middle on large hydraulic shocks. When we lower the plate to the ground, the vibrations resonate off structures and formations, sending a series of echoes back. You know, like a fish finder. Each object sends back a very unique series of waves to our sensors and depending on the item's specific density, the plotter charts accordingly."

"The denser the material, the darker the image the plotter prints," Carlo says, describing the printout Clive is looking at. "Nothing in nature produces a right angle, and as you can see—"

"Those are pretty damn big!" Clive blurts out. "What's with the lighter shading on the inside? Are they full?"

Carlo shrugs and shakes his head, "We got no frickin clue."

"Is that a liquid?" Clive asks.

"There's something in them, we can't tell for sure what. The tank's shell is so dense; we can't get a clear picture of the inside." George sits down at the keyboard and types several commands, bringing up several new images for Clive to see. "There they are.

There's a *hell* of a lot of dirt and rock between them and the surface and it sure looks like they have something in them." He hits another key and a new image is displayed. "You see this." George points at the screen.

"Why is that blurry?" asks Clive.

"It's moving," Carlo says.

"I don't know about you, but we sure as hell *don't* have any shovels!" George crosses his arms over his chest and looks at Clive.

"Moving? What could be...I gotta call this in." Clive realizes that this situation is far more complicated than what he had expected. Considering all the potential risks involved, he phones into his office. He confirms with the office that the EPA has been notified and one of their inspectors is en route to Evergreen. "He might as well grab a room for the night and call the sheriff, just to be safe," Clive explains to the girl in the office. "We don't have enough daylight left so we're all gonna head back to town, and can you call Mitch Hollister and have him bring his big excavator up to the old fire road just outside Eagle's View for first light tomorrow. Tell Mitch he'll have to walk the machine into the site from the road. He'll know what he needs to do. Oh, and we also need to find out who owns this piece of land."

***

I'm scared and so alone, surrounded by all this. Robbie, where are you? It's so dark and strange, this place. My belly aches and my heart cries out for you. Josh can you hear me? I can feel my soul as it tries to escape, escape from this place. It can't...it's trapped. I'm trapped. Am I dying? Is this how it feels? How did this happen? Robbie, Josh, can anyone hear me? The light is fading, it's getting dark. Oh God, can anyone hear me? Oh, this must be just a dream. This can't be real.

Help me.

U.S. Department of Justice
Federal Bureau of Investigation

CHAPTER FOUR: Dig Them Up
Present Day

The following morning, George and Carlo meet with Clive and Mike, the agent from the EPA, at the diner attached to their motel. "How far off the road is the site?" the EPA agent asks George.

"Just under ten miles, and with the ATV, travel time is about an hour," George replies.

"My office was able to confirm that several old mines have operated on this site," Mitch says. "The girl in our office is trying to find out who the current owner is. We have dispatched a local excavation contractor. He should be onsite by the time we get up there."

"I hate old mines," Mike says. "We had one a year or so ago, what a pain in the ass! You can find everything from old machinery to drums full and half full of almost anything. Some of these old mines even did smelting onsite. What a mess that is! When we finally got into the damn thing, we found crates of dynamite all over the place, not to mention the dozens of rusted drums of mercury and sulfur. There were no real regulations back then, so decommissioning a mine meant taking what you could and leaving the rest behind. I've never seen one with tanks this big before."

During their conversation, George went over some of the details of a similar situation they had during a survey in Texas. They found a tank buried on a ranch that contained hundreds of gallons of toxic chemicals. During the removal, the tank ruptured, and the contents contaminated several acres of land. Several people working on the recovery required hospitalization.

"We *never* get to find some wise guy's stash of money in the ground! Remind me to bring my lead boxers," Carlos says.

With their meeting over, the men drive up to the site, and while en route, Clive receives a call from the excavator operator Mitch Hollister. "Hey bud," Mitch says. "I'm up here. You want me to start walking the excavator or should I wait for y'all?"

Clive tells Mitch to head into the site and get set up. "Just follow the trail these guys made, and you should see their rig eventually. Watch for bears. They told me they had to chase a couple away over the past couple of days."

"What the heck's going on up here, bud? I got a call from your office and all they told me was to get up here for dawn," Mitch asks, then takes a sip from his coffee.

"We got an old mine to dig up. A couple of surveyors found some buried storage tanks. Damn things look like they are full too. Looks like this could get real messy. The EPA guy is here too."

Mitch shouts, "Overtime, buddy, git 'er dun, oh-ver-time!"

"Yeah, bud, I hear ya…I don't know, I just got a bad feeling, a real bad feeling! We'll be up there in an hour."

Clive finishes his conversation with Mitch as he stares at the sticker on the back of the EPA service truck: *Keep America Beautiful.*

As the convoy of service trucks arrives at the cutout where Mitch unloaded his excavator, Clive suggests that the trucks should now be able to drive into the site. "Mitch's 330 CAT will have blazed us a pretty good road. That should save us some time."

The EPA agent assumes the lead, explaining that they have to presume there is an environmental hazard present; therefore, his agency has jurisdiction here. "Trust me boys, I sure hope there's nothing up there, but if there is, I gotta make sure we're all safe."

When they arrive at the location, the EPA agent introduces himself to Mitch and they discuss what has to be done. "It looks like the first tank is twelve feet deep, and the other is another ten feet down. We have no idea how old they are, and hell, they could even be leaking. I want you to expose one of the top corners of this tank. Can you position your machine far enough away from the top to protect it from crushing?"

"I can only reach out about ten feet and that's if I'm parallel to the tank. I should be able to dig deep enough. Can I see that?" Mitch looks at the printout, checking the size and locating where the tank should be. "I'll cut a pit, say twelve feet deep and large enough to give you access to the top corner of the tank, but it will take some time. I have to step back the sides of hole or shit's all gonna cave in."

"Take these, and I need everyone to put on these coveralls." The agent passes each man a pair of white chemical suits. He points to a flat rock approximately one hundred feet from where they will be digging. "We have to be very careful, assume the worst. There could be gas pockets down there. Clive, can you take this equipment and set it up over there? You said you were searching for nat gas deposits?"

George nods. "From what the team back at the office just told us, we could be sitting on a huge deposit."

The agent opens another case and inserts a series of probes into the ground.

"What are those things?" George asks.

"These're supposed to detect the presence of heavy metals and other contaminants. They work great in sand, clay, and soil, but really suck in rocky ground. Welcome to Montana! Once I have the last of these set, you can start to dig."

The agent gives Mitch the signal to start. Mitch slowly raises the boom up, then lowers the bucket to the ground.

The excavator's engine revs as the bucket contacts the hard ground. Mitch starts to strip the shallow layer of topsoil. With a full bucket, Mitch rotates the excavator and dumps the contents into a pile.

"Heavy liquids rarely flow up, but let's keep an eye on what he's dumping, just in case. Help me set a couple of these monitors over by the pile," the agent tells Clive. They set up two more stations to monitor the debris pile, which is growing fast.

As the excavator digs deeper, passing six feet, large shards of rock and small boulders appear. The bucket's strong metal teeth tear chips into the rocks as puffs of white smoke swirl into the air.

"Hold on, stop, stop!" The agent frantically waves his arms to get Mitch's attention. "I need to test the air down there right now! We've had a couple of big sparks off the rocks you just pulled out. George just told me that they found some natural gas deposits around here." Carlo lowers one of their ladders into the hole and the agent climbs down. "It smells a bit down here but that's to be expected, stirring the ground up like this. This meter detects most explosive gases. Clive, what does the meter on the red tripod read?" Clive walks to the pile, checks the reading, and shouts back, "five thirty-two and twenty-one hundred!"

"Thanks. Those reading are fine and we're good down here too! I'm coming back up." The agent motions to Mitch to resume digging.

Standing with him at the hole, Carlo points to the various colored tripods and asks, "Your gear, what does all this shit do?"

The agent explains, "I'm checking for flammable and noxious gasses. Methane is my biggest concern and if we hit that, boom, no work tomorrow. The ground plugs and this box will let me know if we hit anything caustic or corrosive. When their alarms go off, we clear out!"

"Why?" Carlos asks.

"Corrosives or caustics are normally accompanied with some form of poisonous vapor."

"Great, and me here without my lead boxers. I tell you, man, we don't get paid enough for this shit."

The final foot of material will have to be removed by hand to ensure they do not damage the tank. The men struggle to use shovels and their bare hands as they lift and remove the final rocks and gravel. "I hit something. Sounds like I got it!" Carlo shouts as a metallic twang echoes from the hole. With each shovelful removed, the top of the tank becomes visible. Carlo brushes off the last few chunks of gravel and rocks and comments, "Is that what I think it is? Looks like a shipping container. Aren't those…that ain't no tank, it's a freaking container! What the fuck is that thing doing way out here?"

"Clive toss me down the red test box. And the rest of you guys can climb out now," the EPA agent shouts. "The container appears to be in pretty good shape. This looks like, I don't know, some kind of identification numbers, or what's left of them. The metal is in great shape, probably an old ocean container."

"Yeah, those things are made with corrosion-resistant steel," George says.

"Well nothing's leaking. I need the box from my truck marked VideoScope," Mike says to Clive.

Clive lowers the large black case to the agent. "I can use this to see what we have inside there." Flicking open the latches on the case, he takes out a large drill and a can of spray lube.

"What's that for?" Carlo inquires.

"The lube keeps the metal cool as the drill cuts into it. No sparks. Then I can insert the scope into the hole and that monitor will show me what's in there. The scope has both video and air quality probes on it, kind of like a drain snake a plumber uses to check for roots."

"Gotcha, I'll just be watching from over here...um...behind this," Carlo says quietly as he hunkers down behind the track of the excavator.

The drill bit's sharp teeth squeal as they contact the container's hard metal surface. Holding the drill in one hand and the spray lube in the other, Mike begins to drill through the top. There's a loud clunk as it breaks through the surface. "Okay, that's better." He inserts the probe into the hole.

"Whoa, you might want to come up here and look at this!" Clive shouts as the data from the probe lights up the monitor.

"What the hell is that?" The agent asks as he adjusts the camera focus and stares at the monitor along with the others.

"George! Holy crap, you okay man?" Carlo shouts. George has just collapsed onto the ground beside the excavator.

U.S. Department of Justice
Federal Bureau of Investigation

CHAPTER FIVE: We Need Help
Present Day

Exiting the conference room, FBI Supervisory Special Agent Christopher Banks and the other team leaders have just concluded their monthly field review with the director of the Behavioral Analysis Unit. Banks joined the bureau in 1995 and found his place in the BAU shortly thereafter. His current team has been together for the past two years. Based in Quantico, VA, they respond directly to the requests of local law enforcement agencies. Their cases can involve serial killers, multiple murders, child abductions, and terrorist activities. Solving these cases requires efficiently developing an accurate subject profile.

As he reaches his office, his cell phone rings. "Agent Banks, my name is Mark Wilson, sheriff of Evergreen, Montana. Thank you very much for taking my call."

"Good morning, Sheriff. I've been expecting your call. Our field office in Salt Lake emailed me the details of your situation. I'm not sure what assistance we can offer you at this time. With the current lack of any physical evidence, I hope you can understand my hesitance. Dispatching my team at this time is probably premature."

"What do you mean? You have the file, don't you? You've seen those images. What more do you people need?"

"Sheriff, I have seen the file."

"Agent Banks, something terrible has happened in my community. I don't have the people or the resources. This is a damn good town. Kind, good people and now I have four men in the hospital. One even had to be airlifted! This stuff just doesn't happen here. They said your team would need my invitation to come to my jurisdiction. You have the pictures. I am begging you, sir. We need your help!"

The level of desperation in the sheriff's voice causes Banks to pause a moment before speaking. Banks considers his response as he scans a map of Montana, paying particular attention to the federal lands near Evergreen. The site's location provides Banks with his solution. The proximity of the crime scene to a national forest places the case in the bureau's jurisdiction. "The property appears to border onto a federal land preserve," Banks says.

"Yes, I believe it does."

"Sheriff, that's all I needed to know. I will have our communications liaison get in touch with you right away."

Banks taps the window in his office and motions to the two agents on the other side to come in.

***

"And you will make seven." Those are the last words she heard as the man placed the cover back onto the end of the wooden crate. Trembling, the three-and-a-half-year-old Cree Indian girl had been abducted from a park near her reservation four days earlier. Bound, and with her cries silenced, not a sound radiates from the pickup truck. The heavy bags of feed placed around and on top of the wooden crate insulate her cries. All she can do is wait.

The ease by which he can find them, then disappear, pains him more and more. At first, they struggle. Then they realize there was no *lost puppy* or *small bird that needs a friend*. The terror he sees in their eyes as they understand he has fooled them gives him no pleasure, nor pain. It is just part of the process; her captor says to himself. *Keep them safe.*

It is always the same, however, no matter how gentle or soft he is with them as he closes the box. Their screams and the look of terror in their tiny faces, "No...Mommy, Mommy, I want my Mommy...Mommy." He has no choice but to cover their mouths. Once they are in the box, they will be safe. He doesn't have to frighten them anymore, and there is no need to cover their mouths.

No matter the time of day, or even the day of the week, with a tired caregiver or in a crowd, he can always find someone who is forgotten or ignored. Sometimes they are even in danger and how could he just walk past? He remembers a certain little boy in a car, on a stifling hot day. Alone in that car...the door wasn't locked. The poor child was too young to get out by himself. What type of person would do that? He opened the car door. The smallest, the ones who are quiet and withdrawn, they disappear so effortlessly. It only takes a moment.

He can find them anywhere: the park, the shopping mall, their backyard. Just off by themselves, unattended and ignored for a moment. It's done so quickly. He especially finds it comforting when he finds a small group of children; perhaps they are there together or not. He will see one who is sitting off alone, or wandering off, just far enough. He finds them arriving from the group home or the orphanage, out for their weekly trip to the mall. He watches as the social workers fumble and try to keep track of all those little ones. There are times when he doesn't even have to approach them. They will come to him, eager and curious about something he's holding. There are so many of them, especially the shy little ones who are just looking for someone to play with, just a little attention. With his friendly face and his voice, it only takes a moment.

U.S. Department of Justice
Federal Bureau of Investigation

CHAPTER SIX: Puzzles and Challenges
Present Day

Sitting in the team's common room, Agent Eric Torres finds himself stumped once again by the team's technical advisor. "Okay, I give up. Explain it to me. How did McClane and Zeus do it?"

"You have two jugs. First, fill the five-gallon jug. Empty the water into the three-gallon jug. What do you have?" Torres' partner Martin Sanders says.

"Two gallons left in the five-gallon jug?" Torres responds.

"Now if you empty the three-gallon jug and pour the two gallons from the other—"

Sanders gets cut off by Torres, "Brilliant, of course. I hate puzzles."

"You just hate the ones that challenge you," Sanders says and chuckles.

Martin Sanders is one of the bureau's top computer analysts. A gifted programmer, he was asked to join the bureau shortly after he was caught hacking into the system. He uploaded a virus into the system that simply contained his resume. He addressed it *To whomever is in charge.*

"I have something special coming in just for you, pally. Cherkoff said she's got one that's sure to stump you!" Torres states as he leans back in his chair and grins, prepping Sanders for a little surprise he and fellow agent Paulina Cherkoff have cued up. "She texted me from a specialty game shop in Montreal, 'No way can he solve this one!' So be warned, pal, when Cherkoff and Lee get back, the game's on!"

Sanders nods and gives Torres a familiar *we'll see* look.

Banks summons the pair to his office.

"Sanders, I need you to recall Cherkoff and Lee. We leave for Montana in twenty. Get them the first charter out from Montreal. This is a bad one."

"Is there ever a good one?" Sanders says. Each team member carries his/her go bag with them always, ready to mobilize on a moment's notice. Sanders texts both agents. He notices that the small plaque Banks displays on his desk has been moved. Each member of the team is an astute student of observation and the human condition. Sanders is blessed, cursed, with an eidetic memory so clear and powerful he notices even the slightest changes. "What's with your plaque?"

The plaque reads: *In very dark places, we will, at times, see a moment of light. Our choice is to decide if it's a way out, or the headlight of an oncoming train.* These were the words that were spoken by one unsub shortly after being brought into custody for the execution-style killing of two families in California. Their investigation would uncover that the unsub had been horrifically abused as a child by both his father and mother. He had been repeatedly tortured and his mother injured him terribly one day after she found he had wet the bed the night before. When she discovered he had hid his bed sheets, she tied fishing line around his genitals, making sure he would not make the same mistake ever again.

***

The team has had very little time off over the past few months. Lee and Cherkoff have taken this current break between cases to enjoy a shared hobby, extreme triathlons. The two-day, 226-mile race begins at Mt. Tremblant, Quebec, Canada. The race begins with a 165-mile cross-country mountain bike race, followed by a sixty-nine-mile paddle and swim, and wraps up with a grueling fifty-two-mile double marathon across the rugged hills surrounding Quebec's most scenic ski areas.

Thomas Lee, the latest addition to the team, was recruited by the FBI, specifically the BAU, shortly after 9/11 and has been with the team for just two years. Competing as a team in the Grand Prix de Mt. Tremblant, a very strong bond between him and Cherkoff has developed over their past few races. With each race, both the mental and physical challenges they've faced together have brought them to the breaking point or "the wall," as it is called. Lee is constantly amazed at the grit and determination Cherkoff possesses. Only five feet tall and 120 pounds, many men have underestimated her. Banks often comments, "If you ever wonder why the bureau has done away with minimum height/weights as prerequisites for hiring, I give you but one answer: Paulina Cherkoff."

"How many followed you this time?" Lee asks Cherkoff, while they each try to clean some of the mud off their arms and legs.

"Only two. Once they realized I was heading off the trail, they stopped. At least this time we weren't that far into bike race. Better now than the last five miles of the marathon. Sanders said that there's a jet waiting for us at Mirabel Airport and something about meeting up with the rest of the team in Montana. It pissed me off, just a bit. I was just getting into the rhythm."

"You dropping out of a race, on the last day? I believe that could happen, just like I believe Sanders will get stumped by that toy you bought him!" Lee teases Cherkoff as they finish collecting their gear and head to the airport.

U.S. Department of Justice
Federal Bureau of Investigation

CHAPTER SEVEN: Sanders
Present Day

In Quantico, Agent Banks instructs Sanders to arrange a video conference, connecting all members of the team, later in the day. "Here, I need you to look through this while the rest of the team is in the air." Banks hands the entire case file to Sanders, a move that catches Sanders off guard. The main case file always accompanies the team. Team briefings, whether in the conference room in Quantico, a local police station, or some other location, have always been presented by Banks to the whole team. Releasing information to the group at once ensures that no member of the team can develop a biased opinion. "I need you to look through the file and do what needs to be done. Call me on the plane when everyone is in the air."

Sanders continues to make the arrangements required for the agents. Both the team's private jet in Quantico and a charter from Mirabel Airport, just outside Montreal, Quebec are standing by. With his tasks complete and Sanders finally alone, he opens the case file and attempt to make sense of what he is looking at. The main case folder contains two identical bureau folders, with only one exception. Attached to one is a printed label *Sanders: Your Eyes Only*. Inside this folder, he finds an envelope with his name handwritten by Banks.

He places the folder down, just for a moment, pausing to decide—open the envelope or continue through the file? Sanders decides to inspect the file first. He finds various pictures of a rural setting, each photo marked with GPS coordinates and an identification number. He's pleasantly surprised. The images could be used as postcards and are not the typical gruesome crime scene shots he had expected. There is a total of twenty-five photos, mostly aerials.

There's also a list containing names: Marshall, George; Di Pastori, Carlo; Anderson, Ron; Hollister, Mitch; Hemming, Clive. Each person's title and emergency contact information is attached to the inside cover of the folder. Sanders notices that the names include members from two federal agencies: the US Forestry Service and the EPA. Stamped across the entire page in red bold type:

FAMILIES TO BE NOTIFIED.

The list totaling seven men has an additional list that totals well over fifty people to be contacted. So much for just "next of kin" being contacted, Sanders thinks.

One photograph catches his attention as he sifts through the pile. A massive excavation site has exposed what appears to be a large storage container. The pit dwarfs the large excavator and men standing near the site. On the back of another photo is a yellow sticky note that reads, *Open your envelope now*, also handwritten by Banks. "All right, boss," he says to himself, and opens the envelope containing a letter and several additional photos and instructions.

Martin:

I figured that you would look through the file first, holding off opening the envelope. Since joining our team, your unique ability to read between the lines is an asset our team benefits from every day. Your ability to control the flow of data and the press will be greatly challenged with this case. The team will be briefed together as usual at the appropriate time.

I apologize that you must see these images before the rest of the team. I have no other choice, and as this case plays out, you will understand. The remoteness of this location will present many challenges for our team and is unlike anything our team or the bureau has ever dealt with before.

- Banks

U.S. Department of Justice
Federal Bureau of Investigation

CHAPTER EIGHT: When Paths Cross
November 1963

"Today, November 22, 1963, the country is in shock. President Kennedy is dead. 'The president is dead.' This statement has just been released by a priest who was at the president's side," announces the broadcast on televisions and radios across the nation.

"Wow, shame about Kennedy, man." Charlie chats with Oldson, as he continues to pump gas into Oldson's tank. "Deer or elk, what's it gonna be this time? How long you gonna be up there?"

"Usual two weeks, and with any luck, I'll bag a few of each." Oldson pays cash for the gas and checks the tie downs covering the contents in the back of his Ford F250 four-by-four, before heading back onto Route 93 South.

US Highway 93 extends from the Canadian border near Eureka Montana in the north, south to Wickenburg, Arizona. It winds through the mountains and valleys, national forests and Indian reserves in Montana on its way south. Passing through towns both large and small, traffic along Route 93 is busy at times, but today, only a few cars have come into view and no one is stopping to pick up Terri or her boyfriend, Josh.

"I see one coming down the pass now. Baby lift yer skirt and show off them legs." Josh grins and heads off the road just out of sight. Terri rolls the hem of her dress up just enough.

A few moments later, a pickup slows down and pulls to the side of the road. Rolling down the passenger's window, the driver leans over and asks, "You need a ride?" The smell of cigarettes and leather come from the cab of his truck. Terri quickly assesses the man, his height; he looks very well groomed. She can feel the warmth radiate from inside the truck. Smiling back at him, Terri nods and as she tosses her bag into the back, the driver notices Josh coming toward the truck. Terri's bag is just resting on the tarp placed over the center of the truck's bed. The driver gets out and pushes it under the cover. Standing face to face with Josh, the driver takes the bag from Josh's hands, placing it under the tarp as well.

Terri and Josh get in the passenger door as the driver walks around to his door from behind, closes it, and pulls back onto the highway.

Josh looks at the driver. "Hey man, what a sight you are!"

Nodding, the driver looks over at the pair. "You didn't need to pull that little trick. I would have stopped either way."

Feeling guilty and a bit embarrassed, Terri and Josh hold hands, and listen as Telstar plays softly on the radio.

"Man, we've been trying to catch a ride for most of the morning. Thanks, man," Josh exclaims as the pair nestle into the soft leather bench seat.

"It's pretty late in the season to be hitchin'. Where are you two going?"

"Been trying to make our way to California, meeting some friends we're gonna stay with," Terri answers.

"I can take you both as far as Idaho Falls." He lights a cigarette and offers one to each of them. Sitting closest to the driver, Terri gladly accepts and passes one to Josh.

She takes a deep drag from her cigarette and exhales. "I'm Terri and this is Josh. This truck is so warm." Josh reaches past Terri and shakes the driver's hand.

"My name is Oldson."

"Old-Son?" Josh says.

"It's pronounced ole-sun. Ole-sun." His deep voice repeats each syllable several times, making sure they understand. Terri folds her arms across her chest as she raises her cigarette to her mouth. The leather seat squeaks as she tries to get comfortable.

Josh places his left arm around Terri and gently pulls her a bit closer. Josh looks at Oldson and, smiling, says, "Ole-son…that's real cool name, man." He kisses Terri on the forehead, squeezing her just a bit. Looking around the interior, he notices a gun rack with rifles, and packed behind the seats are several denim bags. A wineskin sways as it hangs from a hook. Josh asks, "You goin' hunting?"

Oldson replies, "No."

Josh and Oldson speak for a while as Terri falls asleep. Josh does most of the talking as Oldson watches the road, nodding occasionally, acknowledging something Josh said. "Hell, her old man's drunk half the time and my old man wants me to go sign up for 'Nam and get all shot up like he did. Neither one of us are farmers so not much we can do in Beulah! Her mom left Terri and her little brother with her dad one day. She said she had to go to the store or something and never came back. Terri pretty much raised her little brother."

Oldson frowns. "Where's her little brother at now?"

"He was only three, so the state took him. Their dad gets real mean when he drinks and a few months ago, things got bad, man! So damn bad that the neighbors called the sheriff. Her old man got in a fight with both deputies that arrived, and he ended up getting shot and then put in jail. A lady from the county came and took her little brother away. She cries about him a lot, her little brother, I mean."

"No grandparents or relatives that could've taken the boy? Surely some relative could have been found, to protect him and take him in?"

"Nope, just Terri and her dad, and with Robbie gone, we figured. what the hell." With a shrug, Josh looks back in the direction of the Dakotas giving it a salute with one finger.

The radio crackles with static while Oldson searches for a station. Reaching for the radio, his right

37

arm brushes over Terri's leg, pulling her skirt up slightly and exposing her just a little. From the corner of his eyes, he sees that Josh is unaware and Terri is fast asleep.

"When did you two eat last?" Oldson asks.

Josh twists his mouth to one side, "I dunno, we found some berries where we crashed last night, man, probably yesterday?"

"That's not very much to eat. You two still growing and all, need more than that!" Josh smiles, nods his head as Oldson suggests they stop at a diner in Lakeside, the next town. He's curious as to how the couple ended so far up Route 93 if they were heading to California from North Dakota. Josh explains they caught a ride with a trucker who was heading to Montana. They made a deal to help him unload and made some money for their efforts.

"We had no idea how far north this guy meant when he said he was going to Rexford. We've never really been out of Beulah, only field trips to Bismarck but that's about it. We found a great place to unpack and spent a couple of days camping. Real private, man, if you know what I mean."

A voice breaks through the static on the radio. "Acting White House Press Secretary Malcolm Kilduf announced that President Kennedy died at approximately one o'clock central standard time, roughly two hours ago."

Oldson switches the channel and the announcement is drowned out by the voice of Johnny Cash singing "Ring of Fire."

"The diner in Lakeside has the best burgers on this road," Oldson says as he grins and lights a cigarette.

U.S. Department of Justice
Federal Bureau of Investigation

CHAPTER NINE: The Provider and the Game
November 1963

Pulling off the highway and into the dirt lot, Oldson parks close to the diner's entrance. As the pickup bumps along, swaying back and forth as it enters the parking lot, Terri wakes up.

"What's going on?" she asks softly.

"I've been told this place has the best burgers on the highway," Josh smirks as he reports to Terri.

Oldson frowns just slightly, staring at Josh as the young couple exit the truck.

Inside the diner, they're greeted by a waitress and sit at a small table by the window. Josh and Terri sit across from Oldson.

"Three eggs, sunny-side-up, bacon, and toast," Oldson says before he sits down. He also takes the newspaper the waitress offers. Terri excuses herself and heads for the bathroom, leaving Josh and Oldson alone.

"We have a couple of friends out in California and they said we could crash with them for a while so…" Josh makes small talk as he looks out the diner window. Only Oldson's truck and one other are in the parking lot. "Man, meeting up with you, it's gonna save us a ton of time."

Oldson just listens to Josh as he explains their plans, smoking his cigarette and nodding occasionally.

"Not too many people run these roads this time of year, just loggin' trucks and hunters." Oldson stubs out his smoke, lights another, and hands one to Josh.

"Thanks, man."

"That feels so much better!" Terri says as she sits back down. "I feel ten pounds lighter—all that road dust and grime gone." The waitress returns with their order. "Oh man, does that smell good."

Topping up their coffees, the waitress leaves the bill and heads to the counter. Josh and Terri devour their meals. Terri finishes before Josh. Oldson notices juices from the burger dripping down from the corner of her mouth. He reaches into his pocket to remove a handkerchief and gives her chin a gentle wipe.

"Mmm, thanks." Terri says as she grins nervously and slides a bit closer to Josh.

Oldson places the handkerchief on the table, folding it neatly, then returning it to his pocket.

"I'm going to need to try a few more burgers down this road, but so far this one was the best I've had," Josh says.

Oldson says nothing, just continues to finish his meal. He stares into Terri's eyes, then glances down, admiring her delicate fingers.

After they finish eating, Oldson lights a cigarette and offers one to Terri, then Josh. While he holds the bill in his hand, he asks, "Now how are you gonna pay your share?" He addresses this question directly to Josh.

"I got some cash, man. What do we owe?" Josh answers as he looks at the bill clenched in Oldson's hands.

Oldson replies, "I like to play this little game at mealtime. You see the back of my pickup? That black tarp, tied down all neat. You guess what's under there and, well, lunch is on me." Oldson lifts his coffee cup to his mouth, drinking the last mouthful. Crushing his cigarette into the ashtray, he waits for Josh's answer.

"What happens if I guess wrong?"

"If you answer wrong, then you pay the entire bill. To sweeten the deal, I'll even add the top two bills in my wallet." Oldson opens his wallet to reveal several crisp ten-dollar bills.

"How am I gonna know if I guess right?"

Oldson stands up. "I'll tell you."

Josh turns his head and looks out at the truck.

"We'll pay our own share!" Terri reaches for the bill, taking it from Oldson. "There, and thank you, that was the best meal I've had in days."

After leaving a tip for the waitress, the three head out and walk to the truck.

Looking at Terri, Josh whispers, "What the hell was that all about?"

The skies have clouded over, and the air is getting cool. From the parking lot, the winding highway below frames the lake on this late autumn day. As they walk to the truck, Josh notices the pickup sways a bit. It's probably the wind coming from the west. The truck rocks gently as the wind fades. As Terri slides into the truck, Josh glances at the tarp. He gets in and, closing the door, he turns and looks back at the tarp again. *What is under there?*

There's almost no traffic. Most people are at home watching CBS and the wrap-up of the events in Dallas earlier in the day. Oldson informs Terri and Josh that he was planning on stopping near Missoula for the night. He has camped at a very nice location about half an hour north of Missoula in the past. There is a lake and the fishing is very good. If they can get there before it gets too dark, they could set up camp. Pulling off the highway and onto a dirt access road, it is another fifteen minutes until they reach a small open area next to the lake where they can set up.

"Sun is gonna set fast, so you two go and find some wood," Oldson directs Josh and Terri, so they head off in search of tinder.

"I just can't get over how pretty it is up here. These trees are so big, baby," Terri says as Josh collects more fuel for the fire. "It's too bad though." Terri pauses as a small tear rolls down her cheek. "I just hope he's alright."

Josh drops what he has collected and turns to hold Terri. Safely in his arms, Terri buries her face into his neck. "Robbie is fine. He's safe. Your dad's not gonna hurt either one of you ever again."

"You're right. I know he's better off now; I just miss him so much. I don't know what would have happened if you weren't there." Josh holds both sides of Terri's face and kisses her on the lips. He lowers his

43

hands down her back as their lips and tongues caress. As their bodies embrace, one of the buttons on Terri's dress opens exposing her cleavage. "Josh, I'm not scared when I'm with you," Terri says softly and together they pick up the wood and return to camp.

U.S. Department of Justice
Federal Bureau of Investigation

CHAPTER TEN: The Campsite
November 1963

Oldson had placed their bags in a small pile in a clearing near his truck. They see him down at the water's edge casting a line into the lake.

Josh makes a fire pit and lights the camp fire. "This looks like the best place to set up." Josh motions to Terri and they pitch their tent. "Give me a hand here."

"Does that help?" Terri smiles as she reaches around Josh's waist placing her right hand in his pants. "Oh, you meant the tent…sorry, baby." Terri giggles and slowly removes her hand, raising his shirt. Her lips trace a line over his belly and up to his nipples. Josh, very distracted, tries to finish with the tent as Terri continues to play.

Terri reaches for her bag and removes a joint. She lights up, takes a long, deep hit, and passes the joint to Josh. A small bag of weed was part of their payment for helping the truck driver a few days before.

"Come over here," Josh says. He raises the bottom of her skirt with his hands, exposing her bare ass. He lowers the top of his pants pressing his body toward her. Terri raises her hips as she feels his body penetrate hers. Moaning, she bends down to hold her ankles in her hands. Watching the lake, Josh holds Terri's hips as he thrusts deeper and deeper, gently slapping her ass. She can feel his erection growing harder inside her. A warm rush flows deep within her body as Josh reaches around and squeezes her tightly in his arms. She twists her body around taking Josh's tongue into her mouth as their climaxes subside.

Oldson returns to find the pair swaying slowly in front of the fire. Holding up a small catch of three fish, Terri offers another joint to Oldson who notices the loosened button on her dress and glimpses the outline of her breasts as he stands beside her. He takes a toke and passes it back to her. Placing the fish down on a nearby rock, and using a long-serrated knife, he slowly cuts into the skin of the fish. The tip of his blade runs red as he slices open the belly of each fish.

Widening the cut, the glistening intestines spill out onto the rock. Oldson reaches into the cavity and pulls out the rest of the organs. He wipes the flesh clean with his hand. Putting aside the guts from each fish, he finishes cleaning them. Pausing slightly over each fish, he draws a circle in the air with his knife. Terri and Josh are paying no attention as he reaches into the pile and removes the hearts from each fish. Placing these aside, he watches as a couple of drops of blood drip from his hand. He throws the rest of the guts directly onto the fire. Reaching down, he finds a few pieces of wood, which he uses to support the fish over the flames.

Oldson walks back to his truck, and, from behind the bench seat, pulls out several denim bags. "It looks like you both worked up an appetite," Oldson says as he returns from his truck. "You know how to pitch a tent, at least." Oldson tosses one of the bags, containing his tent, to Josh and motions for him to set it up. He empties the other bag, pulling out a frying pan, pot, and several tins. "Set that up for me, right over there." Oldson points to a flat area just beside his truck. "I'll get dinner ready."

"Come on, babe, give me a—"

"I'm sure you can handle that yourself," Oldson interrupts Josh.

Josh shrugs and sets up the tent alone. Terri sits back down and watches Oldson prepare their meals. "You don't have to rough it just because you're in the woods. Meals are more than just sustenance. When you have been forced to do without, you realize that you should make it special when you have the time." Oldson describes to Terri what he's doing as he prepares the meal. "Pan-fried potatoes with red onions, seasoned just right. Go so well with fresh trout." Oldson places large potatoes slices into the oil bubbling in the frying pan.

Once the fish are cooked, the three sits down around the fire. Oldson has provided them with camping plates and cutlery. He has also cooked rice, completing the lovely meal in a very short time. With his left hand, he passes a plate to Terri, then Josh, keeping one himself. Stopping them before they start to eat, he announces, "We must honor those who are about to give their energy to us." Passing one raw fish heart to Terri and then one to Josh, he takes the third.

47

He raises it to his lips and slowly chews then swallows the heart.

Yuk, Terri thinks, trying not to show her disgust. Paralyzed for just a moment, she watches Josh hold the heart in his hand. Dangling it over his mouth, he chimes, "Whatever you say, man!" Josh eats the heart, copying Oldson's ritual step for step but adds a peace sign as a toast. Josh teases Terri, taunting her with the heart just before devouring it. "Come on, baby, what's the matter?"

"Asshole," says Terri quietly as she closes her eyes and quickly swallows the warm heart. Not chewing, just downing it whole.

As Oldson continues to explain, his voice grows sterner. "The energy from the fish is now in us, and as it gave its life to feed us, we must always remember. Our lives and our souls are enriched by that which came before us. We, the predator, stand to eat our prey which fought so well. As the victor, we honor your life. For each who falls, one remains on top."

U.S. Department of Justice
Federal Bureau of Investigation

CHAPTER ELEVEN: Temptation
November 1963

The trio spends the balance of the meal relaxing and discussing plans for the morning. With just over four hundred miles to reach Idaho Falls, Oldson says, "If we get an early start and leave by nine, I can drop you off by nightfall. With any luck, you should be able to catch a southbound truck or train."

With the warm glow of the fire and the warm feeling in their stomachs from their feast, Josh lifts Terri up and, placing her on his lap, he wraps both arms around her waist. He kisses her gently on the neck and squeezes her waist just enough to make her sigh. Terri can feel his erection grow as she sits on his lap. Squeezing his hand in hers, she kisses him back.

Oldson walks to his truck to check that everything is tied down, secured and ready for the morning. After wishing Josh and Terri a good night, he retires into his tent. His eyes are fixed on Terri as he zips his tent shut.

Josh and Terri kiss and cuddle by the fire. Quietly she asks, "What did you think about grace?"

Josh raises his eyebrows and replies, "I don't know, babe. In a way I get it, you know, with the grass and the fresh mountain air. Hell, it's all pretty, spiritual. It's them and us. It always has been and always will."

He slowly spins her around and, as they face each other, he opens the remaining buttons on her top.

"Josh, you didn't see the look he gave you when you were playing around with that heart," Terri says as his fingers caress her breasts and tug at her nipples. He moves his hands under her skirt. She moans and holds the back of his head in her left hand, pulling his hair through her fingers. Josh holds her in his arms, stands up and carries her into their tent. Laying her down on their sleeping bag, he slowly removes her top and her skirt as she pulls his shirt off and unbuckles his pants, tossing them on the ground. Kissing her deeply on the mouth. Terri rolls on top of Josh, pulling him to her just a bit at first, moaning as she lowers herself onto him. The warmth from his body and the feeling of security she feels when she's with Josh makes her almost forget the world they left behind.

The moonlight reflects off the lake and fills their campsite with a cool blue light. The campfire flames die leaving the red glow of the embers. A breeze sways the trees. Josh wakes up and gets out of the tent to find a suitable place to relieve himself. "Shit!" Josh says as he stumbles into the puddle he just made.

Oldson's pickup truck begins to rock slowly. The springs squeak as the truck moves from side to side. Curious, Josh walks over to the side of the truck.

Oldson has parked the truck in the clearing, behind cover from the access road. With Oldson's tent set close to the truck, Josh walks slowly as not to disturb anything or make a sound. He stops at the back of the truck and puzzles over what Oldson has under the tarp. He reaches over the truck's tailgate and tries to lift the tarp. The tie-downs are placed with military precision and are very taut, allowing no slack in the tarp. Josh walks to the driver's side and leans over the tarp, his back now facing the access road with the truck between him and Oldson's tent. He releases one of the straps holding the tarp down.

With both hands on the strap at the base of the tarp, Josh attempts to pull on the loose end. The knot is tied tightly but releases easily. He removes the strap and whispers, "Yes…now what's under here?" He reaches for the corner of the tarp and lifts it up, "What the fuck? Bags of potatoes and rice, that's it?" he says as a bead of sweat drips from his forehead onto the bag below. He notices his hand tremble slightly. As he starts to lace the strap back into place, the truck begins to rock again, and a soft bumping noise breaks the silent night air.

Josh drops the strap and steps back from the truck. He listens for where the sound has come from, but there is only silence. Shaking his head, he continues to tie the tarp back down. With the final loop secured, Josh places the loose end of the strap back where it had been.

"What are you doing?" whispers a voice behind Josh.

Josh gasps as he turns around. Terri smiles back at him.

Josh sighs with relief. "You scared the crap out of me." He looks back at the truck. "Just bags and bags of food—rice, potatoes, and seeds. Let him try that *what's under the tarp game* now!" The couple returns to their tent and Josh leaves his shoes outside to dry off.

Oldson steps out from behind a large group of rocks where he had been watching Josh. Walking over to his truck, he inspects the tarp and the tie-downs. Glancing over at the young couple's tent, he removes the strap. Folding the tarp back, he looks at the bags. He places his hand on the top bag, slowly shaking his head. He places the tarp back not securing it with the strap. The wind is picking up now as he walks back to his position behind the rocks to wait with his tools. The loose end of the tarp flaps with the wind.

Hearing the tarp, Josh sits up and looks in the direction of the noise.

"What's the matter?" Terri asks him.

"Damn it, the strap came loose."

"You better go fix it." Terri lays back down, slowly falling back to sleep.

Josh is positive he tied the strap securely when he peeked earlier, but he decides to do as Terri asked and walks to the truck. Without warning, Josh feels a rope around his throat as his feet lift off the ground. The rope cuts into Josh's throat as Oldson pulls even tighter. Josh attempts to scream, his hands grasping desperately at his throat. Oldson jams one of his knees into the small of Josh's back forcing Josh down. Blood vessels in his eyes burst as his eyes roll back, his body convulses and contorts, then goes limp. Oldson reaches around, opening Josh's mouth, and shoves in a cloth.

Oldson stands up, walks to the truck and lowers the tailgate. He lifts the tarp. Quietly moving several bags out of the way, he exposes a large wooden crate under the bags. Oldson walks to where Josh is lying. He bends down and lifts Josh up. With very little effort, Oldson tosses Josh over his shoulder and carries him fireman style to his truck. He props Josh up on the edge of the tailgate. Removing two pieces of rope from his pocket, he swiftly hog-ties Josh. Oldson opens the end of the crate and shoves Josh's body in. The effort needed to stuff Josh into the crate surprises Oldson, but he shoves harder. With the tarp secure, Oldson returns to his tent and falls asleep.

U.S. Department of Justice
Federal Bureau of Investigation

CHAPTER TWELVE: Breakfast
November 1963

As the sun rises, warming the air and waking Terri, she rolls over to embrace Josh. Realizing he isn't there, she stretches and begins to get up. The smell of coffee wafts from outside the tent. She finds Oldson packing. Oldson greets Terri with an enthusiastic "Good morning!"

"You too," Terri says. "Have you seen Josh?"

Oldson says, "I think I embarrassed him. I caught him playing with the tarp in my truck...I asked him if he wanted some coffee, but he just walked on down to the lake. You know how boys get when you catch them red-handed. In fact, he could hardly say a word."

"Damn him, he just had to look. I'm so sorry about that. You've been so nice and everything. I told him to just mind his own business."

"Don't you worry about it, just boys being boys, you know. I guess I'll just have to put something else under there then."

Oldson gives Terri a cup of coffee. She holds it tightly against her chest. The steam rising from the cup forms little droplets of water on her face. "This is so good. There's something about coffee, it's just...thank you for everything. We haven't eaten so good for days." They smile at each other and gently tap their cups. They talk while the sun rises over the lake.

She finishes her coffee, and asks, "Which path did Josh take to the lake?"

"Not exactly sure." He hands Terri a cigarette and packs up the rest of the camping gear.

"Can you give me a hand with my tent? That way, when Josh gets back we'll be ready to go."

Without hesitation, Oldson tells Terri to relax and let him do the work, giving her time to wash up.

"You go take a swim. The water is so fresh and cool. He's probably down there anyhow." Terri agrees, thanks Oldson, and starts for the lake. "Remember we gotta be out of here by nine if you want to get to the Falls tonight, so don't play too much!" Nodding and smiling back at Oldson, she runs down the trail leading to the lake.

***

At the edge of the lake, Terri takes off her sandals and walks into the water. The water is much warmer than she expected. Looking around, she decides to strip and quickly slips into the water. Terri swims just off the shore. Treading water, she glances around looking to see if Josh is nearby. *Josh, where the hell are you?* The lake is nestled between mountains to the west and south. The area where they're camping extends to the lake near two trails leading into the forest. Not seeing Josh and finishing bathing, she gets out of the water and begins to dry off. Hearing footsteps, she turns and yells, "Josh...Josh, is that you?"

"Just me...you decent?" she hears Oldson's voice echo. "So, you found that boy of yours?"

"I'm really getting worried about him," Terri says. "Once I've dried off I'm gonna go look for him. Damn it! He had to mess around with your truck. I warned him, I said let it be, let it be..."

"It's alright, don't you worry about the truck, that's all forgotten. These woods are pretty big and you going off looking for him by yourself, that's a bad idea—end up with both of you lost. Hell, he might even be back at the truck by now. You dry off and let's check the campsite. If he still isn't there, we'll go look for him."

Terri continues to scan the woods as they walk back. "If we got to go search for him, we need to do it right. I'll get my rifle from the truck, just in case. There are bears out there. And we best leave him a note, if he manages to get back before we do, it'll let him know which way we went and to stay put." When they find that Josh has not returned to the campsite, Oldson opens the passenger's door of his truck and grabs a pad of paper. "Here you write him a note and I'll get my gun." Oldson removes his rifle from the rack as he places a wineskin over his neck. Terri takes the pad and begins to write.

She shakes her head. "I am so sorry about all this. I'm just so pissed at him right now! He can be so immature I just want to—" Terri stops for a moment when Josh's duffle bag catches her eye and immediately realizes something is very wrong. The morning air is still, the only sound the click Oldson makes as he checks the chamber of his rifle. "His shoes! Why are they still here?" Her voice trembles while she bends to touch his shoes tied to his bag. Terri looks up at Oldson. He stands by his truck with his rifle.

Oldson steps forward and quietly explains, "Josh was pretty upset when I caught him at my truck. Hardly could keep his feet on the ground, and just bolted off. Terri, just calm down, I'm sure he's just fine." He steps closer to her.

Terri shakes her head frantically reaching for the ground with her hands, "Where, where did he walk? Show me, show me, there's nothing, I don't see anything, where!" The earth near their campsite reveals no footprints. Terri is screaming at Oldson as she steps back. "Oh god... what did you do?" Her voice trembles as she attempts to speak. "Josh! Josh! Where the hell are you! Josh!" Terri gasps as her fears have taken control and she attempts to bolt.

Oldson places his rifle down. "Terri, it's alright, you have to be calm now. You're the strong one! Don't be frightened, please! It will be alright, I promise. Look, you're not making any prints in the ground either. Even my boots hardly make a trace. Just please, calm down. We can figure this out together. Finish the note and let's go look for him."

Desperate to believe what Oldson is saying, Terri slowly calms down. *Where am I going to run? He's right, he must be right, Josh is just being Josh.* Holding her hands across her chest, her breathing returns to normal. Oldson offers his handkerchief and a drink from the wineskin.

"It's a little strong, but it'll help your nerves."

Terri nods nervously as she takes the wineskin and steadies her hand, taking several sips. "You're right, he's just being Josh. I'm sorry."

U.S. Department of Justice
Federal Bureau of Investigation

CHAPTER THIRTEEN: Team Briefing
Present Day

With a gentle tap on the shoulder, the flight attendant wakes Cherkoff and Lee and informs them of their scheduled video conference.

Sanders is facilitating the conference call from Quantico. He has set up the connection between both jets. "Everyone is here, sir," he says to Banks. "I have just sent copies to Cherkoff and Lee."

"Martin is it taken care of?" By addressing Sanders by his first name, Agent Banks creates an immediate hush in both planes.

"Yes, roughly three hours ago. The release went out to all of the major networks."

"Good," Banks says.

"I can count the number of times you have called him Martin on the fingers of one hand and still have enough left over to get that old sixties feeling! What the hell is going on?" Agent Sandra Jenkins asks Banks. She is the final member of the team and second in seniority.

"Two days ago, a pair of surveyors working in Montana discovered what, at first, appeared to be buried storage tanks. They found them on the site of an abandoned mine. They followed procedures for dealing with this and alerted the EPA, forestry service, and the local sheriff." Banks instructs the team to bring the first set of images up on their tablets. "As you can see, the topography is extremely rugged, and the site is very isolated. The local officials decided to excavate a small section at first, for fear of collapse."

"What is that? Is that a shipping container?" Lee asks.

"Yes, heavily reinforced and it connects to a second, buried deeper," responds Banks. He pauses to allow the agents to view all the images.

"How long have they been buried?" Jenkins asks.

"Unknown. However, the initial investigators believe this site could be at least ten years old. From what we know, the first container was roughly twelve feet underground and the second even farther. When the top of the first was exposed, the agent from the EPA, Ron Anderson, followed procedures for inspecting an unknown substance within a closed environment. A video camera was placed through the top of the container."

"Have they excavated the second container?" Lee asks Banks.

"At this point, all work has stopped pending our arrival. The EPA agent inspected the interior of what we will refer to as Container One. Sanders can you show everyone the first set of images."

A pop-up window opens on the main video screens in both planes displaying the image Banks had requested. At this point, he turns the discussion over to Sanders.

Banks sits back to observe the reactions of his colleagues seated across from him despite the fact his team is accustomed to viewing a wide variety of crime scene photos.

"The EPA agent was the first to view this, and as you see, this was not what anyone had expected," Sanders says. "This image gives us a bird's-eye view of the inside of the container. This angle gives a good view of what we have to deal with. However, when they lowered the camera deeper into the container and panned around…and started to view the walls—this is why we are here."

"Oh my God!" Jenkins raises her hands to her face momentarily to shield her eyes. A marine for over twelve years and one of only a few women ever crowned top sniper, her shriek is unexpected and sends shivers through each agent.

"Sorry, folks. I should have warned everyone. It gets worse, if you can believe it. I've been looking at these for the past couple of hours. Getting used to it, I guess." Sanders stops talking, allowing the agents to take in what they are seeing.

Jenkins asks Banks, "Are these drawings or pictures?"

"Believe it or not, just drawings," replies Banks.

"Has anyone entered the container?" Lee asks, his eyes focused on just one image.

"No.".

"Have they verified—"

Banks interrupts Lee. "We have no physical evidence, just these images. The local sheriff made an impassioned plea for our help. The actual location of the site is flanked by federal land and with the limited resources the local sheriff has at his disposal, I authorized our deployment. Until we get boots on the ground, there's no telling what we will find in there. If this is what it appears to be, we need to be the first on the scene. I instructed the sheriff to have his men secure the site until we arrive."

"Where exactly in Montana is this?" asks Torres

Cherkoff adds, "This stuff always seems to happen in Montana, and how many…have all the people on this list seen this?" Cherkoff holds a copy of the list containing the names of the surveyors, federal agents entitled: *Families to be Notified.*

"The EPA agent was working the video equipment, and his monitor was in plain view of the others working at the site. The closest town to the site is Evergreen, with a population just over six thousand," says Sanders. Banks instructs Sanders to read a press release he prepared before they left Quantico.

Cherkoff shakes her head. "We'll be able to keep the wolves at bay?"

Banks says, "Enough to keep them occupied and allow us to profile this case."

Lee holds his tablet, still displaying the picturesque Montana scenery. He leans toward the video screen and states, "I've personally witnessed one of the darkest days our nation went through. I saw people on fire, jumping to their deaths. My partner died right before my eyes, but this—this is truly messed up!"

"This case is unlike any the bureau has ever had to deal with. More than ever, we must not let our emotions sway our focus. We have our procedures. Follow the procedures to the letter, and they will work. Even there," says Banks as the team focuses on the images. "When we land, Lee and Jenkins, I want you to interview the witnesses at the hospital. They're quarantined and Sanders, as usual, has worked his magic. The hospital staff are cooperating to help maintain the cover story. Keeping the witnesses away from their loved ones is unfortunate, but necessary. Torres and Cherkoff, process the crime scene. The mobile lab should be onsite when we land and at your disposal. We have an enormous amount of evidence to collect to develop this profile. This complex was discovered by chance, and without the surveyors working here, all this would still be hidden. Sanders will release another statement to the press shortly after our arrival."

U.S. Department of Justice
Federal Bureau of Investigation

CHAPTER FOURTEEN: Two More
Montana 1960

Oldson carries the last bag to the cart. His figure casts a faint shadow on the ground through the twilight air. He climbs into the tunnel and drags the cart and its contents underground. Oldson is dressed in jeans, a shirt, and boots. He piles the bags, stacking them just so, with the others he brought in earlier. Oldson turns and uses the cart to block the tunnel's entrance. At his desk, he sits and opens the long drawer, taking out a notepad. Placing it on the desk, he opens it and reviews his notes from two months prior.

Glancing back at the bags, he records the quantity of each item he has brought in. He opens another drawer to remove a sketch pad. He slowly draws a picture of the bags as they lay on the floor. In intricate detail, he takes the time to draw the subtle wrinkles in the bags, their labels, and even the loose ends of twine at each end. Reaching down, he lifts an unmarked burlap sack. He carries it to his workbench.

He puts this bag down and opens one end. The contents spill out, revealing several large rubber tubes, ten-mm needles, a trocar, and a large metal hand saw. He also removes four large metal bowls, a scoop, and several large spoons from the bag, which he places on the bench. The bowls, scoop, and spoons are all made from stainless steel. So clean, they brighten the room with their reflection of the light above. Oldson puts everything on the bench, in order, and in its proper place. Three bowls are in the shape of a triangle, the fourth just off to the right. Carefully sorting through some hoses, he places them according to diameter beside the bowls. Oldson inserts the saw in a long slot in the left edge of the bench.

With his work area organized, Oldson walks to a hatch in the floor. The lights in the ladder-way illuminate the steps down into a shaft. The vertical shaft is four-foot square and connects the two shipping containers. Several years prior, he had purchased and buried them, forever sealing the main exit of the old mine, entombing its contents, now buried deep under twenty feet of dirt and rocks. Located deep within a large plot of land, the mine had been abandoned for decades. Several shafts and vents are the only means of access now. The deepest shaft within the mine extends one thousand feet below the surface, carved through layers of rock and shale. Oldson discovered the blue gas and methane deposits several years ago. With some minor modifications, he converted a diesel generator to use the abundant supply of natural gas, powering enough electricity to run water pumps and a series of electric lights in the containers and throughout the mine.

Self-sufficient and well-stocked, the complex allows Oldson to work in this isolated location day or night.

He is eager to inspect the results of his last visit, just two months ago. He enters the second room. With a gentle flick of a switch, he turns on the light illuminating the area beyond the window. Pleased with what he sees, he inspects the surroundings. Gazing into the chamber, which was the main office and lobby of the top shaft area of the mine, a large colony of bats hang from the ceiling above. The light disturbs the bats, causing them to take flight. Their black wings reflect the light with a blue sheen.

The remnants of decaying mine equipment, old wooden storage boxes, and various other memories of the past daily activities of this mine, now lie motionless in the light. The office, shop, and workers' areas are now forever sealed behind the glass of the container. The view through his window frames a world frozen in time. It is illuminated by two floodlights. Mounted on either side of the window, the lights face into the mine, illuminating the darkness.

Oldson installed four long fluorescent fixtures on each side of the window to aid in his work. The air temperature inside the mine is a constant sixty-nine degrees Fahrenheit, and, coupled with a moderate humidity level, provides the ideal atmosphere for the fungi and mushrooms that grow in abundance. A wide variety of insects' scurry when the lights are turned on. The skeletal remains of a small animal lay close to an old wooden chair. The chair, tipped to one side, is slowly being consumed by fungi and rot. The rate of decay is accelerated within this environment, a pleasing byproduct of his hard work. In some cases, items only leave faint outlines of their existence after the insects and molds have had their way.

The tenacity of the fungi and molds, and their ability to survive, even thrive, amazes Oldson. In between his visits, the fluorescent lights had burned out, but the plants still grew with the limited light coming from the small vent holes that dot the mine's interior. With the bulbs replaced, he makes sure to record in his book the replacement date for the bulbs. "Can't have you in the dark like that," he muses to himself.

The creatures in his underground landscape come to life as the light shines. The warmth coming from the floodlights contrasts the cool blue light from the fluorescents. He can sense the anticipation, from the other side of the window, of all the creatures, big and small. "Play nice…be patient," he says to the window. Three rats, their eyes wide and their pupils tiny as the light catch their eyes for the first time in many days, cover something on the ground as they feast.

Throughout the mine, there are several sources of natural light. Pinhole streams of sunlight come from small cracks and fissures. Some holes are only as wide as a human hair but the light they produce contrasts against the darkness. They also serve as natural ventilation points. Oldson debated whether to install lights farther into the mine, eventually deciding against the idea. With the work area hermetically sealed, he keeps the threat of contamination to a minimum. He designed the housings that cover the floodlights. Two metal boxes, welded inside the container, house the flood lights. A panel, that is only removable from inside the container, allows only him, access to change the bulbs.

In his design, Oldson has ensured the complex allows for easy access and maintenance of all systems, without disturbing anything past the glass. Oldson holds one of his notepads, his attention drawn to the center of the area just beyond the glass. Marveling at the progress of his work, Oldson makes careful notes as he continues to monitor the mine.

***

Oldson climbs up both ladders and back to the surface. He walks to where his truck is parked on a ridge near the entrance to the tunnel into the container. He gets in his truck and drives a short distance. Stopping in front of a large rock, he edges the front bumper to it and, with the truck in low gear, pushes it, exposing a metal grate that covers a hole in the ground. He gets out of the truck, unlocks the grate, and lifts it out. The grate covers a vertical shaft lined with wood that empties into the mine. Oldson reaches into the truck's bed and opens one end of the large wooden crate.

He reaches into the box and drags out one burlap sack, followed by another. Placing the first sack onto a wooden panel, he lowers it into the mine. When the panel reaches the mine floor below, Oldson releases one end of the rope and, pulling on the other end, he retrieves both the rope and panel. With the sack safely on the mine's floor, he peers down the shaft. Several rats already eagerly sniff at the burlap, tugging and chewing at the fabric. "You are eager today!" he comments as he watches the activity below. After replacing the grate and lock, he moves the rock back to its place and returns to the entrance.

U.S. Department of Justice
Federal Bureau of Investigation

CHAPTER FIFTEEN: One, Two, and You Make Nine
1961

The most recent additions are located just less than twenty feet from the window. In short time, the rats have chewed a series of pear-sized holes in the sacks. Several pieces of dried potatoes spill out of the holes and a small pile of rice forms a pyramid beneath one hole. The mushroom spores that Oldson made sure were mixed into the sack are also now being tracked around by the rats. The precision and efficiency of the rats as they devour the contents of the sack is accelerated today by the welcome blast of light. Some of the burlap will be taken by the female rats for nesting material and, in the end, nothing will be left or wasted. Satisfied with what he has seen, Oldson returns to the first room. He moves several bags from the pile to his workbench.

He stacks six bags, two of each: dried potatoes, rice, and mixed seeds. He carefully mixes different quantities from each bag on the center of the workbench. Once the mixture is to his liking, he places the mixture in an empty sack. Repeating this procedure several times, he now has six bags piled near the exit of the container. Oldson records his work and documents every detail in his notebook.

He also takes the time to place two fresh chicken eggs into a carton. He counts quietly, "One, two, and, finally, you, make nine." The carton is carefully stored in a tight plastic box, which he keeps in the file cabinet. The bags are taken out of the container and placed in the back of the truck. Oldson turns all lights off in the containers as he exits, leaving only the fluorescents on to illuminate the mine. The hatch, which had been used as a cart, is now back in its place, securing the entrance.

Driving his truck back the short distance to the location of the shaft he used to lower the other sacks into the mine, Oldson delivers six more bags. Repeating the procedure, moving the large rock and grate, he drops the six bags into the mine through the shaft. They fall one after the other down the fifteen-foot drop through the shaft and the twelve feet to the ground below. With the bags disposed of, Oldson returns the rock to its proper place and after spending a few moments securing items in the bed of his truck, he drives away.

***

The mine floor is alive with activity as the rats climb over one another and race to inspect all the bags. The two bags lowered into the mine earlier are nearly empty, just large holes remain, torn in their sides. The remaining bits of the bags are being fought over by several rats. The final six bags that Oldson had just finished dropping into the mine are nearby. As the echoes of the heavy bags slamming into the mine's hard floor subside, more rats have scurried out from the tunnels and into the light. Their shadows cast in the light of what appears to be a giant tug-of-war as each rat fights for its share. Two figures in the distance cling to one and other. Their scent catches the attention of several brown rats, which quickly race to investigate.

A large group of rats focus on the figures. Slowly the rats, with their noses twitching and tasting the air, reach the tiny feet of a young boy and girl. The pair, clutching onto one another, are terrified as they feel the bristles and whiskers of several rats touch them. They cry and scream, "Mama, Mama." The high pitch of their screams echoes into the darkness of the mine, causing the rats to retreat, but only for a moment. As their cries for help go unanswered, the only sound that remains is that of the clawing and chewing made by the rats that have stood their ground.

Too young to completely understand what is going on, all the pair can do is instinctively hold onto each other in hopes that someone will answer their cries. Dressed in pants and a long sleeve shirt, the boy is three and a half years old. The girl, three years old, is wearing similar clothes. Both had been abducted by Oldson earlier that week. The girl was taken first and the boy a day later, from different cities. Their clothes intact, they have no visible marks or evidence of injury. For the time, the rats seem more interested in the contents of the bags that Oldson dropped before leaving.

The girl's eyes search for something familiar; her mother's face or a toy. All her tiny, tear-filled eyes can see is the darkness and the decaying history sprawled out in front of her. Her voice softens with each cry of "Mama…Mama…Mama." Her tiny hands tremble as she faces the little boy. They have managed to work their way free from the bags they were held in. As the rats bit into the burlap, the children escaped and ran from the bags to the office. The office, once alive with the daily business goings-on of a working mine, is now home to a different workforce. Located in the main lobby of the mine, the office houses the decaying remains of several old tables and chairs. They are slowly being consumed by the relentless onslaught of different species of fungi and mold. For the time, the children are alone, the rats being frightened off by their cries. The boy and girl manage to comfort one another. Their tears slowly subside, and their cries no longer interrupt the quiet interior of the mine.

U.S. Department of Justice
Federal Bureau of Investigation

CHAPTER SIXTEEN: Trails and Scars
November 1963

Terri hands the wineskin back to Oldson. He passes her a cigarette and offers to light it. She places a note for Josh on the windshield to inform him where she and Oldson have gone and for him to stay put until they return. Terri and Oldson walk toward the lake attempting to retrace Josh's trail. "Josh! Josh!" Oldson cups his hands around his mouth amplifying his calls. They chose the trail adjacent to the path Terri took when she went for her swim.

"What are those?" Terri points to impressions on the ground.

Kneeling down, Oldson inspects the rounded groove in the dirt. "Most likely a buck elk that was probably looking for his lady. Trails around here are all runs of some type, deer, elk, and moose." Terri looks back in the direction of the truck, wondering if she should have insisted on Oldson bringing his rifle. He replaced it in the truck when she panicked back at the camp. Oldson looks at Terri and, sensing the situation remarks, "Most things out here are way more afraid of you and me than we are of them. You see a bear, all you have to do is make a sharp, loud noise and they're off. But a bull Moose in rut—"

"Rut?" Terri asks.

"When the male is looking for a mate, they have one thing one their mind and nothing, I mean nothing, will stop them. It's hard not to hear them crashing through the woods, sixteen hundred pounds and eight feet to the top of their shoulders looking for a mate."

Terri shouts, "Josh can you hear me…Josh!" She hears no response. Standing beside Oldson, this man whom she has only known for less than forty-eight hours, she thinks, *Josh, where are you?*

"It doesn't look like he came through here, being barefoot and all." The cover of the trail opens into an overgrown area littered with vines and dense brush. They turn back to follow a trail that branches off in the direction of the lake.

"You two didn't have a fight?" Oldson asks, tones of concern in his voice. "Everything seemed so nice with both of you. Is he like this when…"

Terri stops Oldson midsentence and offers, "When he's in trouble? Oh yes, he'll run! Always does. We are runaways."

Oldson's eyes focus on a tiny tear forming in her eye.

"But living in a small town, there…there just aren't enough places to run. You can't go home. Knowing what's there, just waiting and you know it's there. You can hear it running through your mind as loud as those moose. Damn it, Josh, where are you!" Terri's voice echoes. She yells so loud she coughs as her voice cracks.

She stops, bending at the waist and wretches onto the ground. The remains of her last meal now lie at her feet. Terri motions with her other hand, and signals that she doesn't need Oldson's handkerchief. "I'm okay."

When they reach the lake, Oldson soaks his handkerchief in the water and passes it to Terri as she splashes her face, freshening up as best as she can. She looks out across the lake and watches four ducklings follow their mother, with her attention focused on one little duckling that is struggling to keep up with the rest.

While Terri is kneeling at the edge of the water, Oldson notices a small L-shaped scar on the back of her neck.

"Your scar, something you didn't run from?" Oldson kneels, drinking from the lake as Terri answers.

She rinses her mouth and covers her neck with her hair. "You've got very good eyes. Sometimes you choose not to run so someone else can."

Oldson nods and stands back up. With no sign of Josh on either trail or from what they can see at the lake, Oldson suggests they head back to the truck. "That's why I told you to leave the note. You go off looking for someone when they were just out walking, and when they come back and no one's there, now they think you're the one who's lost. He's probably just sitting back there waiting."

Terri tries to stand but loses her balance. Oldson reaches out and catches her before she falls. "Easy there, you okay?" he asks.

Terri nods. "I guess between the walking and just puking. I'll be okay." Oldson offers her a drink from the wineskin and they head in the direction of the campsite. Terri only gets a few yards up a hill before she feels nauseous again. Her knees buckle as she tries to steady herself. This time Oldson remains back a few feet and lets the scene unfold, not attempting to intervene.

"You sure you're okay? Terri? Terri? You're really not looking that good."

Terri collapses on the ground just in front of Oldson. "Terri? Terri!" Oldson bends down on one knee. He reaches to her neck, checking her pulse. Crumpled on the ground in a semi-fetal position, her body is cold and clammy to his touch. Her pulse is rapid as she pants, unable to catch her breath. With little time to spare, he rolls her over on to her back. Opening her eyes, he checks to ensure all is as it should be. He kneels at her side, placing his hand on her belly. He can feel the warmth of her skin through her clothes. Her panting and gasping start to subside. He pries open her left eyelid. Terri's pupils are wide and don't respond to the bright sunlight. Oldson takes out his handkerchief and wipes her mouth. He clears away a small amount of vomit and hoists her limp body over his shoulder and says, "You don't have to run anymore."

He feels her body resting on his shoulder, its weight, the firmness of her skin and the texture of her clothes. As he stands just over six feet tall and Terri weighs ninety pounds, Oldson negotiates the terrain without any trouble. Back at his truck, he places her on the tarp covering the crate. Inside the cab of his truck, he removes a small wooden case from the glove box. The truck rocks slightly as Oldson opens the case and removes a hypodermic needle and one of several ampules from inside the case. He draws a specific amount of liquid and injects Terri.

Oldson places her body in the front seat of the truck securing her with both sets of passenger's seat belts. Covering her with a blanket, she appears to be sleeping peacefully. One last check. Oldson clears the last of the items in the campsite. Oldson places both Josh and Terri's bags into the back of the truck. He removes one pair of Terri's panties from her bag, placing it in his pocket, before securing both bags under the tarp. As he starts to drive onto the dirt access road, he looks at his watch. "Five minutes to nine, right on time."

U.S. Department of Justice
Federal Bureau of Investigation

CHAPTER SEVENTEEN: Tombs
November 1963

From the corner of his eye, he glances at her silhouette. The way her bodies lies forces him to relive a moment from many years before. "You know, I watched someone die when I was just a few years younger than you. I can still remember looking down at him, his tiny body curled up, just like you are now. A small piece of metal sticking from his neck; how strange, something so small could have caused so much damage. I just stood there, surrounded by rubble and chaos, looking at my younger brother." Oldson mumbles to himself, "He was just looking for food." His grip on the steering wheel tenses, for just a moment.

Oldson drives from the dirt road onto the access road that connects to the highway. Turns on the radio and finds the clearest station. He lights a cigarette while Hank Williams Sr. sings "Lonely Tombs." He adjusts the rearview mirror to inspect the condition of his load. The straps holding down the tarp are tight and secure as the truck jostles over the ruts in the road. "You'll be there by nightfall." He takes a drag from his cigarette and nods at Terri. "You mustn't be scared. This is what must be done. When I saw his broken little body, all of their broken little bodies, it was only a matter of time. This will all be over, over very soon," Oldson continues, his voice just louder than the sound from the radio.

"I failed him, you know. Of course, you do, you have that scar, you understand. Yours, you carry on your neck, mine...mine I cannot cover with just my hair. Our names may identify us, but our actions define us. You must be calm. You will be calm. Just let this happen, for we cannot change what has already happened. Happened so many times and only we, only you, have the strength to endure. We are all capable of so much more. So much more than what we are, but not until we are given to the task can our destiny's story be told."

***

Very disoriented, Terri feels the vibration of the truck as it drives on the highway. *Where am I? What the hell is going on...Josh...Oldson...Josh!* Words race through her mind as she tries to make sense of everything. She attempts to move but can't. Lying on the bench seat facing the back of the truck, she can't see where they're going. Her body won't respond or do what she wants. All she can do is lie there and listen. She feels stoned, but this is very different. Dizzy and light-headed, but the smells of the truck, and his cigarettes, clear her confusion. Terri tries to yell. Nothing comes out. The sun's warmth radiates over her body. "You killed Josh!" she murmurs to herself. Followed quickly with, "I love you Josh."

Terri feels a strange disconnect between her body and her surroundings. Alone and paralyzed, all Terri can do is let this happen. Whatever *this* is. Her mind drifts in and out of consciousness as she tries to listen to what Oldson is saying. His voice is calm, so calm…it terrifies her. The last thing she remembers is the lake and feeling sick. *What day is this? Did we find Josh? Am I hurt?* Unable to answer these questions, she desperately tries to make sense of everything. In an attempt to calm herself, Terri starts to count the seconds that pass. Eventually replacing the seconds with the number of times the truck stops, or turns; *was that just left, or right?* Her fear turns to anger, then to frustration. She can only lay there.

"We are all chained to things both by choice and those that are put upon us. Even when we are doing just what we are supposed to be doing, fate will often step in. Some of those chains are much heavier than others, but you know that. How a moment in time, a fraction of a second, can dictate the course of a lifetime. On its own timetable, we cannot avoid it. Fate will arrive, armed with its most powerful allies. Chaos and confusion can terrify a person. You see, three people standing on a cliff, you light the ground on fire beneath their feet, all three may die, but each will take a very different path to reach it. Sometimes we can only stand there and watch as it unfolds." Oldson talks to Terri as he glances at the tarp covering the large box in the back of the truck.

U.S. Department of Justice
Federal Bureau of Investigation

CHAPTER EIGHTEEN: Cargo
November 1963

Josh has been unconscious for many hours. The smell of vomit and the aches in his neck and back are almost too much to bear. Both his hands and feet are hog-tied in a manner that if he moves, the rope around his neck tightens. With no soft seat beneath him, Josh feels every bump, twist, and turn on this road. The inside of the box is quite dark, and sounds are muffled by the heavy bags placed around the crate. Josh feels a slow transfer of air but sees nothing. Panicking but unable to move, a strange feeling comes over him. *Am I alone?* Josh thinks, as he can sense something. Something is not right someone or something is with him. He's not able to see what it is, but he has a feeling that grows with each second, that he is not alone. At first, it's just a tingle, then another. His pulse quickens as he listens and feels.

He desperately tries to listen for a clue, anything to tell him what it is. The truck shakes and rocks as it drives. Josh strains his neck in a desperate attempt to focus on a sound he believes is very close and perhaps even in the box. First faint scratching, then something panting, breathing, then more scratching...then Josh realizes...*rats!* In the darkness and barely conscious, he realizes he is not alone.

Beads of sweat pour down his face as Josh tries to focus on what is happening. His memory of Terri and Oldson, everything races from his mind as several rats claw and crawl all over him. *Terri!* Josh screams as his memory flashes. *Oh God! Terri, where are you? What the fuck? It's okay, this is a dream, it must be, it has to be. Just calm the fuck down, Josh, you're gonna wake up...it's alright, this is just a dream.* Josh can only hear the pounding of his own heart and feel the burn in his leg as several rats have returned. Their teeth pierce his flesh and tear at his clothes, and he feels the warmth of his own blood as it flows over his skin. Josh tries to shake them off, only to end up tightening his bindings. He must lay still; he must endure.

Josh can feel their tiny feet, whiskers, and even their teeth as they chew into his clothes. How many are there in the box? There's no way to tell. As one crawls over his arms, he shakes his body, throwing the rat off. *Stupid! Stupid...couldn't just leave it alone!* He desperately wishes he hadn't figured out what was going on. He rolls to his left until his body crams to one side of the crate. Not able to turn around, he rolls the other way to find the other side. Trying to get his bearings, while at the same time moving slowly enough as not to tighten his bindings, his body bumps into what feels like a sack. The sack moved just a bit as he hit it. Josh listens—more panting and a very faint sound. A barely audible human voice is coming from the sack. A little boy's voice cries for his mother. His tiny voice scratches and crackles in the darkness.

Josh can offer no other comfort to the boy. He can only say, "You're not alone…it's going to be okay. I'm Josh." As he tries to speak, he feels the gag in his mouth. His voice is muffled, and he can only wonder if the boy hears his voice. His focus now on the boy, he positions his body in a manner to protect the boy from the rats. The rats are, for the time, occupied with something else in the box. This allows Josh time to consider the depth of what has happened. *Who is this boy? What the hell is going on?*

U.S. Department of Justice
Federal Bureau of Investigation

CHAPTER NINETEEN: Hunger and Chaos
November 1963

The truck bumps and jostles as Oldson turns off the highway and onto the access road. Terri is still secured tight to the seat. Her body bounces and lifts slightly off the seat as the truck drives over the rough ground. The warmth of the sun no longer hits her face. Now she can feel the warmth on her back. *What direction? What time of day?*

"Hunger is a truly chaotic state. As a child, when you watch a group of men fight over rotten crumbs and a moldy slice of bread, you realize this. Watching a pack of rats devour an empty cereal box, knowing that there are no grains left inside, but still, they fight for the cardboard. They waste nothing. There are stories from the ancient west, how the Comanche and Apache would break a wild horse. They would withhold water for three days, only offering a small amount on the fourth day. When they finally offered water to the horses, the horses would be theirs. The secret is in understanding the weakness and where the weakness comes from. Until we accept the power of it, the strength and the force of that most primal need will forever remain frozen. Behind, chained, and captive to its every whim until we accept the power it has."

Oldson continues to talk to the barely conscious Terri. He glances occasionally in her direction. Her body moves with the motion of the truck. Is the sedation wearing off? Oldson knows that with each passing mile, their time together is limited. "Is it our environment, our surroundings, that make us who we are and what we do? What we will do? What we must do! 'Work will set you free,' was written on a sign placed for all to see. I always wondered if that philosophy worked for him. My people were herded like cattle, one by one. We were told to identify ourselves. We must wear an arm band with a yellow star. Many followed orders, others chose not to. Either way, the test would always unfold. They would all die; it was just a matter of how. My brother was just four when he died. It was, he was, my responsibility. '*Holde ham sikkert, skjul indtil mørke.* Keep him safe, hide until dark.' Every morning my mother would say these words to me.

"The day it happened we were both hungry. We were hungry every day but that day it was different. The weather had been foul, and we remained inside for two days. We would wait until late in the day to go out. That day, he could wait no longer and, for just a moment he was out of my sight…just a moment. I could not yell his name; I could only look for him. Yelling his name would have meant announcing who we were and that we were there. So, I walked a few meters and came around the corner of a tall building.

He was lying there on a pile of rubble. At first, I thought he was looking for something... walked to him, I bent down, then I noticed his neck and that piece of metal. Having someone taken away...I was to keep him safe. I wish we had more time to talk. This will be the last time we will ever speak. I will miss the sound of your voice..." Oldson looks down at Terri, "...but what has begun we must now finish."

Oldson steers his truck off the access road and turns onto a dirt laneway, which leads to a gate well off the access road. The path is no more than a dirt road blazed into the woods. Oldson opens the gate and returns to his truck carrying a small section of fence. The section of fence that was clipped to the gate now rests in the truck's bed. Oldson gets back into the truck and continues to drive farther into the woods. The four-wheel-drive truck negotiates the very rugged terrain.

U.S. Department of Justice
Federal Bureau of Investigation

CHAPTER TWENTY: Josh
November 1963

Josh and the little boy feel every rut and bump as they are tossed around inside the crate. They bounce and roll around inside the crate as Oldson continues down the laneway.

After the truck climbs up a final steep incline, it levels out and stops a few moments later. Josh feels the driver's door open and close. Then there is a brief silence, followed by the sound coming from the passenger's door as it opens. The truck lifts slightly with the weight transfer as something is lifted out. Trapped in the crate, Josh strains to hear anything, a voice, cries…Terri…Oldson, anything! All he hears is the sobs from the little boy huddled in the bag beside him. The truck remains still, and the only sound Josh hears is the little boy's whimpers. The silence is shattered by the sound of a single shot from a rifle splitting the air.

"What the fuck…fuck! Terri! Terri!" His voice is silent, but his thoughts scream. A few moments later, he feels the latch of the tailgate open, then a bump as it is lowered on to the stops. The truck lifts again slightly—*the bags, he's coming for me, just one hand, if I*

could, just one hand…if I get it free, I can take him! Josh struggles with his bindings as the truck lifts, again, again, and again.

Each time the truck lifts Josh hears more and more. Sounds grow louder as the bags are removed exposing the wooden crate. Josh tries to free his hands. *Do it slowly this time…if I can just…almost…fuck!* His fingers stretch as far as they can, searching for a way to untie the knot. As his fingers reach the knot, he feels the rope pull on his neck even tighter, the stress and strain around his body nearly unbearable as his muscles begin to cramp.

Josh hears footsteps return to the truck. *What was that?* Josh thinks as he hears something being placed on the bed of the truck. The smell of cigarettes wafts through the air. *Oldson.* A tiny crack of sunlight pierces into the crate turning into a blinding light as Oldson unlatches a portion of the top of the crate and removes it. Paralyzed by the pain from the light and his bindings, Josh lies helpless as he feels Oldson reach into the box. The sack containing the little boy is plucked up and out of the box. As he feels the sack lift, Josh tries in vain to keep the little boy safe, crunching his midsection around the sack as it is pulled up into the air. The box is closed as quickly as it opened, latched and dark once again. There are screams in the distance, then they fade away.

One single rifle shot, then silence. Alone in the crate, Josh huddles in the darkness. Even the constant scurry of the rats has vanished. *Where are they? What did you do? You bastard! Terri and…he was just a kid. What are you doing, you coward? He was so little.* Josh can only wonder what has just happened. Safe for the moment, alone in the box, *am I next?* Josh talks to himself, trying to calm down.

***

The truck remains motionless for hours. *Or is it days?* Josh thinks. He has heard no sound, felt nothing, just the aches in his gut. It's easier to count where it doesn't hurt. His body shakes as the chills of shock worsen. Eventually, Josh is rendered unconscious one more time.

U.S. Department of Justice
Federal Bureau of Investigation

CHAPTER TWENTY-ONE: Enjoy the Ride
November 1963

The sound of the driver's door slamming shut and the engine starting wakes Josh. There's something different about the ride this time. Josh concentrates, best he can, and realizes that something is being dragged behind. The vibration from a roll of fence shakes through the truck's frame. Oldson has tied a roll of fence wire and is pulling it behind the truck as he drives, covering any marks left behind. Once at the road, Oldson removes the fence and clips it back in its place at the gate. With the constant noise of the road under him, Josh lies in the darkness. The rats have gone. The boy is gone. He realizes he is alone and can only try to think about Terri and what he had heard.

As the memories of the campsite and their tent start to fade from his mind, he desperately clings to the image of her face. *California.* We were going to meet her friends. *California…California,* he repeats to himself. The temperature in the box has become cold, or is it him? Josh has no idea how long he has been trapped; he only has the aches and pains in his body to remind him of how long this ordeal has been. Unable to control it any longer, Josh soils himself. Oldson drives through the night.

Their trip ends outside Boise, near an industrial park. Oldson parks in a familiar location and removes the tarp, just enough to expose the one end of the crate. After he opens the crate and grabs Josh by the hair, he drags him out.

With Josh's head and neck exposed, Oldson administers an injection into the skin of Josh's neck. The injection immediately sedates Josh. Oldson lifts his body and carries him to an empty boxcar. Gently, Oldson places Josh onto the boxcar's floor. Then he hops into the boxcar and drags Josh to one corner, placing the pair of Terri's panties that he had taken off her into Josh's pocket. He then returns to his truck, retrieves a burlap sack from the back, and returns to Josh.

He reaches into the sack and removes a large rubber hose and a one-gallon metal jug. The jug is only half full and Oldson attaches the hose to the spout. He takes the loose end of the hose and forces it into Josh's mouth and down his throat. Lifting the jug, he pours the contents of the jug into Josh. The water in the jug gurgles through the hose, making Josh's belly swell. Oldson removes the hose and places his tools back in their bag. He leaves Josh there, closing the railcar's door, and returns to his truck. With no idea when or to where this boxcar will be going, Oldson drives away, leaving Josh behind. "Enjoy the ride," he says dryly as he glances back at the boxcar.

U.S. Department of Justice
Federal Bureau of Investigation

CHAPTER TWENTY-TWO:
Boots on the Ground
Present Day

"Oro y plata. Who would have thought?" Lee comments as he looks out the passenger's window. Agent Jenkins drives the SUV to the Community Medical Center in Missoula.

Jenkins raises an eyebrow and looks at Lee. "Excuse me?"

"Oro y plata, gold and silver, is the state motto of Montana." Lee reads. "Sanders sent an update. Some historical data related to this area. All the dangers the miners faced back in the day, and now you look at the images down there. Who would have thought?"

"What was the name of the EPA agent on the scene?" Jenkins asks Lee.

"Ron Anderson, forty-six. It says here he has lived in Kalispell most of his life. He graduated from the University of Montana, Missoula. He has a wife and two children. Oh, he also is a reserve in the marines, based out of Billings. You should probably handle the interview."

"That works for me. We should arrange to take his statement first. It will help with the cover story,"

Jenkins says. "You know, no one would be prepared to witness what they did. Was Anderson ever deployed as a reserve? With his age, he might have been deployed to Kuwait, could help him deal with what they saw."

***

From their vantage point, the evening news crew for KPAX Missoula focuses their attention in the direction of the crime scene. "Ashley, check this out, that thing he's carrying is a cutting torch."

"You're filming this right?" she says.

"Two more just came out from the trailer wearing hazmat suits. Looks like they're the poor bastards that get to go into that thing. Whoa, look at this." Her cameraman turns his monitor, so she can see and focuses the camera on agent Banks. "That guy is pissed. He was talking on his cell, standing right with the sheriff and that guy in the hazmat suit, then turns right away. He really isn't happy about something."

Banks has been talking with the associate deputy director back in Quantico for the past twenty minutes. "It was my decision to make and it had to be done. I am aware of the risks but under the circumstances, this is the right course of action. Agents Cherkoff and Torres are entering the container as we speak. I have to get back to my team." Quickly pressing the end-call button, Banks walks back to the sheriff. "My team and I need to meet with your deputies as soon as everyone is present. Sheriff, your men will play an integral part in assisting my team search the areas around this site."

The sheriff expresses his gratitude. "Agent Banks, I cannot thank you enough. This whole situation is so far out of our league. My town, well, they are all damn good people. People you would be proud to call your friends. There are no Dahmers or Bundys in our phone book."

"Sheriff, this case will even tax the resources the bureau has at its disposal. I will make every effort and take whatever measures I deem necessary to ensure your community does not also become this unsub's victim." The tone of Banks' voice changes as both he and the sheriff look in the direction of the media.

"Thank you." The sheriff shakes Banks' hand and heads out. As the sheriff's car leaves the site, a black SUV drives in the direction of the command post.

U.S. Department of Justice
Federal Bureau of Investigation

CHAPTER TWENTY-THREE:
Witness Interview: Ron Anderson
Present Day

Arriving at the Community Medical Center in Missoula, Jenkins and Lee are greeted by Ewa Wolf, the hospital's director of admissions. "Agents Jenkins and Lee, your Mr. Sanders told me to expect you," the director says. They shake hands with the director, introducing themselves as they walk the corridors of the hospital.

Wolf escorts the agents to a secured section of the hospital. "We have placed the men in this wing. It's isolated from the rest of the hospital. They remain under quarantine as per the instructions our staff received. They all appear to be in very good health, under the circumstances. Mr. Sanders mentioned there was an accident at some old dump site?"

"Thank you very much. Yes, unfortunately, there was a spill, and until we understand what we are dealing with…you can understand our concerns," Jenkins says. "Can you please take us to Mr. Anderson's room first?"

***

Both agents stand beside Anderson's hospital bed. An IV in his right arm treats him for shock. Several lines that run from his chest are attached to electrocardiogram monitors. The monitor displays his current heart rate as well as other vital stats.

"Mr. Anderson, I am Special Agent Jenkins, and this is Agent Lee. We are both with the BAU. I understand that you were operating the video equipment when the site was discovered. Just take your time and please walk us through what happened, and what you saw."

"My office was called out to the site. Hell, you know that already or you wouldn't be here. Sorry, I'm just really, did we really see that shit?"

Jenkins notices his heart rate increase and changes the subject. "Your file says that you're a reserve?"

"Was, I got deployed in the nineties. I saw some pretty heavy shit over there but nothing like what I saw here. We all saw it. That George guy, I think he puked for twenty minutes straight. When we got the top of the damn thing exposed…"

"The container?" Jenkins inquires.

"Yes, our procedures are very clear when we're dealing with an unknown substance contained within a closed vessel. So, I set up my video gear. I asked the forestry service rep to help me with the air monitoring equipment, so I could start drilling into the damn thing. I was worried we were going to hit a pocket of methane or some other flammable gas. I told Clive, I think that was his name, 'Watch that gauge!' Once the drill bit started to bite through the metal, just one spark and well…we wouldn't be talking right now. So, I got the hole done and I fed through the snake."

"Sorry, did you say the snake?" Jenkins asks.

"Yes, the video camera is attached to a hundred-fifty-foot cable that I can control. I can feed the snake in just like a plumber would do inspecting pipes. I have a joystick that allows me to point the camera in any direction. On the camera head there are several sensors that send back air quality data and LED lights to illuminate the area. The camera's in, no alarms went off, so I turned on the monitor. So, what I had on my monitor was a top-down view of an old desk, the bench, file cabinets, hoses, tools and…those drawings."

"Where were the drawings?" Jenkins asks.

"When I started to swivel the camera head, we could see there were items pinned to the walls. I had Clive feed more of the snake into the container, so the head was probably midway into the thing. There they all were. At first, I thought they were photographs."

Ron composes himself, taking a deep breath. "The detail, it all just seemed to jump off those walls. Right in your face. I don't even remember how many there were. I turned the camera just a bit more. What kind of animal does that? That's when George collapsed, and all hell broke loose. After that, it's pretty much a blur."

Lee motions to Jenkins to look at the monitor. Ron's heart rate flashes 112. Concerned for his welfare, Jenkins says, "Please, just try to relax. At that point, the call was placed to the sheriff's office?"

Ron takes a sip from a cup of water. "Yes, no visible EPA issues, that's for sure. Tell me, you being FBI agents, shit like this, you've seen it before? This is a small town. Small even for Montana. Who could have done something like this? You don't even see this shit in the movies."

Jenkins pauses for several moments as she plans her answer. Her reaction when she saw the images from this crime scene still very fresh in her mind. "This is a very unusual case and no I have, *we* have not seen anything like this before. Our job is to develop a profile, with your help and the other witnesses. What you saw, and the evidence we discover, will allow us to find whoever is responsible for this. For an unsub—"

"Unsub?" Ron interrupts Jenkins.

"Unknown subject," replies Jenkins. "For this unsub to go unnoticed for this length of time, the chances of his being local are extremely low. This location served as his dumping ground."

Ron is relieved by the agent's opinion that his glimpse into the world of a sociopath isn't the norm and he can go back to his daily life without fearing that anyone he knows could be capable of committing something like what he has seen. "Mr. Anderson, thank you again for your time."

U.S. Department of Justice
Federal Bureau of Investigation

CHAPTER TWENTY-FOUR:
Ashley Blair Reporting
Present Day

Ashley and her cameraman have been watching the events unfold both in the media area as well as the closed-off crime scene. The technicians who delivered the mobile media center have finished hooking up the generator and bringing the center online. The techs explain to the members of the media that the center is there to provide power and communications. The center is also equipped with washrooms, a galley, and other conveniences. While a tech is talking to the reporters, the familiar sound of incoming text messages buzzes in the air.

Ashley and her cameraman have moved just outside the media trailer and are waiting for her cue. From her earpiece, Ashley hears KPAX Channel Eight news anchor Matt Clark's voice. "Now in other news, our very own Ashley Blair has been following a very disturbing story, developing outside Evergreen. Ashley, what's happening up there?"

"Thank you, Matt. I have been here since this story broke. What I know so far is that workers uncovered what officials are calling an illegal dump operation that used this location. I haven't been told what exactly is behind those barricades and as you can see, everywhere you look there is another person wearing a hazmat suit. It's quite the sight. Within the past few hours, several large tractor trailers have arrived, delivering into the secured site as well as providing a media center over there." The camera pans to show the FBI media center.

"Earlier this afternoon, I tried to get a comment from Sheriff Wilson, but I was told all comments are being handled through the FBI at the request of his department and there is a press conference scheduled here at the media center early tomorrow."

"Ashley, can you tell us anything about the men who uncovered this site? Do we know where they were taken?"

"All of the workers were taken to Community Medical Center in Missoula and are being held for observation. One of the workers was overcome and had to be airlifted with non-life-threatening injuries and, from what I understand, he is expected to make a full recovery. There has been a lot of activity here at the site since our arrival. Over the past several hours, workers have erected a large white tent over the opening of what was the excavation site. Two workers wearing white hazmat suits entered this area approximately forty minutes ago. Just prior to their going in, another worker was seen entering with what appeared to be metal cutting torches." As Ashley reports, the station displays pictures of oxyacetylene torches.

"Some very fascinating things happening there, indeed. Thanks again to Ashley Blair, reporting live just outside Evergreen."

The station breaks to a commercial.

U.S. Department of Justice
Federal Bureau of Investigation

CHAPTER TWENTY-FIVE: Carlo Di Pastori
Present Day

"Who's next on the list?" Jenkins asks Lee.

"We have George Marshall, the surveyor who had the mild heart attack, and his associate, Carlo Di Pastori."

Jenkins scrolls over her tablet bringing up the background information on the company the men work for and the file regarding the survey site. "It says here their firm was contracted to survey an area of approximately fifty-two hundred square miles."

"That's almost five times the size of Rhode Island!" Lee exclaims.

"Sanders also provided us with the dates and data from their firm, showing the grids that they have already covered." Jenkins continues to review notes on her tablet as the agents walk to Carlo's room, located at the end of the hallway. After brief introductions, Lee and Jenkins begin their interview. Considering the area where they were working, the surveyors may have had the best opportunity to notice something, anything out of the ordinary, during their work.

"We are sorry to hear about what happened to Mr. Marshall. Have you had a chance to speak with him?" Jenkins asks Carlo.

"Only for a moment as he was being wheeled in. He was pretty shaken up. His face was a mess. Lots of blood, when he collapsed. He must have hit his head on the track of the excavator. He got a pretty bad gash. I think the doctor said he was going to need some stiches," Carlos says in his deep Brooklyn accent. Standing at six feet four and weighing just shy of three hundred pounds, Carlo fills his hospital bed.

"We understand that you, with the other witnesses, saw the images in the container," Lee says. "You and Mr. Marshall have been working out there for what, six months?" Carlo nods. "We are very interested in not just what you saw at this site, but if you can recall anything out of the ordinary that you might have noticed during travel to and from the various areas. Anything that you might have seen that struck you as odd, out of place, no matter how insignificant it might seem."

"This is the largest survey I've ever worked on. The area may seem vast but geologically, it's a scale thing. The bosses want this whole thing done in ten months. After our first week, well, shit, we told them they were freakin crazy. So, the geo team back in Kalispell started to focus us in certain areas to best utilize our time. Each week we would get an updated dispatch from the field office."

"The roads in and out of your work areas, is there a lot of traffic, any vehicles, people you recall seeing?

Anything out of the ordinary, a person or a vehicle perhaps, no matter how insignificant it might seem?" Jenkins inquires.

"Seeing people? Have you seen the site?" Carlo comments as he tries not to laugh. "We're working in the goddamn bush! It takes us a couple of hours just to get to the edge of nowhere. As for traffic, sure, Department of Fish and Game trucks, hydro and forestry crews mostly. Lots of campers. It's a regular sportsman's paradise out there! Our dispatch wants us to cover thirty square miles per day, out there." As he glances out the window in his room, he directs the agent's attention to the scenery. He shakes his head a bit and says, "Some days, we're lucky to get five square miles covered."

"What happens then? How does your dispatch deal with that?" Lee asks as he looks out the window.

"They get pissed off, you know. They're working off freakin satellite maps, sure it has all the topography. They don't see all these freakin' trees, brush high as your fucking head! Not to mention all these creeks and rocks. You get the picture? So, you know, it is what it is. We do our daily uploads. They get to see what we've done and then they choose whether to modify our dispatch or tell us to *hurry the fuck up, get it done, do what you can!* It's all big out here. The land and the problems, when things break down, you just aren't around the corner from the local garage."

"So, you have to be pretty self-reliant out there?" Jenkins asks.

"Yeah, I don't think Triple A comes out this far. Don't get me wrong, it's beautiful out there but we just want to get our job done and get the hell home. Enough of this Daniel Boone shit." Carlo raises his hand to his forehead as he looks at Jenkins and Lee.

"I can imagine there aren't many decent pizza joints around here," Lee says.

"Absolutely! I haven't had a decent espresso in…I can't freakin remember! I know George is getting a little wound up too, probably part of the reason he collapsed. If we just keep hammering it, we'll be done. We'll be the fuck out of here and back home. That's what I say. Past couple of months, finally dispatch has been getting the picture, if you know what I mean?" Carlo tips his head slightly to one side as he looks at Lee. "For a while, we were being sent all the fuck over the place. Go here, then way the fuck over there. Back and forth, but all of a sudden, they started to keep us in one main area for a week, then move on."

"Why the sudden change?" Lee asks.

Shaking his head, Carlo leans back in his bed raises both arms in the air and replies, "The client. The developer said we might be on to something. Who knew?"

"You take care and thank you very much for your time. I'll see what I can do about hooking you up with a Starbucks." Lee shakes hands with Carlo.

As the agents are leaving Carlo's room, an alarm sounds over the PA system calling, "Code blue isolation two-twelve, code blue isolation two-twelve," the alarm repeats as several nurses rush past the door to Carlo's room.

"Nurse, what's going on?" Jenkins says to one of the staff members.

"Room two-twelve is coding," the nurse answers Jenkins.

"What patient is that? Nurse!" She tries to get in one last question as the nurse heads out of view. All she and Lee can do is follow quickly down the hall.

U.S. Department of Justice
Federal Bureau of Investigation

CHAPTER TWENTY-SIX: Command Post
Present Day

A command post has been set up at the crime scene. The area surrounding the excavation site has taken on the appearance of a military installation with the arrival of numerous government vehicles, sheriff's cars, and dark SUV's. The most recent arrivals are several large white trailers decaled with the FBI seal and logo on their sides. Along with the sheriff, fellow witness excavator operator, Mitch Hollister, has remained on the site. The sheriff enlisted Mitch to help set up a decent access road into the site, preparing for the onslaught of support vehicles needed to manage this complex crime scene.

"The more we bring in here, the more they want to know," Sheriff Wilson says to Banks. "One of my deputies just told me that two more news vans just pulled up. I told him to corral them with the others, as you directed."

"Good, thank you. Our field office from Salt Lake informed me that our media center should be arriving soon. The agents assigned to it should have it set up and be operational shortly after it arrives." Banks told the sheriff to have his men organize an area off the perimeter of the crime scene for the media to gather. The location, roughly half a mile from the site, offers an unobstructed view of the crime scene while at the same time keeping the media out of their way. Under Banks' directions, this is the only access to the site the media will have.

"When do you expect your team will be entering into the container?" the sheriff asks Banks.

"Our engineers will inspect the stability of the container as soon as they give us clearance to enter. Soon, hopefully. Agents Cherkoff and Torres are standing by and ready to go."

Cherkoff and Torres have been inspecting the exposed sections of the container, recording whatever information they can. Faded numbers are just visible on the corners of the container. Everything they collect is immediately sent to Quantico. Torres says, "Sanders, along with those numbers, the top of the container measures eight feet across by thirty-five feet long, and the techs fed the camera snake eight feet in when it touched the bottom."

"That's a very old container," Sanders says. "They were replaced in the late sixties when international standards changed. I'll try to run the numbers but, unfortunately, there was no standard format for coding and identifying back when that size was used. I'm forwarding this e-mail, complete with the specs and a few pictures. You guys be careful, please."

"You're telling me this thing could be fifty years old?" Torres says.

"At least forty," Sanders says. "They were built to withstand the rigors of ocean travel. Corrosion-resistant coatings inside and out were applied to most containers then and now."

Understanding that they don't build things like they used to, and judging by the exterior of the container, both Torres and Sanders agree that the container could have been buried for at least twenty years. "But until you get into the damn thing, we're all just guessing." Sanders wishes them well, forwards the pair a series of files containing historical data pertaining to the property, and hangs up.

Torres scrolls through his tablet examining the various lease agreements and property deeds for this parcel of land.

Agent Banks walks to where Cherkoff and Torres are setup; he walks in as Torres reviews the property's title history. "From these records, it looks like no one owns this land right now. The last owner, Lyle T. Harding, died two years ago. He was from Illinois and owned this five-hundred-acre parcel for the past fifteen years. Looks like he died without a will and no one has come forward to challenge the state's claim on the land."

"The engineers have signed off on the container's structural integrity. They're torching an access hole into the top right now. You two get suited up. I want you to be ready to go inside as soon as they have the access set up. Jenkins and Lee should be on their way back and I want to go over what we have when they get here. When you're in there, be careful, and keep in contact with the surface."

U.S. Department of Justice
Federal Bureau of Investigation

CHAPTER TWENTY-SEVEN: George Marshall
Present Day

A surgeon comes into the hallway where Jenkins and Lee have been eagerly awaiting any update on George's condition. His scrubs are wet with sweat and he uses a cloth to wipe his brow as he says, "It was close. He suffered another cardiac episode. We changed some of his meds. For now, we have him sedated. He's resting."

"He's going to make it?" Jenkins asks.

Massaging the back of his neck with his right hand the doctor winces slightly. "Time will tell. Unfortunately, Mr. Marshall is a very sick man. He has several blocked arteries and he needs surgery. However, in his current condition he wouldn't survive. Until he is stronger, we can only wait. I understand that you need to speak with him. Right now, that is not possible."

"Of course, please keep us updated and, if there's any chance, we really need to speak with him as soon as possible. Thank you," says Jenkins, then sends a text to Banks with an update.

***

Looking at his tablet, Banks reads the text from Jenkins, and types, *finish as fast as you can we need you both here asap.* Earlier, Sanders sent him a detailed set of historical drawings of the mine. The site was actually two separate mines for many years until a massive explosion and resulting cave-ins forced the owners to abandon their claim. The property was sold off in the late forties and all mining operations subsequently ceased. The drawings show a labyrinth of shafts and tunnels that meander everywhere. *A confined space, with only one viable exit, wonderful,* Banks thinks to himself. The agents who enter the container will have to wear breathing apparatus and a safety tether, just in case.

The most recent news from Sanders back in Quantico isn't good. Speaking with Banks, Sanders explains his findings, "Sir, there just aren't enough numbers and there was no, I mean *no*, standard format back when that size of container was used. I did manage to figure out where the thing was made using the partial serial number. It was manufactured and owned by a Norwegian shipping company and sold off as surplus. That company still exists, and from what they can tell me, those units became obsolete and were cycled out as scrap or sold."

Banks listens to what Sanders says, scrolling over the images and files on his tablet. "When we get inside, we'll finally have a better picture of how old this site is, and how recent the visits have been. I sent you the latest release for the press. They'll want to see this."

U.S. Department of Justice
Federal Bureau of Investigation

CHAPTER TWENTY-EIGHT: Clive Hemming
Present Day

"The forestry ranger, Deputy Clive Hemming. Looking over his application, he lists hunting, fishing, and orienteering as his hobbies. He was in the Boy Scouts too." Lee reviews the information Sanders has provided.

"He's lived here all of his life?" Jenkins asks Lee.

Nodding, Lee comments as he shows Jenkins Clive's current ID. "Yes, he's so young, even this picture."

"I know, he has such a baby face. I can only imagine what his reaction was. Living here all his life, then witnessing what he and the others saw." Jenkins opens the door to Clive's room and they both walk in. At his bedside, they shake Clive's hand as they introduce themselves. "How are you doing?" Jenkins voice is soft as she asks Clive.

"I'm fine, I guess. The doctors here haven't told me a damn thing or said very much except I'm here for observations. I feel fine! I don't understand what's going on. They took all our stuff. My iPhone, everything!"

"Have you had a chance to speak with your parents?" Jenkins asks Clive, although she already knows what the answer will be.

"No. One nurse, one doctor, and that's been it. Like, don't I get one phone call?" Clive smirks at the agents.

Lee chuckles and sarcastically replies, "You would have to be arrested for that to happen, not a witness. I'll see what I can do about getting in touch with your family. Is there a girlfriend we can let know you're alright as well?"

"Yes, Sandi. That would be great, thanks. How is that surveyor, George? Is he going to be okay?"

"We haven't spoken with him yet, but his partner said he should be fine, banged up a bit and had to get a few stiches. He should be fine." Keeping the conversation as low key as he can, Lee continues the interview. "Your file says you've lived in Evergreen all your life? You must know pretty much—"

"Everyone in town? You bet."

"Tell us about your hometown," Lee says, looking at Evergreen through the hospital window. "I grew up in Brooklyn and, man, what I would have given to have had a backyard like this. We hardly knew our next-door neighbor's name. I bet you know every inch of those woods out there."

"Damn straight! Whenever you aren't working you go hit the trails," replies Clive.

"Working for the Forestry Service must also give you an excellent chance to locate some new hot spots?" Lee brings up an image of the Evergreen area on his tablet as he asks the question.

"For sure. I do patrols mainly, campsite checks making sure nothing is wrong. I also work with the maintenance crews on the fire roads." Clive's voice gets quiet as he speaks, "Can I ask you a question? That stuff, those drawings we saw, it was all a torture chamber or something? At first, it just looked like a bomb shelter. There are a lot of survivalists living out here. We have some real *believers*, end-of-the-world types, but when that camera focused on those drawings, especially the little boy, who would do that? Especially on the monitor, it all looked so real."

"I can't comment on what happened inside there but as our investigation unfolds, the details, any detail that you can remember, and especially what it's like to live around here, will help us build our profile. This unsub has come and go over a very long period of time, undetected." Clive's eyes widen as Lee continues, "Your knowledge of the geography will help us understand how our unsub managed to pull this off for so long." A look of pride comes over Clive's face as he listens to Lee's comments. "Are there any roads or trails into that property that aren't listed that you might know of?"

"Just the old fire road. There are some fairly big animal runs that crisscross that whole area. Those would be too rough for even my truck. The fire road doesn't even get winter service."

"It's not plowed at all?" Lee asks.

"The gates at the entrance to the fire road get chained up November first and we don't open them up again until spring." Clive points to the image of the map on Lee's tablet.

"The chain is it locked?" Jenkins asks.

"No, just dummied. We just wrap it around itself, so it looks like it's locked. That's not a problem is it?" Clive asks, somewhat concerned. Lee just looks at Jenkins.

Lee and Jenkins leave their cards with Clive and head to a room normally used by doctors meeting with family members.

U.S. Department of Justice
Federal Bureau of Investigation

CHAPTER TWENTY-NINE:
Familiar and Comfortable
Present Day

Their interviews so far have taken just over four hours. "How do you manage to slip in and out of this area, for what, forty years? And unnoticed?" Jenkins asks as she shakes her head in disbelief.

Lee says, "You don't, especially if you only have access to the site for what, six months of the year?" Jenkins nods in agreement as Lee continues, "Look at this place: there's his only way in or out. Once he gets them in there, there's nothing, no one for dozens of miles."

"Just him and them," replies Jenkins as she looks at the images from the crime scene on her tablet.

Lee traces his finger over his tablet and says, "Most abductors kill their victims within the first twenty-four hours, yet he manages to get them here—"

"Yes, okay, so let's assume his victims are still alive when he brings them here. To pull this off, what do I have to worry about, what do I need? What would make me stand out?" Jenkins says.

"He's mobile, probably a large RV of some type."

"You're going to need supplies, gas," Jenkins says.

Jenkins and Lee study the satellite photos and the crime scene photos Sanders sent them. Glancing through the images, Lee holds his tablet up for Jenkins to see what he's looking at. "Look at this, the images from inside the container. Check this out. There's the workbench. Everything has a spot, the bowls, those tubes and this, these slots. They look like knives or something sharp enough to make those marks was placed there, maybe? Okay, what, I've seen that look before, what's on your mind?" Lee asks Jenkins.

"When we catch this guy, you know just as well as I do, these people have seen him, he's come and gone at will, just another guy in a camper. How are they going to…" Jenkins grits her teeth, "This town, they all know, like the kid said, *everyone*. This place will never be the same."

U.S. Department of Justice
Federal Bureau of Investigation

CHAPTER THIRTY: Opportunity
1962

With his meeting over, Oldson gets into his truck and starts to drive out of town. He makes sure not to miss any of the sights in each town. Each town is the same, every time. The steeples of the churches, towering icons that can be seen long before the town comes into view. The town hall and the town square attempt to compete with the churches as meeting places. The larger cities have more of these places to offer. To the trained eye, it only takes a moment to find what he's looking for. There she is, waving her tiny hands in vain as she tries to get the attention of her sitter, standing just a few feet away. No attention. Not for her. Not this time. Her sitter is too busy dealing with another child's scuffed knee.

Oldson slows his truck down, parking it beside the town square. The lady who is dealing with the teary-eyed child with a scuffed knee stands with her back to the little girl. Two other children stand beside the lady, each tugging at her sides, "I need this!" "Fix…now!" The other children yell, and the overworked caregiver with just two hands can only do so much.

There you are, alone and unprotected, it only takes a moment…then you are gone, Oldson thinks as he walks across the sidewalk. All the daytime activity and the chaos in the square, just a few more steps and you will have what you want—attention! Oldson reaches down and it is done. *As fast as knees get scuffed and attention is lost, and then so are you.*

Quietly, Oldson picks up the little girl. As always, the surprise of his action catches the girl off guard. She attempts to call out, but with her face pressed tightly into his chest, she cannot make a sound. He holds her tight enough, so she cannot move, but not too tight to cause too much alarm. Walking back to his truck, he opens the driver's door and gets in. The girl is just the right size, small enough to fit on his lap, her face still at his chest, her little legs swung over toward the passenger's seat. Oldson turns the truck on and as he drives away, he glances in the rearview mirror. *Still too busy and not enough hands*, he thinks as he watches the lady deal with the three other children.

Ten minutes have passed since he left the town square. Judging by her weight and height, Oldson figures that she must be three. Oldson figures the girl's weight is about half of one of the sixty-pound feed bags in the back of his truck.

With the steeples of the town still visible in his mirror, Oldson finds a convenient place to pull over. Oldson looks at her, her tiny frame as she sits there, unable to move. He notices what the problem was. An untied shoelace; it's still undone. When the little girl struggles, Oldson needs only to squeeze just a bit tighter and her struggles fade.

He reaches for the glove box as and he collects his small wooden case. With one hand holding the girl, the other hand is free to do what needs to be done. He opens his wooden case lying on the passenger's seat. Inside the case, he picks up an awaiting syringe, primed and ready to be used. Oldson inserts the needle into the little girl's arm and depresses the plunger. Placing the syringe back where it belongs, he closes the case.

U.S. Department of Justice
Federal Bureau of Investigation

CHAPTER THIRTY-ONE: One Rung at a Time
Present Day

Jenkins and Lee have just returned from Missoula. Their two-hour drive has given them ample time to talk about the interviews. Since the team landed in Kalispell, this is their first view of the crime scene. They park beside the command post and are greeted by Banks.

"Sanders texted us a few moments ago—*they're in*. How are they doing?" Jenkins asks Banks.

"The engineers reinforced the container and installed a couple of ladders to give them access," Banks says. "It's not great, but for now it will have to do. Cherkoff and Torres just got inside. We have a video feed in the command trailer hooked up live."

"I see the media circus has finally arrived in town," Jenkins says.

"Sanders will be releasing a new statement shortly. We were waiting for the media center to arrive from the Salt Lake office," Banks explains as he leads Jenkins and Lee into the team's command trailer.

***

Cherkoff and Torres each take a few moments to get accustomed to the full-face masks and the suits. The initial claustrophobic feelings subside as they walk into the covered area around the perimeter of the excavation site. Cherkoff and Torres walk to where a ladder has been placed. Technicians have installed a large white tent over the entire excavation and Cherkoff and Torres take a few moments to discuss their plans before climbing down the ladder into the pit. Their Tyvek suits are equipped with both a breathing apparatus and a closed two-way communication system. The breathing apparatus also provides limited ventilation throughout the suit.

"How are you feeling?" Cherkoff asks Torres.

"Good, takes a bit to get used to the mask. Ready whenever you are." Adjusting the last couple of straps on his mask, Torres follows Cherkoff to the first ladder.

Several ladders have been set up to allow the agents safe access into the hole. At the bottom lies the exposed container. An access hole, measuring five feet square, has been torched into the top of the container. One final ladder leads into the belly of the container.

"Can you hear me? Check." Both Torres and Cherkoff test the audio between themselves and Banks back at the command trailer.

"We can hear you both just fine. Take your time, keep in touch, and be careful," Banks instructs.

Cherkoff takes the first steps down the ladder and enters the container. "You both need to watch where you're walking in there," Banks says. "Even though the container is sitting on rock, we don't know how safe the floor of the damn thing is. The engineer told me metal in the top was in great shape, but he could only speculate as to the rest of the containers condition." *One rung at a time, don't look down,* she thinks as she slowly reaches the floor of the container. Not usually bothered with heights or ladders, perhaps the added weight and restricted mobility of the suits has caused Cherkoff's reaction. The support techs have also lowered several lights to provide proper illumination of the scene.

Torres works his way down the ladder and reaches the floor. Both agents are standing together at the bottom, silent, as they attempt to come to terms and process what they're seeing.

"Oh my god!" Cherkoff's voice crackles in the eerie silence and is the only sound heard over the com. She turns slightly, shining her flashlight on drawing after drawing pinned to the walls. "He was right," reports Cherkoff, her tone somber.

"What? Who was right?" Banks asks Cherkoff.

"The ranger, Clive, he said these looked so real, like photographs. The detail is incredible." Her flashlight shines on a drawing of the inside of the container. The drawing shows a man's hands holding a large tube, placing it into the mouth of a child. "The child is bound to the bench; the tube is in the child's mouth and his left hand holds the end of the tube. The child's face is not very detailed, but everything else is…he's even included cigarette ashes on the bench top. He's drawn the detail of the clothing, but the face is blank.

No eyes, nose, just the mouth drawn on a blank oval, like you would see in a beginner's sketch book. Everything else is photo quality."

"Cherkoff, look at this!" Torres points to the drawing. "The face in this drawing has been erased. There are impressions in the paper; they're faint, but they're still there."

The drawings on the walls range in size and subject. The largest appears to be eighteen by twenty-four inches. Cherkoff walks slowly around the container's floor, mesmerized by the images, eventually reaching one of the drawings that prompted the sheriff to contact the BAU. "He took the time to draw this." Her fists clench slightly.

U.S. Department of Justice
Federal Bureau of Investigation

CHAPTER THIRTY-TWO: His Studio
Present Day

Torres stands with Cherkoff, the drawing, a series of four sketches, presents an image from inside the second container. This extremely detailed series of sketches appears to be layered, time-lapsed portraits. The agents now see details they missed earlier. "On the border of the drawing, he has printed *after four weeks*."

They're looking at a drawing of the second container's contents. The container's wall appears to have been modified to include a window into the mine. The artist has drawn a picture of a child lying on one side. The child appears to be a very young boy lying in a pile of rubble. The drawing shows a silhouette sitting in the container, in front of the window, looking in the child's direction, watching as the boy's remains decompose into the ground where he lays.

"This bastard has even drawn the whiskers on the rats!" Cherkoff shouts.

Torres taps Cherkoff on the shoulder and motions her to join him as he inventories the furniture located in the container. "You take the desk. I'll check the file cabinet."

Torres opens the top drawer of the four-door legal-size file cabinet in one corner of the container. Inside the drawer is a series of newspapers. Each newspaper is wrapped in a protective plastic. "These are from all over the place—*The Calgary Herald, The Quad City Times…*" Torres photographs the drawer and documents how the papers were stored. "It looks like the earliest is from 1961 and 1983 is the latest. I've got a total of twenty-five, no, twenty-seven." Torres doesn't remove the papers from their protective covers.

In the third drawer from the top, he finds a collection of tools—knives, a large mortar and pestle, and some type of press. With no idea what it is, all Torres can do is document and inventory the items.

Torres snaps several more photographs as he opens the bottom drawer. He discovers three plastic cases, each containing an egg carton. He carries them to the bench and opens each up. The first two are full, eggs remain inside, unbroken but dried up. The final carton has only three eggs, again unbroken but dried. "The label on the crates says *Thompsons' Chicks*. In a way I'm kind of glad we have the suits on. They look …"

Cherkoff walks over to where Torres is and looks over at the crate and comments, "Pretty revolting!"

Both agents take extra care to ensure that they document how every item was placed and where. A large workbench, roughly five by eight feet, is in the center of the container adjacent to the hatch in the floor. "Everything in here appears to be very clean and well organized. This workbench has places for everything. Tools, bowls, slots to store knives, and it looks like they've been used a lot." Torres describes the bench top with numerous cut marks like what you would see on a butcher block.

"There's what looks like a hatch on the floor beside the one end of the bench. Looks to be about four feet square and it's secured to the floor with two flat steel bars. The bars slide…I have the hatch open." Torres shines his flashlight into the darkness, illuminating a ladder-lined square tunnel that leads down to the second container.

At the other end of the container, Cherkoff has been taking inventory of the desk and its contents. "This desk reminds me of my first-grade teacher's desk, same design. With three drawers on the right side and one long narrow drawer over where your legs would go." She opens each drawer. "Lots of notepads and a couple more sketch pads. This one here, look at this." Torres walks over to Cherkoff as she reads the title, *Dietary Supplements for Primates and Other Hominids*. "What do you make of this?" she asks, holding the book in the air.

Torres shakes his head and motion to her. "Something for Sanders."

"These notes are handwritten, but they all to appear to be in some form of code. Sanders, he'll have his hands full." Her comments are directed to Banks as she speaks over the com.

"Oh Christ...Fuck!" Cherkoff screams as she opens a sketch pad that she recovered from the desk, trying not to drop the book as her hands tremble.

"Cherkoff, talk to me. What's the matter?" Banks asks. His voice calm but concerned. Cherkoff walks to where Torres has been examining the bench. Standing with Torres, she slams the sketch pad on top of the bench. "The unsub had several of these sketch pads in the drawers in the desk. I found this one by its self. Look what he's done." She opens the pad on the bench. "There are...picture after picture, all these kids. Some have just one child, then there are drawings that are just a collage. They're all the same, different faces but the same scene...rats covering their dead bodies as they lay in front of that goddamn window. I really need some air right now!" Cherkoff drops with procedure, leaving the pad on the desk and heads for the exit. Climbing rapidly to the surface and pushing her way past the tech at the top of the last ladder, Cherkoff storms her way to the command trailer, ripping her respirator off her face as she walks to the trailer. She is forced to stop, almost in the middle of the compound, and vomits uncontrollably. She doubles over, grasping at her gut as her stomach empties.

Banks instructs Torres to leave and head for the surface as well. "Come on out. Get out of there and take a break!" Banks quickly heads to meet Cherkoff. Arriving at her side, the first thing he notices is that both of her hands are trembling and, as she looks up at him, her face is ghostly pale.

"I'm alright. That was just too much. I know what you're going to say, so save your breath." Cherkoff slowly calms herself. "I know, emotions in check, our head's in the game at all times, but Jesus Christ." She clenches her fists as she speaks.

"Talk to me, what was it?" Banks says.

Torres has also reached the surface and is standing with both agents. In his hand is the sketch book that caused Cherkoff's reaction. Instinctively, he opens the book to the page, and without speaking, he shows the sketch, another time-lapse-style drawing, its handwritten title, *4th at 1-21 days*. Another very graphic image of a child, his body in various stages of decay, has been drawn in incredible detail. Banks leads both Cherkoff and Torres into the command trailer to go over their findings thus far.

U.S. Department of Justice
Federal Bureau of Investigation

CHAPTER THIRTY-THREE:
An Update for the Media
Present Day

"Did you see that? Ashley, check this out." Her cameraman is shouting, wanting her to look in the direction of the command trailer. "That agent down there, that one—she just came rushing out of the tent and puked her guts up all over the place!" He focuses his camera right on Cherkoff's face. "Whoa, she really doesn't look good. I don't know what the hell they found down there but look at this." He swings the camera monitor, so Ashley can see Cherkoff's face. The commotion from the scene below has also grabbed the attention of the other media in the area. Noticing this, Ashley grabs her cell phone and dials into the station.

"Hi, it's Ashley, not bad, but things are getting kind of hot up here. Has the research department found who owns this place yet? Great, yes, I got it now. That's a great idea; we'll see what we can do. They have us pinned into this tiny area, corralled like livestock. Yes, six, and again at eleven. We'll be ready." Ashley hangs up and continues to read the recent texts and e-mails from her producer. "All they could find is historical, nothing current."

"What? That's impossible; you're telling me our *super-geek* in the tech department is shooting blanks this time?" Ashley looks over to her cameraman as he speaks and shrugs.

"Mr. 'If You Need It, I Can Get It' only could get us this," she replies and passes him her tablet.

Her cameraman shakes his head as he reads the file the office received from land registry. "By the looks of this report, he's been out-geeked by somebody, and there's a lot of information missing here," her cameraman announces.

"Are you sure about that?" she inquires.

"You bet, especially if this property is being expropriated. When did that FBI guy say the press conference would be?"

Ashley looks at her watch and replies, "Should be any time now."

"Shit, she's still puking down there," says her cameraman as he looks back to where Cherkoff and the other agents are standing. "I got an idea, give me a minute. He should be home."

He quickly dials a number. "Hey, it's me, listen I need you to do something right away. I need you to call your brother, the one that lives in Helena. He still works at the Capitol Building right? Here's what he has to do…"

***

The monitor above the podium in the media center is turned on. Ashley and the various other members of the press have taken their seats. Craving answers and armed with a series of questions, she quickly checks her tablet one last time before turning it off.

A video recording is being played on the monitor. "Good morning. My name is Supervisory Special Agent Christopher Banks. At this time, I would like to provide an update on the status of one of the witnesses."

"So much for question and answer," Ashley quietly says to herself.

"I regret to inform you that, Mr. George Marshall succumbed to his injuries. Mr. Marshall worked for Deep Image and was the lead surveyor working on this job site at the time of the discovery. An autopsy is currently being performed and until we have the results, the cause of death at this time is unknown."

The video ends and a still image of the FBI shield remains on the monitor. "That's it? That's all you're giving us? Come on now, you've got us all crammed in here like sheep, that's the best you can do?" Ashley says. A sentiment, judging by the reaction of her fellow reporters, is shared. Her cameraman signals her to come to where he's standing.

He pulls Ashley to the side and close enough so that only she can hear, "I just got this from my brother in-law, the one who works at the Capitol Building. I asked him to ask his buddy who works in the Archives Department to check the hard copy title registration. There's nothing, it's gone."

"What?"

"No mortgage, no lien, no title. No record of present owner whatsoever. The hard copy is gone. Hell, you could squat there, and no one could do anything to you. From what his buddy told him, it looks like the file has been that way for years. Your guess is as good as mine, but I know one thing, someone is hiding something big."

"And now we have a dead guy."

U.S. Department of Justice
Federal Bureau of Investigation

CHAPTER THIRTY-FOUR: Alabama
November 1963

In a warehouse on the outskirts of Birmingham, Alabama, two workers, Troy and Jimmy, get ready to start their day. The sounds of The Kingsmen's "Louie, Louie" can be heard playing on the radio over the loud speakers. "They left it at door ten," Troy instructs the Jimmy. The two men are forklift operators and an empty railcar has been placed against door number ten and waits to be loaded. The second worker opens the warehouse door. Using the forklift, the other worker slides the heavy steel door open. The high-pitched squeal, metal binding on metal, echoes through the warehouse, a sound worse than nails on a chalkboard.

"Now just how the hell did you get in there?" Jimmy's voice echoes, as the door opens and exposes a barely conscious man.

Josh lies inside the empty boxcar, his shirt bloody, as two men drag him out into the warehouse and to the office. Dazed and dehydrated, Josh is unable to explain how he got there, or for that matter, where he is.

"Looks like you've been in a fight son. You're all scratched up and it looks like you lost a lot of blood too. Hell, if you won the fight, I'd sure hate to see the other guy," Troy says, as the stub end of a cigar dangles from the corner of his mouth. His overalls cover a sweat-stained shirt. The men inform Josh that hopping rides in train cars is trespassing and he could get in big trouble. As they talk with him, something in Josh's pocket catches Troy's attention. "What the hell have we got here? Panties, and what the hell's on them? Is that blood?" Troy decides to call the police. "You just sit tight and relax. Jimmy will take care of you. You make sure, he don't move, ya hear me?" Jimmy nods.

Troy retreats to an adjacent room to call the police. The other man remains with Josh, offering him a cup of water. "Yeah, you better get over here. We got us a real pervert here. He's all covered with scratches and blood and has some lady's panties still in his pocket. He ain't goin' nowhere!"

After hanging up the phone, Troy returns to the room where Josh is. Josh has started to become agitated as he looks at his hands. His hands, arms, and face are all covered in scratches. Josh can only shake his head as he looks at the panties, unable to put together what has happened. "Where am I?" he asks the men.

"You're in Deed's Warehouse, son." This only adds to Josh's confusion. All he remembers is being in Montana with Terri. Josh attempts to stand but the men push him back in his seat. "Terri! Terri…I got to go find her…let me go…" he screams at the men, who now forcibly restrain him in the chair.

"You need to sit right down. We got help coming for you."

When they ask him who Terri is, Josh just holds his head in his hands and says nothing.

***

The sheriff arrives at the warehouse. As he enters the office, Jimmy greets him, calling him by his first name. He tells the sheriff how they found Josh as they walk to where he is being held. "We got us a real hippie here. Found him in that railcar. Sheriff, it looks like one of them free-lovers. Take a look in his pocket."

"Let me see what you have in your pocket." The sheriff reaches into Josh's shirt pocket and removes a blood-stained pair of girl's panties. "What do you have to say about this? Who'd you get these from?"

Josh stares at the panties, desperately trying to figure out what is going on and where they came from. "They look like Terri's."

"And just who the hell is Terri?" the sheriff barks at Josh as he inspects Josh's clothes. "You got one heck of a lot of blood all over you, son. Is it hers? Whose panties are these? Where'd you get 'em son?"

Pulling at his hair, Josh pleads, "My girlfriend, Terri. I've got to go find her, she's ..." His eyes search the room wildly as he grasps for answers.

The sheriff places the panties on the table in front of Josh, then instructs Josh to empty the rest of the contents of his pockets onto the table. As Josh places the items on the table, the sheriff says, "Son, you in a heck of a lot of trouble now."

He reaches down and picks up a bag of marijuana. The sheriff turns Josh around, pushing him facedown into the table. With his night stick, he spreads Josh's ankles and pulls Josh's hands around his back. Josh attempts to struggle but is quickly over powered by the sheriff. After he has placed handcuffs on Josh, he pushes him into the chair. The sheriff opens the bag and with a sniff of the contents says, "Hooey, you doing this shit? No wonder you're confused."

"They're hers. I know, I've seen them before, you know," Josh says.

The sheriff asks Troy, "The boxcar he was in, where'd it come from?"

Troy explains that it was shunted down from Birmingham previous night and before then, who knows.

Josh takes a sip of water as his voice cracks, "Terri and I, we were hitchhiking to California from North Dakota."

As Josh tries to explain, the sheriff laughs and says, "You a heck of a long way from California, boy! All I know is you've been found trespassing in a railcar. You got blood all over you, this little bag of mary-wanna and, oh, I mustn't forget, panties. Now get up! We gonna have us a little ride."

The sheriff thanks the men as they help him take Josh to the squad car. As the sheriff drives back to the station, a restless Josh tries to tell him about Terri and where they were. He cannot recall enough details, just fragments, only adding to the sheriff's skepticism, who tells Josh he had better start getting used to the idea of them handcuffs as he was going to jail, probably for a long time. In disbelief, all Josh can do is sit quietly and try to remember what had happened.

"Oh, man...think...think," Josh says to himself staring out the window of the squad car. He remembers Terri and the campsite and making love. The sounds of the squad car's tires as they bump over cracks on the road remind him of the sounds from the train. The rhythmic *click-click, click-click* echoes through his mind.

He quietly asks the sheriff, "What day is it?"

The sheriff informs him it's the twenty-sixth of November.

U.S. Department of Justice
Federal Bureau of Investigation

CHAPTER THIRTY-FIVE: His New Home
November 1963

When they arrive at the police station, Josh is placed in a holding cell. The sheriff hands Josh a cup he can use for water and tells Josh to strip. He removes all his clothes, revealing numerous bruises, cuts and scratches all over his body. The sheriff takes a series of photographs eventually handing Josh a pair of county overalls to wear. Josh's clothes, as well as the contents of his pockets, now evidence, bagged and tagged.

The sheriff tells Josh to "make yourself at home…You might as well get used to it; you gonna be here awhile." The sheriff leaves Josh and walks to his office, carrying the evidence bags. The sheriff picks up the telephone on his desk and dials the county prosecutor. He explains Josh's situation. "Looks like he's done beat the hell out of some poor girl. God knows what else he did to her. Real pervert type." The prosecutor assures the sheriff that he will do his job and make sure Josh gets his day in court.

The sheriff hangs up the phone, smiling. He reclines his chair, reaches into the evidence bag, and pulls out the panties. He holds them in his hands for a few moments, his fingers playing with the fabric. He places them back into the bag.

***

In his cell, Josh sits on the bed. A thin mattress over a steel spring frame supports his weight. A small stainless-steel sink, mirror, and toilet are the only other things in the cell. The holding area has two cells and Josh is the only prisoner. He looks at his forearms covered in scratches. The marks and light bruises on his arms were obviously made by a person. Josh has bruises in the shape of a person's hand and scratch marks leading from them.

He stands, walks to the sink, and pours some water into the cup the sheriff gave him. Josh drinks cup after cup of water but his stomach immediately knots with pain causing him to throw it back up. Josh lifts his head from the sink and looks at his reflection in the mirror. He stares at his bruised and scratched face, desperately searching for the missing days. Without money and with no family to call, the reality of his situation weighs heavily on him.

***

The following morning, Josh wakes up as the deputy slides open the sally-port in the cell door. Josh stands and takes the plate of food from the deputy. On the plate is one very overcooked egg, one piece of white toast, and a pile of grits. With both hands, he hungrily downs everything on the plate and drinks the cup of warm coffee.

The sheriff and the prosecutor know that Josh will be charged with possession of a controlled substance. Coupled with the fact Josh admitted to bringing the drugs into their county from out of state, he's facing a lengthy sentence. If they can find his victim, the charges will be much more severe. The blood type from stains on his clothes will be compared to his own. Josh will be fingerprinted, booked, and formally charged on Monday. The sheriff and deputy will have the balance of the weekend to piece together whatever they can find. The prosecutor assured the sheriff that: "He'll be serving time for the drugs and I'm sure his victim will turn up somewhere."

U.S. Department of Justice
Federal Bureau of Investigation

CHAPTER THIRTY-SIX: Josh's New Friends

"Marty, I want you to go through all them missing girl cases," the sheriff says. "Look for anyone found without their panties and had their finger nails all broke. You start there...and Marty, if you need to drive up to Birmingham, you do it. If he killed one of them girls, you need to get on this."

Marty has been a deputy for only a few months and is as eager as the sheriff to find answers. He starts to look through reports and files. His investigation turns up several possibilities, which he and the sheriff will investigate.

Josh is interrogated by the sheriff and his deputy. They question Josh for several hours, focusing on two unsolved cases involving the murders of young women whose bodies were found in different locations around Birmingham over the past several weeks.

"You know, Marty, this here mary-wanna can get you in a heck of a lot of trouble, just look at poor old Josh here. He can't help himself, can't remember, look at him. Josh!" the sheriff bellows. "We have figured it all out. Tell him what you just told me, Marty."

"Well, sheriff it would appear two unidentified girls were found—"

"Their bodies were found, you mean," the sheriff says.

"Yes, their bodies were found. One was raped. She was left naked in a ditch near, get this, a rail siding," Marty explains.

The sheriff says, "Near a rail siding, in Birmingham? You following where this is going, Josh? Tell us some more, Marty, help the boy out!"

"Yes, sir, Sheriff, the victim was a twenty-one-year-old college student. She had been reported missing a week earlier. With her fingernails broken and bloody, she had obviously put up quite a fight!"

The sheriff looks directly at Josh as he speaks. "Go on, Marty. You keep listening, Josh."

"The other girl, her body was found just two days ago. Now, she was a twenty-year-old prostitute. She was also found near a rail siding in an industrial park in Birmingham. She was found wearing only her bra and shoes."

"You see, Josh, it don't matter to me what you can remember. Marty here did all this fine police work. And It will be finer police work when we match the blood on your clothes with those girls'." The sheriff pats Marty on the back, knowing just how pleased the county prosecutor will be when he gets this information. The sheriff leans his chair in closer to Josh and speaking in his deep southern drawl relates his version of the chain of events.

"I tell you what I see here, boy. Hitchhiking, I believe you. You were hitchhiking. Terri, now I don't know who she is. Hell, that might just be the name of that prostitute up there in Birmingham." The sheriff abruptly stops talking and breaks out into laughter slapping his knee with his hand. "It just dawned on me, Marty. We're the only two friends poor old Josh has right now. And what I also know is this story has three possible endings, just three, and not one of them has you walking outta here."

The sheriff is sitting face to face with Josh across a small table.

His voice is intimidating and loud. "You!" the sheriff says as he points at Josh. "You met one of those girls. Y'all did your mary-wanna smokin,' having your free loving. Then things got a little out of hand, now didn't they, boy? Things got a little rough, a little wild even, like animals. The next thing you know, you've got a dead girl on your hands, her blood all over you! You raped that girl and killed her!" The sheriff points to a picture of the prostitute after slamming it on the table.

Josh looks at the picture of the young girl, beaten and lying facedown, next to the train tracks. Her body has a yellowish tone and is covered with bruises, cuts and scratches. Josh shakes his head wildly repeating "No, no, no...I couldn't!" Holding his mouth, his stomach retches, and he vomits on the floor.

The sheriff stands up in disgust, looks at Josh. "Damn it son, now look what you've gone and done. Marty's gonna have to clean all this shit up." The sheriff bends over and looks Josh right in the eyes, his face close enough that Josh can feel his breath. "Now, you just tell us how you killed this poor thang and it'll be alright. Damn it boy, the Lord's the only one that's gonna be helping you now."

"Sheriff, you have to believe me I didn't hurt anyone. I, we, we were camping. Camping with Terri, there was a lake and, oh God, there was someone." Josh raises his voice as bits of his past start coming back. "He gave us a ride."

"And just exactly where did this guy pick the two of you up?" the sheriff says, his tone sarcastic.

"I can't remember. You must believe me! I'm telling you the truth!"

"You didn't happen to catch this fellow's name?" inquires the sheriff, as he pretends to hold a pad and pen in his hand. "Now what did this, man look like?"

Josh can only shake his head, unable to recall any details.

"You're all alone boy. Your Terri, whoever she is, you see, it don't matter. Once we match the blood stains on your clothes with those dead girls up there, Terri, well, that won't matter no more."

Josh weeps as he covers his eyes and lays his head on the table. "I'm innocent. I didn't do this. Please, oh God, you have to believe me. I didn't kill anyone. Please, please…"

"You see, son, Jimmy and I are your only friends right now and when the prosecutor comes walkin' in here tomorrow it is ova. I mean son, it is ova!" The sheriff continues quietly, "You tell me now and I can help you. That prosecutor comes in here, shit, he's gonna have just one thing on his mind—strapping your ass into a chair and turning on a little switch. You'll get that 'good-ole' feeling working its way through ya, until all them juices in your eyes boil and then split right open! I tell you what, with the evidence we have on you right now, you just be glad you ain't black…hell, you'd already be dead."

The sheriff and Jimmy continue with the interrogation as Josh sits rigid with fear.

Josh stares down at the photos of the dead girls. Their bodies brutally violated and displayed in front of him. Focusing on their faces Josh shakes his head wildly and exclaims, "That's not her! That's not Terri, not Terri. I don't know who these girls are. I've never seen them, ever. My girl, her name is Terri." His heart races as he speaks. Trying to stand up, Josh's body goes limp as he falls to the floor.

U.S. Department of Justice
Federal Bureau of Investigation

CHAPTER THIRTY-SEVEN: One Phone Call November 1963

The next morning, the prosecutor arrives at the station. He asks to see the prisoner. The sheriff and Jimmy talk with the prosecutor about their interrogation.

"Did he make his phone call?" the prosecutor asks Jimmy.

"Yes, sir."

"Who did he call?"

"Called his daddy up in North Dakota. Here's the number."

"How did that go?"

Jimmy says, "I gave him the phone once it started to ring. Then I hear him say, 'Dad, it's Josh, I'm in trouble...Dad...Dad,' then he hands me back the phone. I ask him what happened and he kinda looks up at me and says, 'He hung up.'"

The defendant's family not accepting his phone call for help only reinforces the prosecutor's belief that Josh is a criminal.

Jimmy stands at the door, while the prosecutor and the sheriff sit at the table across from Josh. The prosecutor places a large stack of files and papers on the table in front of Josh. He opens the file on top, and hands it to the sheriff. The prosecutor cups his hand over his mouth and quietly instructs the sheriff, "He needs to know this."

The sheriff leans across the table and says, "I'm gonna give you a chance. A chance to make things right, right now, that I know you didn't give that girl up there in Birmingham. Ya see son, I'm gonna ask you just this…the chair or the chamber? What's it gonna be? You see this paper, this here little form right here. If the prosecutor here puts a little old check mark here, eeelectric chair. See that box right there, this one? You're right. I knew you could figure that one out. Lordy, boys, we got us here a regular wizard. You guessed it, gas chamber!"

The sheriff and Jimmy grin at each other as the prosecutor says, "The sheriff and Jimmy have done some amazing police work here, tracking down where you were and all. Hell, they should have been home with their families and not having to follow your twisted sick little path.

"Josh, I assure you, as sure as you are sitting right there, while you're in our custody and awaiting trial on the drug charges, the sheriff will have been able to link you to one or possibly both murdered girls." The prosecutor leans into Josh as he explains. "We will be in front of the judge very soon, and you'll be facing serious charges for your drugs. I will also be informing the judge that more charges are pending…charges of a heinous nature." As the prosecutor speaks, the sheriff hands the prosecutor a small slip of paper.

"I have been telling these…I've told the sheriff and his deputy I didn't hurt anyone. Those girls, I haven't even seen before. I was camping with my girl, Terri. Why won't anyone believe me?"

The prosecutor inspects the piece of paper. "The sheriff tells me you don't even know who the president is! Josh where were you when President Kennedy was shot?" Josh can only shake his head in disbelief as the prosecutor continues, "Hell, you have to be the only person in the country that doesn't remember where you were! You expect us to believe what you're telling us when you can't even remember that." The prosecutor looks at the sheriff and Jimmy as Josh sobs. "When we get the results in from the blood on your shirt, we'll have found your Terri."

U.S. Department of Justice
Federal Bureau of Investigation

CHAPTER THIRTY-EIGHT: The Workshop
November 1963

Oldson arrives back at the location where he left Terri and the little boy. He parks his truck in the usual spot. His tire tracks have again been obscured by dragging the fence roll behind the truck. Walking to the tunnel's entrance, he makes his way into the first room. Inside he finds Terri and the bag lying where he had left them. Before he left, he secured Terri. He hog-tied her in the same manner as he had done to Josh; if she struggled the ropes would tighten. He also tied the bag containing the little boy to the loop in the rope connecting her ankles to her neck. If the bag ever tried to *get away*, it would only further tighten the noose around Terri's neck. "Looks like you two have been playing nice," Oldson comments as he looks at the pair on the floor.

Terri is unable to scream. The gag Oldson placed in her mouth muffles any sound she tries to make. From his file cabinet, he removes the plastic box. Opening it, he takes out the egg crate. He counts methodically as he inspects the egg crates. Oldson then places two fresh chicken eggs into the crate. "No more surprises," he whispers as he closes the crate and gently secures it in the box. He replaces the box in the cabinet and files two newspapers in chronological fashion. The paper with Kennedy's assassination on the front page is in front. Each newspaper is wrapped in cellophane and a metal hanger suspends them from the rail within the drawer. A total of five newspapers are stored in this manner. Oldson caresses the spines of each paper before closing the drawer; resting beside the cabinet is another stack of newspapers.

His workbench is ready, properly stocked and the necessary tools in their respective places. Oldson removes a fresh handkerchief from his pocket and wipes the edge of a large carving knife. With the reflection of his face in the blade, Oldson reaches for a sack placed on the bench. He removes the last two tools that he must use to complete this process. Oldson walks to where Terri is and unties the bag containing the little boy. Terri can only watch and listen as she lies on her side as Oldson carries the boy to the workbench.

The top of the bag has twine bindings which he removes. He takes a cloth from his back pocket and ties it around the boy's face, shielding his eyes from the light. Oldson lowers the bag. The boy, who is sitting very still, only trembles slightly. The warmth of Oldson's hands, the first human contact that the little boy has had since he was abducted, provide comfort to the boy, but not for long.

In a soft voice, Oldson says, "This will make you feel much better and it won't hurt. Quiet now…be still…" The boy struggles a bit as Oldson takes a small hose and places it down the boy's throat. The boy's hands try to push at the hose. Oldson smiles, the image of the boy reminds him of the struggle a small frog made trying to get a fish hook out of its mouth just before being used as bait. "This is for you!" Oldson exclaims as the hose is pushed further down his throat. With the tube in place, Oldson reaches for a nearby bowl. The contents, mixed carefully and moistened with water, are ready for use. Holding a large syringe in one hand, Oldson draws up the mixture and injects it into the tube. The process is repeated many times as Oldson observes the boy's tummy swell as it fills.

"That wasn't that hard, now was it?" Knowing the boy was very hungry, the food and water he just received would be welcome. Oldson removes the feeding tube and wraps the boy back up in the bag.

U.S. Department of Justice
Federal Bureau of Investigation

CHAPTER THIRTY-NINE: Final Touches
November 1963

Terri has only been able to watch what is going on. She feels Oldson's hands around her waist as he lifts her to the top of the bench. Her legs hang over the edge as she sits facing Oldson. Her body trembling as tears drip from her eyes. Oldson gently dries her face and walks to the other side of the bench. He keeps a firm grip on the rope at her back and when he reaches the other side of the bench, Oldson loops a rope through it and to the base of the bench. Terri cannot move, she can only sit, her head tilted back and her mouth ready to receive. Her profile takes on the appearance of a baby bird in a nest as Oldson tries to feed the tube into her mouth.

She tries to turn away, but this only causes him to hold her face. Pulling down her chin, he opens her mouth and slides the hose down her throat. She gags at first, trying to cough it back up but Oldson continues putting pressure on the hose until it reaches its target. "Sorry this isn't a warm fish dinner, but you need this!" He draws a full syringe from the bowl and injects the contents into the tube. Careful to not hurt her, he watches her belly as it too swells as more and more gets pumped in.

A strange sensation radiates from her stomach. A curious feeling comes over her. Terri is not uncomfortable, but it did not hurt and in a strange way, she feels content. She's not able to taste what she just ate; all she can do is sit. Oldson removes the feeding tube from Terri's throat. As it draws out from her mouth, he gently wipes her lips with a cloth.

With Terri hog-tied to the table, he walks to the desk, sits down, and scribbles some notes in his journal. He glances at her profile and picks up a sketch pad. He relaxes in his chair and, facing Terri, he starts to draw. Tears begin to run down her cheeks as her muscles scream. Her bindings force Terri to remain still; the slightest movement tightens the noose around her neck. Terri remains motionless, the perfect subject.

The details of his drawing are quite remarkable. He captures the little pattern in her skirt, the frayed end of the ties that bind her wrists. It takes him about an hour to produce a near photo-quality rendering of the scene in pencil. She watches as Oldson stands up, picking up the little boy. She strains her neck to watch as Oldson and the boy disappear from her view. The sounds from his footsteps fade as he exits the container. Unaware of where she is or what is going on, she sits on the bench, unable to move. When Oldson returns, he walks to Terri and releases her from the bench. She feels him rubbing something on the ropes. The smell is familiar. It is the same odor that came from the tube when he pulled it out of her throat. Oldson smears the last of the bowl's contents on Terri's bindings. With the bowl clean, he picks up the empty bag from the bench, places it over Terri's head, and tucks it under the rope around her neck.

U.S. Department of Justice
Federal Bureau of Investigation

CHAPTER FORTY: Oh God
November 1963

She feels her feet lift off the ground as he picks her up and carries her out of the container. The temperature changes and she realizes she's outside. He carries her from the mouth of the tunnel to where a large rock has been recently moved. He places her on the ground. With her bare feet on the cold ground, she feels something lift up her skirt. Oldson places a board between her legs, turning it sideways so it becomes a seat. She tries to move but the rough edges of the plank scrape against her thighs. She feels a rope in front and behind her, as her feet leave the ground. The cool autumn breeze gives way to a still, heavy feeling as she is lowered into the mine. Oldson is standing across the opening into the shaft. With the rope over his shoulders, he slowly lowers Terri into the mine next to where the bag containing the boy lays.

Within minutes, the rats sense the food hidden inside the bag and smeared over Terri's bindings. From all directions, the rats swarm the bag, chewing and gnawing at the fabric until it gives way. Terri shrieks as several large rats crawl over her legs and chest. One stands on her neck. She feels the warmth of its breath as it begins to sniff under the bag, covering her face. She struggles to her knees, ignoring the choking of the rope still bound around her neck. But only for a moment, then she falls back to the ground amid the crawling mass of rats.

The metal grate is lowered back into place and locked. Protected from the world outside, now secure in their new home, she hears a grinding screech and the air flow change as Oldson's truck pushes the rock back to its resting place atop the grate.

The rats force their way under Terri, who's lying on the ground, and nose into the ropes. She hears the terrified scream of pain from the little boy lying behind her. In a mad horde, the rats chew and bite, making no distinction between rope and human flesh. The rats begin to make progress, devouring the rope, but not before Terri suffers numerous painful bites on her wrists, ankles, and neck as she frantically tries to loosen her bindings. The scent and taste of fresh blood only excites the rats' chewing frenzy. They chew and bite at the rope, devouring it quickly. The rope begins to loosen. She violently swings her arms around in front of her, throwing most of the rats to the ground. She grasps at her face, tearing the cloth away. Her eyes are open to her new home.

Terri and the little boy are trapped, surrounded by darkness where only a faint light in the distance outlines. *Is that a door?* There's just enough light to illuminate the mine's main room. Dark tunnels and the outline of a room are just visible. Terri's eyes search for the little boy. His screams are her only guide as she crawls to where he is lying. Terri claws her way over the hard ground. "Oh God...oh God. No...no!" she screams as her hands touch the remains of a small human skull.

U.S. Department of Justice
Federal Bureau of Investigation

CHAPTER FORTY-ONE: Evil Bad Guys 0 Me 1
Present Day

In the command trailer, Banks sits with the other members of the team. Cherkoff is still shaken from the images the unsub drew. Her complexion is still pale as Torres hands her a cup of water. The sheriff and the excavator operator are with Jenkins and Lee in an adjoining room. "It is very organized, and surprisingly clean," comments Torres as he describes the container's interior.

"As soon as you're both ready to go back in there, we need you too." Cherkoff nods as Banks instructs them to continue. Both agents begin the process of getting back into their protective suits and, after a communications check, return to the first container. Banks remains in the trailer to monitor their progress. His cell phone buzzes. He answers, "Sanders, what's going on?"

"How is Cherkoff? What happened?"

"What do you mean…how did you"

"Turn on channel eight," Sanders instructs Banks. "You need to watch their live update." Banks turns the TV to channel eight and watches as Ashley Blair describes "… a frightening scene that has just taken place here. It appears that a member of the FBI's team was just overcome. We're not sure what happened, but as you can see, something has made her violently ill."

Banks resumes his conversation with Sanders. "She's alright—she needed some air. They're recovering some more notepads, newspapers, and sketch books. Torres said most of the notebooks are in some sort of code. I'll send you those items as soon as they're ready to go. Do your magic!"

"Check your tablet please," Sanders asks Banks, who opens the new file. "You see the tracks? It took some time to enhance the images, they're barely visible on the satellite image. I have arranged for a tech to come out from the field office with a drone to help you navigate to where they are. With all the brush and topography, even if you were standing on the path, chances are you wouldn't even notice. They end around the ridge behind the excavation. Those marks work their way out to an access road."

Banks agrees with Sanders observations and is pleased with this new information. "Great work."

Sanders turns to one of his computer screens, and with a click of his mouse, his digital score board reads, *Evil Bad Guys:0, Me:1*

U.S. Department of Justice
Federal Bureau of Investigation

CHAPTER FORTY-TWO: Site Access
Present Day

"Sanders has found what appears to be the route the unsub used," Banks says to Cherkoff and Torres.

"There has to be another hatch. I'll check when we get back into the container," Torres says.

When they get back into the container, Torres is focused on the walls. He sees an outline of what looks to be a hatch and two small areas for hands. "I think I've found the exit hatch." With a little effort, he removes a small door, roughly four feet square, revealing an L-shaped tunnel on the other side. He leads the way and both agents climb into the tunnel on their hands and knees.

"It feels like we are going up an incline," Jenkins reports over the com.

The tunnel leads to the surface and as they exit, Torres looks back toward the entrance. "He's used an old vent shaft. It's tucked into a small outcropping of rocks. There's lots of brush around it too," Torres says.

"It's really clever. There's so much overgrowth here, you could walk right by and not even notice it," Cherkoff adds. "We're heading back in."

Crawling into the container and through the tunnel, they follow the path that the unsub must have used many times. The agents notice the rails and what remains of an old ore cart. "The unsub probably used this to bring in his supplies. It even has a brake. Looks like it still works too," Torres explains.

Ready to enter the shaft connecting both containers, Torres leads the way. The tunnel connecting the containers is concrete; it appears to be made from sections of sewer pipe with a metal ladder attached to each section. The agents notice several industrial-style light sconces clad in a metal cage. As Torres climbs down the ladder, the light from the container above shines on the floor below him, illuminating a portion of container two. When he reaches the halfway point, he notices the ladder has a retractable section, like you would find at the bottom of a fire escape. Torres pulls on the lever that releases the final section, extending it just above the floor. Both agents traverse the ladder and reach the floor.

They pan the container with their flashlights. A large pile of bags sits in one corner, piled almost floor to ceiling. "There are bags of rice, dried potatoes, and a bunch of different seeds," Cherkoff reports. In the center of one side of the container is the large window and, placed in the center of the container, a single chair and a light is hung from the ceiling above the chair.

"There doesn't appear to be any access from here into the mine. These walls are solid, and by the looks of things, even more reinforced than the first container," Torres reports as he hits the wall with his hand.

Cherkoff photographs the contents and placement of every item in the container. She pays special attention to the chair and where it is with respect to the window. She stands behind the chair and takes a photograph representing the perspective from the chair looking at the window. Then she stands to one side and places his flashlight directly on the window, the beam illuminates a portion of the room on the other side. The light cuts a narrow path into the darkness. Cherkoff moves in closer, focusing the flashlight's beam and slowly pans to the left, then to the right.

"Anything?" Torres asks.

Cherkoff shakes her head. "Hard to see anything. We need more light. There's something there but I just can't make out what it is, wait…oh no."

U.S. Department of Justice
Federal Bureau of Investigation

CHAPTER FORTY-THREE: Trapped
November 1963

The faint light in the distance has suddenly become blindingly bright. The main room has been illuminated for the first time, revealing what the darkness kept secret. The mine is lighted from only one end. She sees the long fluorescent light tubes that frame a shiny rectangle, a mirror. The image in the mirror eerily amplifies her surroundings. Terri reaches to her ankles and frantically removes the rope. The little boy cries out as the rats' crawl over him. The rats have torn holes in the sides of his clothes and the rope around his wrists. From the corner of her eyes, she sees the office. Terri scoops the boy into her arms and runs into the office. The old wooden door, with its hinges seized, won't move. With both hands, pressing all her weight against it, she forces the door closed.

With the boy in her arms, she cradles his little head in one hand, gently rocks him, and whispers, "Don't cry, it's just you and me...I'm Terri." She gently wipes the little boy's face. He can't be more than three years old. He's dressed in faded jeans and a lightweight T-shirt. Terri places the boy on top of the desk. Outside the office, she sees the rats fight for the balance of the fabric and rope. The main room has four tunnels branching out into the darkness. *We must have come down through that,* Terri thinks as she inspects the hole in the ceiling, which glows an eerie blue. The pale blue moonlight slipping around the boulder hints at the wooden frame around the shaft's exit. The hole in the ceiling is centered over the floor of the main room. "It's so high, and there's nothing to stand on," Terri speaks to the little boy.

There must be something. "Shit, move, damn it." Terri grunts at the desk as she pushes. "Come on, Terri, you can do this, you have to do this." No matter what she tries, the desk won't budge. "These chairs are done, and the little table is rotten too." A soft, moss-like fungus covers the top of one table and is growing onto the next.

"We have to find us a way out of here," she tells the boy. Through the window, the rats have calmed down. She decides to open the door. Squeezing her fingers through the opening, she pries it back, not all the way, just enough for the boy and her to wiggle through. The boy holds her hand tightly and won't let go. In the main room, the rats are more curious than aggressive. Some raise their heads off the floor, almost standing up as they sniff the air. Terri waves her hands wildly, shouting, "Go on…get out of here! You heard me, shoo!" The rats, surprisingly, obey her commands and disappear into the darkness. The main lobby of the mine, roughly thirty-five feet across and sixty feet long, is flanked at one end by a large metal wall. In the wall is a mirror, three feet off the ground, approximately four feet wide by six feet long.

Although she's only clad in her skirt and top, the air is surprisingly warm. She is unable to see where the light is coming from, just that it frames the mirror. She turns to face the mine and the dark square holes, the shafts that extend into the distance. With the sound of the rats and running water, she feels a slight breeze. *Down here, how can that be?* The pair walks to where they were lowered into the mine. Terri strains her neck to find a handhold or anything else they could use or reach the mouth of the shaft. Without warning, the entire room is black. There's no light. Only darkness surrounds her once again as her heart races.

The little boy screams hysterically, frozen with fear and surrounded in darkness. Terri rubs her eyes, squinting to adjust her vision to the darkness. Her hands, the little boy standing beside her, gone, only the darkness and the sounds of the rats as they scurry fill the air. Terri frantically tries to retrace her steps back to the room. *Oh, my God.*

U.S. Department of Justice
Federal Bureau of Investigation

CHAPTER FORTY-FOUR: Separated
November 1963

Frantically, Terri reaches for the little boy's hand. Their fingers brush past and finally connect. She reels him into her with a tight grip and with her right arm stretched out, she tries to find a wall. Anything that will help lead her and the boy back to the office. "Calm down, calm down, calm down," she repeats to both herself and the boy, but her voice cracks with fear. "It's just over there, come on…hold my hand. Oh God, please don't let go. Don't let go!" Afraid the pair might get separated in the darkness, she picks the boy up and cradles him in her left arm. He grasps her neck with both arms squeezing so tight Terri must force him to loosen his grip. She says soothingly, "Not so tight, it's okay, okay…shh-shh."

Eventually, she finds a wall and manages to grope her way back into the office. Her eyes start to adjust to the darkness. The only light source comes from tiny pin holes and fissures dotted throughout the mine. The room is so dark she can barely recognize the outline of the boy holding onto her. She bumps into the desk and searches with her hands for the edge. She tries to remember what the room looked like just a few moments ago. "Where's that chair? Shit! Now the table…okay, this is the soft one." Terri places the boy on top of the desk. "I'll be right back. I'm just going to close the door, so you'll be safe,"

"No, no," he wails as she tries to release his hand.

"Sweetie, I have to close that door. I'm not leaving you, I need to close the door sweetie, it's okay." She continues to talk to the boy while she feels her way to the door and back. Mission accomplished, Terri returns to the little boy. She feels his tiny body tremble as he sits beside her, in near total darkness. She cups both her hands over her mouth and quietly whispers to herself, "Josh…" In the background, she hears the scratches and hisses as rats scurry around. The little boy grabs at her and buries his face into her side. Terri caresses his forehead, remembering many times when she did this for her little brother. "We're safe. I know you're scared. I won't let anything happen to you." She squeezes him tightly to her.

The desk, can I move it there? Is it high enough, can I even move it? How far is it? Where was the shaft? I couldn't even budge the damn desk and everything else is too rotten.

"Damn, this isn't fair." Terri cries quietly as she presses her weight against the desk. *Nothing, it won't budge.* She traces the outline of the desk with her hands and finds a corner. "Don't be afraid. I just want to see if I can lift this a bit. Damn."

U.S. Department of Justice
Federal Bureau of Investigation

CHAPTER FORTY-FIVE: Teddy
November 1963

Terri and the boy sit in the darkness, unsure of know how long they have been there. *Has it been hours or days? I'm not hungry enough for it to have been days.* The traces of light that barely shone in the darkness have now been replaced by bright spears of light. Their eyes have not yet fully adjusted to the darkness. Faint outlines and darker shadows of unrecognizable objects surround them. Judging distance is, for now, impossible. For the moment, at least, the air is warm, and they are safe within the office. From the office window, Terri looks into the main room.

In this surreal environment, so dark, the tiniest dots of light amplify and cast strange silhouettes in the void. The little boy rests his head in her lap. Her fingers stroke his forehead and run through his hair. If she concentrates, she can see the main room where the walls connect from shaft to shaft. There's the distant sound of running water from deep within the mine. Except for the two missing panels of glass, the window provides the same view the men who worked here years before would have had.

It was right there, she thinks as she looks where she and the boy were lowered into this place. *He closed it.* She remembers the sounds and how the draft changed. *We're sealed in.* Trying desperately not to cry, Terri searches her memory for anything she saw when this place was lit. Anything she could use. Did she see a way out? *Why is it dark now? Did he turn the lights off? Is he gone?*

"So now...just where are you from, little guy?" She talks in a soft voice to the boy but there's no sound or response from him. Not sure what's going on, where Oldson is or what happened to the lights, the more Terri struggles to answer questions in her head, the more confused she becomes. A sudden wave of fear envelopes her as the full gravity of her situation sinks in. Fists raised to the ceiling, she screams, "Let us out of here, you bastard!" Her screams make the little boy cry. Terri stops screaming and comforts the little boy, whom she has arbitrarily decided to name Teddy. "Shh...it'll be okay, Teddy, I promise," Terri repeats this over and over in a motherly tone. Teddy finally calms down and falls asleep. Terri hears a noise outside the room that sounds out of place. *Oldson?* Her body tenses as she tries to figure out what it is.

In the main room, near the outline of one of the shafts, something moves. The motion catches her eye. Terri, careful not to disturb the boy, stands, leaving him behind on the desk, and moves to the window. She feels her heart racing. A figure, then a second, followed by a third and a flash from the shaft's opening. She only hears the sound of their feet as they come out into the room. Their panting echoes within the silence of the mine and sends cold shivers down her spine. Instinctively, she places her weight against the door and continues to peer through the window for the figures in the darkness.

Cornered in the office, she considers trying to move the desk in front of the door but decides that her efforts would attract their attention before she could barricade the entrance. She hears their feet as they move around. They come close to the office, but then move away slightly, then return even closer. She hears them sniff the air and their quiet low-pitched grunts as the three figures prowl the area. Terri is reminded of an article she read in the *National Geographic* about how wolves hunt together in packs. She's sure these three creatures are on the hunt now, sure that they're hunting for her and Teddy.

Close to where she hears one of them, she also notices the familiar sound of several rats. Suddenly, shrills break the silence. She sees the outline of two of the figures as the rats shriek. Then the sounds from the rats go silent. Terri stands motionless after seeing what she had just witnessed. Two figures are fighting over what must be a rat they have just killed. One of the figures is possibly two feet high; the other is a bit smaller. They appear to be eating the rat, ripping it open, trying to get the largest portion. She also sees the silhouettes of several rats near the pair awaiting any missed scraps that might be left behind.

For the first time, Terri sees their full outlines and realizes what they are. Tears fill her eyes and stream down her cheeks. Her legs tremble so hard, she almost collapses. Slowly lowering herself to the floor, she braces the door with her body. Terri stares at the little boy laying a few feet from her.

The three figures on the other side of the door just breathe, grunt, and finish their meal. In this new, dark world sounds have become her brightest color. The two figures huddle together, each tearing pieces off the rat and quickly eating their share. The largest figure notices another rat, and without hesitation, pounces on it. With a quick grab, a twist, and a sharp crack, the neck of the rat breaks. Before the legs stop twitching, the three figures grab and tear at the body. The sound their teeth make as they carve into the flesh and the smell of the fresh kill has caused the other rats to scatter. The trio tears pieces of flesh from the bones, quickly devouring everything. They even eat the bones, leaving little waste behind. With their meal finished, the figures lose interest with the office and, satisfied by their shared meal, they leave the main room and disappear into the darkness.

Her attention is suddenly drawn to the sound of the third figure, off to the right of the office, as the sound of its panting and grunts reach the other side of the door. Terri feels the door start to open as it pushes in. She widens her stance and braces the door with her shoulder moving the door back into the doorframe. *Bang!* The creature rams the other side of the door. Terri slams her weight onto the door. The door opens a couple of inches but sticks on the uneven floor. Terri hits the door so hard it jolts the figure on the other side and sends it rolling onto the floor in the center of the room. The figures in the room are now frozen in the darkness, looking in her direction.

U.S. Department of Justice
Federal Bureau of Investigation

CHAPTER FORTY-SIX: Charlie's 76
November 1963

Oldson stands in his *observatory*, as he prefers to call it. His fingers trace the outline of his latest sketch. "Welcome. You're home. You're safe. No more running." He switches off the lights and climbs the ladder to his workshop. Reaching the surface, he pulls the hatch shut, leaves the tunnel, and gets in his pickup. Oldson drives back to the access road, covering his tracks. Two dead elk lie in the back of his truck. He turns onto the road and heads for US 93.

By sunrise, he has arrived in Eureka where a familiar voice asks, "Just two this time, Hank?" Oldson smiles at the gas station attendant, pays cash for his gas and a carton of cigarettes.

For the past ten years, Charlie has run his little two-pump, Union 76 gas station at the north end of Eureka. Like the sign says, *Last Chance for Gas*, as his station is the last stop before the Canadian border. One air hose, water, a small store, and a single-bay shop make up the balance of Charlie's 76. He calls most customers by their first names. The ladies all seem to be named "Darlin" and the men "Hank." Charlie, as always, is dressed in blue coveralls. An oil-stained white cloth hangs from his left pocket, and he thanks "Hank" for the business.

"When you gonna be back?" Charlie asks.

Oldson looks in the direction of the mine and back to Charlie. "A month or two and should be able to bag another couple by then."

U.S. Department of Justice
Federal Bureau of Investigation

CHAPTER FORTY-SEVEN: Keep This Secret
Present Day

Banks and the other members of the BAU have returned to the command post after spending the past several hours resting at their motel in Evergreen. The first order of business is a meeting with the sheriff and his men, followed by a meeting to deal with inquiries from the ever-anxious media present at the site. The media presence has grown. At least ten vans, with their satellite antennas reaching into the sky, are parked around the media center.

"So far, they've respected the barricades. Hard to corral that many," the sheriff explains to Banks. "My deputies are doing the best they can, but with the property being so large, and most of the fences in various stages of neglect, it's just a matter of time until someone tries something stupid."

"We're about to deal with that issue right now," Banks says to the sheriff. He then sends an e-mail to Sanders instructing him to advise the media of the morning briefing scheduled to take place in thirty minutes. As Banks walks into the command trailer, a tech hands him a clipboard. He looks down at the pages, which detail what has taken place at the site during the past hours.

"Good morning everyone. On behalf of myself and the other members of my team, Sheriff, I wish to thank you and your deputies for your assistance thus far and going forward. Your help is vital to the success of this investigation. This crime scene covers a vast area, and with the increasing numbers of the media people gathering here, patrolling and maintaining a secure perimeter will require more security. At my request, the National Guard has been mobilized and should be arriving shortly to assist. Late last night, members of my team confirmed the presence of human remains."

The news, though shocking, isn't what's most troubling.

This dark, hidden secret that has gone undiscovered for so many years, is finally being unearthed. The sheriff's team present at the meeting each look at one another as Banks continues to describe details of this gruesome discovery so close to their homes. "The unsub has travelled into and out of here many times. There are limited routes into this site and I have asked the sheriff if he would coordinate a comprehensive search in areas that we believe the unsub used. Sheriff, please …"

"Thank you, Agent Banks. Mr. Sanders has sent me a series of maps." One of his deputies hands out copies as the sheriff continues, "As you all can see, this area where we are going to be searching is vast. This son-of-a…this unsub, travelled through here many times. He has come and gone as he pleased and with any luck, we'll find that he left something along the way. We have a hell of a lot of ground to cover, and with the help of the National Guard, if it's out there, we'll find it."

The meeting over, Banks and the other members of the BAU speak privately. "There are lights and switches down there, but none of them work. There are no visible wires, outlets, anything, we are assuming the UnSub concealed them within the walls of the container. These lights get their power from somewhere." Torres continues to describe what he and Cherkoff discovered. "We scanned what we could with the flashlights. There has-to-be a power source, another container, something, somewhere. I just hope they can find it." He looks in the direction of the sheriff and his men.

During the night, the Salt Lake office delivered several drones with video cameras and several walk-behind, ground-penetrating radar units capable of viewing objects buried deep underground. The ruggedness of the terrain will make the search difficult, but not impossible. The techs on scene have also placed portable lights into each of the containers to aide in the investigation, while at the same time minimizing contamination of any possible evidence. Banks knows it would have been much easier for Cherkoff and Torres if the lights were installed prior to their entry into the containers, but he could not risk damaging or disturbing anything. His agents must be the ones to make first contact.

Jenkins and Lee will help with the ground search and have enlisted the assistance of Deputy Ranger Clive Hemming. They arranged to have him released from the hospital in Missoula during the night.

"How are you feeling this morning?" Lee asks Clive.

"Not too bad. It was good to hear from my mom, not so worried anymore. What's the plan?"

U.S. Department of Justice
Federal Bureau of Investigation

CHAPTER FORTY-EIGHT: The Media
Present Day

At the far end of the crime scene, Banks has arrived at the media center and makes a brief statement to the press.

"Agent Banks! Ashley Blair, Channel Eight News. Can you give us an update of the agent's condition following the incident here late yesterday?"

"Her condition is fine. The environment, perhaps the nature of the confined space, caused her reaction," he replies.

"Have your people been inside the mine, and, if so, have they recovered anything?" another reporter asks.

"The witness that died, do you know the cause of death yet? Is it true that all of the witnesses are in intensive care?"

Question upon question continue as anxious voices overlap.

Raising his hands to calm the anxious crowd, Agent Banks' tone is firm. "This is an extremely complex site, and until our engineers can certify the safety of this structure, I am not going put anyone else at risk or attempt to remove any items. My team has been examining the architecture of this mine and its location on this property. From what we are told, these tunnels stretch out for several hundred feet, with possible pitfalls and other hazards. At my request, the local detachment of the National Guard has been mobilized to help patrol the area and to keep it secure. Your cooperation with this is greatly appreciated and your stations will be receiving a formal statement later this afternoon from our office in Quantico."

Several members of the media press for one or two last questions, but to no avail. The press conference concluded, Banks has always understood how the media can both help and hinder any investigation. The need of every reporter to *get the story* can, at times, put everyone at risk. "Yes, it's their job, but it's mine to make sure we're all safe," he has said many times throughout his career. He never avoids a question, rather choosing diplomatic and carefully worded responses. Insticntevely, he knows when and where to place the punctuation, and what talking points to either use or leave out.

U.S. Department of Justice
Federal Bureau of Investigation

CHAPTER FORTY-NINE: Back into Hell
Present Day

Banks returns to where Jenkins, Lee, and Clive are planning. They are examining satellite images Sanders provided, the same images that helped Sanders discover the route the unsub apparently used when he came to the site. Jenkins explains, "This path worn into the ground, when you stand on it, you don't see it. Look, these impressions are visible from above." Clive's face takes on a somber appearance as he looks at the photo.

"We are going to walk this route, all the way back to the access road," Lee says.

"That's pretty rough shit right there." Clive points to several areas on the photograph. "He drove through that?" The forestry department has also provided the team with detailed surface maps to aid in the search. "Even a stock four-wheel drive would have problems getting up and over that." Clive shows the team an area where a creek traverses through the hills. "It'll be hard enough to walk."

Jenkins looks at Lee and shakes her head a bit. "Maybe we should let our adventure racers take this one…" Jenkins points at Cherkoff and Torres in the distance. Cherkoff and Torres are leaving the command trailer, wearing their hazmat suits and putting on the respirators as they walk to the container's entrance. "On second thought, we'll stay up here," Jenkins concludes, as the agents and Clive leave the command area and begin to inspect the route taken by the unsub.

***

"You ready to go back into hell?" Cherkoff asks Torres, who nods, and the pair start their way down the series of ladders. The technicians are completing the final connections for the lighting system. This will provide Cherkoff and Torres with their first clear view of the mine's interior. Several other techs are setting up the equipment that will process the mapping data received as the various teams scan the ground. From the command trailer, Banks will be able to see a map of the site appear as the data is transmitted from the field radar equipment.

"This monitor will show you what the ground radar units see, and the plotter will provide you with a hard copy." The tech gives Banks with some last-minute details on how the system operates and remains with Banks to interpret the data. The sheriff's voice comes over the radio in the command trailer, "Agent Banks, we are about to start. Everyone is here." The sheriff is in charge of the ground search. "Each team consists of three people and each team is equipped with a mobile ground penetrating radar unit. The teams will span out from the excavation site in a circular pattern." Banks acknowledges the sheriff as the ground search begins. With the National Guard's arrival, the sheriff has teamed members of the guard with his deputies.

The sheriff also informs Banks that he has explained to each team their need to exercise extreme caution as they survey the land. "The possibility for cave-ins must remain paramount in everyone's mind," the sheriff said. "What information we have about this site is mostly historical and outdated. No need for any more victims here. Mr. Sanders has also provided us more recent survey data of the property via Deep Image."

The area being searched covers approximately four acres. The data has already started to display on the monitor in front of Banks. The mine's interior starts to form. A large area in front of the second container appears to have several shafts or tunnels attached. "The shade will get darker if the depth changes." The tech explains to Banks what he's seeing, "That area is probably a vertical shaft at the end of the tunnel." Banks cross-references the images with the historical map of the mine from the US Geological Department. As the mine slowly takes shape on both the monitor and the plotter, the vast scale of this underground complex is becomming apparent.

Banks updates Cherkoff and Torres. "The main room outside the lower container is at least eighty feet across by at least that long. The surface teams are dealing with some rough terrain changes."

"We're just about finished in Container One. We'll be heading down into number two shortly," Torres announces.

U.S. Department of Justice
Federal Bureau of Investigation

CHAPTER FIFTY: Container Two
Present Day

Cherkoff stands next to the workbench and says, "So he does what he does to them here. How does he get them into the mine? There has to be an access point into the mine, somewhere." Both agents finish in Container One and head down the hatch into a very well illuminated second container. Several high-power lights, placed on stands, are set up. One unit stands in front of the window and Cherkoff proceeds to turn on the switch.

A white, blinding light immediately off the window. As she adjusts the lights, their beams penetrate deep into the room in the front of the container. Torres stands beside her as they see for the first time what their flashlights could not show them yesterday. "Oh my God."

"What is it?" Banks asks.

"A crap load of rats just took off into the tunnels," Torres says. "Hundreds. You're right. That room is huge. We can see what looks like an old office. There's moss and mold everywhere."

"It's not what I was expecting. And the bones we saw are human. What's left of them. I can see what looks like several femurs, twenty feet or so into the room," reports Cherkoff.

"What's that in the middle there?" Torres points at an opening in the ceiling. "I think we found the access, roughly thirty feet or so in front of the window. There's a square opening, probably another vent shaft."

"How far from your location is it?" Banks asks.

"Thirty feet, dead center from the window," remarks Torres.

Banks, in turn, instructs the ground team closest to that location to look for evidence on the surface. The ground team finds a large rock. And as they scan the ground, an image of a vertical shaft displays on the monitor and plotter in the command trailer. "The ground team found the shaft. It's covered with a large rock, and we are working on getting it removed," Banks informs Torres.

"So, he just, what, dropped them in there?" Cherkoff asks Torres, a look of disgust covers her face. "And let the rats…oh Jesus!" She stops mid-sentence as something catches her eye. "Banks, you need to get down here, right now." Her voice is calm but direct and immediately prompts Banks to leave the trailer. Banks exits the command trailer and heads to the excavation site. When he arrives inside Container Two, Cherkoff motions him to look through the window into the mine.

U.S. Department of Justice
Federal Bureau of Investigation

CHAPTER FIFTY-ONE: Denmark 1943

This is his place. His responsibility. His duty. Jakob, his younger brother. He watched as both his mother and father disappear into the darkness of the night. It was difficult for him to watch them go, standing there as their shadows faded. But this is his place. With him and he has Jakob…his younger brother. His responsibility. Each time when they would leave his mother would say, "*Holde ham sikkert, skjul indtil mørke.*" Keep him safe, hide until dark. In her soft voice and with a gentle pat on the head, she would leave. This day is not much different than any other since the German occupation of Denmark began. The Nazis patrol the streets checking papers, and, more importantly, armbands. All Jews must wear a yellow armband. To be caught not displaying this means certain and swift punishment. Many Danes try to help the plight of the Danish Jews. Even King Christian X wore the armband in silent protest.

Both his parents work day and night with the resistance. Oldson and his younger brother would hide in the rubble and even the sewers during the day. Protected in the darkness of the night, they would come out to search for food, clothing, anything. Oldson knows that it's so much easier to see a threat in the darkness than during the daylight, the red glow of a soldier's cigarette. It becomes a beacon at night. *Keep him safe. Hide until dark.* These words he will always remember. His mother taught Oldson from a young age to be resourceful and independent.

Oldson and his brother had been unable to leave the cover of their hiding place for almost two days. A cold front brought terrible weather and the boys could only huddle together for warmth. Being cold is bad enough but also being damp and not able to get dry made the past days almost unbearable. His little brother is four and weighs just thirty pounds. Oldson just turned ten and he cradles his little brother in his arms. Oldson always places his brother on top of his lap when the ground is wet, draping his little legs over his own. He can feel his brother's stomach churn and growl. This feeling does not cause either alarm, only when they cannot feel this do they start to worry. Hunger has become more familiar to them than the faces of their parents.

His little brother would stare intently at Oldson as he would tell him a story. Stories that Oldson has thought of, stories of places far away, away from the rubble and chaos that surrounds them. Speaking to his brother in Danish, his stories about *vores sted*, our place, where the boys could fish by the river all day as their parents watched.

"Believe me, Jakob, such a wonderful place does exist," Oldson would tell his brother, and he would hold his tiny hands. "Close your eyes. You can see it, yes? There is Mamma and Papa, oh, and what do you have? Can you see it? You have one. Your first fish; they are so proud of you. I am so proud of you!" His little brother would smile as Oldson recited.

However, today is different. His stories are not helping. Oldson caresses his brother's hand as he speaks, but his restlessness increases. Two days with nothing more than a pinch of rotten bread and a handful of rain water in his little belly. Oldson understands why he is restless, but still they must wait. "It will be dark soon, and the weather is clearing," Oldson tells his brother. Oldson sees from where they are hiding that the streets are wet and muddy. The walking will be difficult, but with so few people in the streets these past two days, their chances for finding food are good.

U.S. Department of Justice
Federal Bureau of Investigation

CHAPTER FIFTY-TWO: Jakob
1943

The evening sky has always provided the boys comfort and safety. The darkness magnifies any problem and the evil things can be seen from far away. The cool grey twilight brings so much excitement as the chaos and the light of day gives way to the quiet stillness of their nights. As the sky darkens and the shadows fade, Oldson senses his brother's excitement.

He tells his brother, "Soon, very soon, it's almost time. We must be very careful tonight. You hold my hand and stay close." As he speaks, his brother looks at him and nods. "It is very wet, and the puddles are deep. We walk and don't run." The streets may appear empty, but at night, sound travels much farther than during the day, so the boys never speak when they are out. Oldson's eyes constantly pan the horizon, around every corner, looking for anything, something. He hears everything, the sounds of the city and the distant sounds of someone walking as a piece of glass breaks under foot.

The boys scurry from one place to the next, keeping their bodies as low to the ground as possible. The rain has brought many creatures out into this night. Oldson finds snails, worms, even a tiny garter snake. *You just have to know where to look.* He thinks to himself. Oldson always makes sure that his brother eats first. Even when their searches result in nothing more than just one snail, Oldson always lets his little brother eat first. This evening's menu is much more plentiful than even Oldson could have imagined. In a short time, both boys find themselves feeling full. *When our stomachs are so empty, it doesn't take much to fill them.*

Oldson carries with him a small cloth bag and as they search, he places the extras in it. Oldson's favorite spots are all turning up a bounty better than expected and the bag is filling up fast. The small end of a loaf of bread, a dead bird, and three bird's eggs and, as usual, the leftovers in the bottom of the ration tins left behind. Apparently, the scrapings at the bottom of the tins aren't good enough for the Nazi soldiers who ate from them.

Their route tonight takes them to the old town square. Shops and cafes once owned by Jews are now vacant and boarded up. In the windows where merchants proudly displayed their inventory, now only wooden voids remain. The scars left on his town, though silent, have a great impact. The boys make their way to the town square, and if their luck holds out, they should be able to fill their bag, then return to where they were hiding.

Oldson looks up at one of the old stores. He can remember when his mother used to bring him there to buy clothes; *it was so long ago…or was it?* The boards on the windows, the word *JUDE* painted across. With his attention for just a moment on the sign, he doesn't notice his brother wander off. Oldson hears footsteps as they run. He turns and realizes the sound he's hearing is his brother. Not able to call out to him, Oldson can only chase after him. The sound of his brother's footsteps is followed by the sound of him tripping, then the crash of his body as it smashes into the ground.

Oldson runs around the corner of a building and sees his brother's tiny body lying on a pile of broken bricks. He sees the rock that his brother tripped over. Oldson knows he must not scream or cry out. He bends down to his brother's side. His brother's little body shakes violently as the sound of his last breath of air rushes out of his mouth. His little body lying facedown on the pile, Oldson turns his brother over and sees the damage. The piece of metal sticks through his throat and Oldson can only watch as the life drains from his brother's eyes. They cloud over, and he is gone.

Oldson places his brother on his lap and holds him as he has done so many times. His little legs on his, his arm around his tiny waist, and his hand caressing his hair. He pulls the piece of metal from his brother's neck, pausing briefly to look at it, then places it on the ground. His tears provide his only comfort, as he holds his brother in his arms.

U.S. Department of Justice
Federal Bureau of Investigation

CHAPTER FIFTY-THREE: Not Alone
November 1963

Terri and Teddy remain huddled together in the office. The creatures in the main room are content, for now. In this dark place, the sequence of events is very disjointed. Enough time has lapsed to make her eyes adjust to the level of light in the mine. Through the tiny streams of illumination, she can see the trio together. They look in her direction.

They crouch on the floor and appear puzzled at what has just taken place. Those strange sounds, the child's cries and the sound of Terri's voice. The largest figure can't ever recall the door moving, let alone snapping back like that.

Submerged in darkness and left there together, Terri and the little boy remain cornered in the office. Terri has watched the figures come out from the darkness of the shafts. They come into the main room to search for food, anything to eat. *They are just children,* she thinks, but they are so wild—their eyes, hands, and faces. The little boy is becoming increasingly restless and his cries get the attention of the figures in the main room. "Quiet, Teddy, it's okay," Terri attempts to console him.

Terri feels the weight of one of the children press against the door, which is followed by grunting as the figure continues to press against the door with all its might. Terri has more difficulty as the figure attempts to breach the door. She feels the weight of the second figure, and then finally the third, pressing against it. Terri has shown Teddy how to climb onto the table using the chair as a step. She motions to the little boy. He scurries to the table and climbs on top.

"Go away! Leave us alone!" she yells in a harsh tone. Almost immediately, the trio freezes at the sound of her voice. The three boys, two Caucasians and one black, stand on the other side. Their grunts have stopped for the moment. Terri speaks again, her tone a bit softer, "Just go away! Now!" Her feminine voice is pleasing, but the harsh tone warns the trio of the possible danger. Such sounds they have heard, a long time ago, but are now foreign. *How long have you been down here?* Terri thinks as she looks in their direction.

The reaction Terri receives each time when she speaks to the trio, no matter the tone or volume, is the same—confusion. *What is this strange thing that makes this strange sound?* The little black boy walks from where they are huddled to the door. The largest of the group stretches on tippy-toe trying to reach the window in the wall of the office. Unable to make himself tall enough, he presses his ear to the door and listens for that strange sound. Terri hears the scratching and scuffling sounds as he moves to the door.

Terri feels the weight of his tiny frame against the door. As he pants quietly on the other side, Terri says,

"I'm Terri." She doesn't understand why she says this. Her heart is racing fast as she tries to digest what is going on. "He did this to you too…" she says quietly, more a statement than a question. There is no reply, of course, only the sound his hands make as they grab for the window ledge. His chipped fingernails and blackened palms are visible as he pulls his face up to the glass. Terri looks at the little boy on the other side. He couldn't be more than seven years old, but in his face and eyes, there is a maturity a curiosity. Terri only stares as he looks at her face through the glass. Again, she softly announces, "I'm Terri. My name is Terri."

U.S. Department of Justice
Federal Bureau of Investigation

CHAPTER FIFTY-FOUR: Hungry
November 1963

The little boy in the office with Terri is becoming more and more restless. His cries start to get louder. Terri motions him to be quiet with a gentle, "Shh." As she waves her hand, the motion startles the boy at the window. He drops down from the window and the trio retreats into the darkness. Alone again, Terri and the little boy comfort each other in the office as best they can.

"Why are you doing this?" Terri says as Oldson's image flashes through her mind. *How long have we been here?* Looking into the main room she watches as several hungry rats search for any remnants of the boys' meal. After watching what the others have eaten, she ponders, *Will I become like them?* The thought of killing, let alone eating, a rat was an absurd thought, until now. The strong aroma of the fungi growing on the table reminds Terri of mushrooms that her family would buy at the store.

She pulls several small pieces of the soft fungi from the table top. "It smells fine," she says to the little boy sitting atop the table. Terri pulls just a pinch of the fungi from the table. Unable to see its color, she can only guess. *Is it brown? No, it's green*, she debates as she lifts it to her mouth. Suddenly, the little boy reaches his hand out, grasping at the air, trying to grab at the food in her hand. Terri stops for a moment, looking at the boy as she thinks, *What would happen to you if I get sick from this?* She decides to give the portion to the boy. He opens his tiny mouth and eagerly consumes the fungi. Like a little bird, he begs for more. Terri gives him a tiny bit more saying, "Easy now…that's all for now."

A small portion would have to suffice. "Time, time, we have to wait." She gently rubs his belly and tries to calm the little boy. Terri opens the office door, not all the way, but enough for her to squeeze through. She tries to remember where she saw the trio grab something from the floor and appear to eat. She motions to the little boy to sit still and tells him, "I'll be right back," as she leaves the office for the main room.

As she disappears into the black, she keeps talking to the little boy. Whether this is done for his benefit or her own, the sound of her voice calms them both as she searches the ground. In the main room, she crouches down where the trio picked at the ground. Her hands feel only the cool floor. She finds a smooth rock and feels its outline. The rock must be at least three feet square, and she feels something familiar on its surface. *Snails, that was what you*…from the corner of her eye, she sees the trio.

They have come to the exit of the shaft right across from where she is. Their grunts echo from the mouth of the shaft. Terri is kneeling at their favorite spot. The tallest in front is pacing, moving his weight from one side to the other. She senses his concern. She isn't welcome where she is. He takes several steps in her direction, only to retreat to the others. Terri stands up and the trio darts off deep into the dark, intimidated by her size. With the trio gone, she kneels down to the rock and finds a snail.

She holds the snail, only about the size of a quarter, between her fingers. She closes her eyes tight as she smashes the snail into the rock. *Aw...yuck. Terri, what are you doing?* She picks the small pieces of shell from the flesh. The fresh meat between her fingers, she opens her mouth and throws the snail in. She doesn't chew, just swallows. Swift and fast. That's it. *What does it taste like?* It happened so quickly she had no chance to experience the taste. *Not as horrible as I thought,* she admits as she searches the rock for more snails. She finds four and then a fifth. She stands up and heads back to the office.

Terri stands at the table in front of the little boy and squishes the snails. His little eyes watch as she picks the pieces of shell from the meat. His little fingers reach to her mouth as she throws another meal into her throat. She divides the next snail between them. With her fingernails, she pinches off a small piece for the little boy, who chews it eagerly. His face only grimaces for a moment as he adjusts to the feeling and taste of the meat. Terri decides to chew the next snail as she eats. The warm feeling of its fresh flesh in her mouth and the rubbery texture cause her to gag, just slightly. With her hand cupped to her mouth, she chews and swallows her food. Having protien in her stomach, finally, gives Terri a strange feeling. Her mind that had been cloudy clears a little and the anxiety of a few moments before, now is calm. With their small meal finished, the pair sits together in the office.

When Terri came in, she could not close the door with the snails in her hands. The door stands ajar. Now, from behind her, she hears the sound of the trio. Closer and closer they approach the office. Terri is on the floor beside the little boy. She turns to the door as the trio, led by the largest, approaches the opening. Their agility and dexterity amazes her. They don't stand upright, though they can when they need to. Their gait reminds her of chimps and monkeys. They walk hunched over, feeling for objects in the darkness with their hands as they move.

When the trio gets to within a few feet of the open door, the leader's pace quickens. Terri leans back slightly as the little black boy reaches the door. "I'm Terri." Her soft voice stops the boy at the threshold. He sits down on his bottom, at the entrance, and tilts his head to one side, staring at Terri. She sees his brow furl as he tries to analyze what he is seeing and the sound of her voice. Though thin, his physique is surprisingly taught. The muscles in his arms and legs are well developed. Over and over, she repeats, "I'm Terri. I'm Terri." The visitor at the door only grunts as he rocks his head back and forth. The boy is frightened and curious as she speaks. Any sudden movement startles the boy and his smaller companions. When she stands, towering over them, at five feet, four inches, they cower, and the leader slowly moves back from the door to the comfort his friends.

U.S. Department of Justice
Federal Bureau of Investigation

CHAPTER FIFTY-FIVE: The Trio
November 1963

The three boys have known only each other and a few other small children who were brought here. They've survived alone and don't remember teenagers or even adults. They were abducted by Oldson when they were very young. Even memories of Oldson, his size, his face, all forgotten now. The trio has been together the past year. The black boy and one of the white boys came here together.

The third boy, who was already here, witnessed other children perish and managed to fend for himself. When he was abducted at the age of four, Oldson had deposited him into this world. He was lowered down the shaft and sat for several days. Beside him on the ground lay another little boy who was, unfortunately, past the point of no return. His eyes were sunken deep, his little belly hung distended. He would die a few short days later. His fate had been sealed when Oldson brought him to the mine.

Oldson had not yet perfected the method for lowering the children into the mine. The rope elevator was not yet in service, so his victims would fall to the rock-hard ground below. The success rate of his captives greatly improved with the addition of the elevator. The little boy, having seen the remains of several victims scattered around him and witnessing the death of the boy beside him, chose to leave the area where he was lowered, and hide. He sought the shelter of the black, the darkness in the tunnel. Escaping from the horrors in the main room, he retreated into the third shaft, only coming out to find snails or the fungi. He would spend most of his time in the darkness and warm air of the tunnel.

From time to time, he would hear sounds coming from the main room. These were at first very frightening but would sadly grow familiar to him. The same scenario would play out over-and-over again. From his perch, safe within the tunnel, he would see the light in the main room change. Followed by a loud, ear-piercing scraping noise. He would hear that noise, then the eventual screams. The crying would slowly fade to whimpers. He would try to muster up the courage to investigate. He even attempted to help the new-ones. However, their fear over-taking their need for survival, eventually, that noise would stop.

He could, once again, emerge from the darkness. There, on the floor, another cold body would be there. He would stare at it for a while then go about his business, looking for something to eat. When the room was quiet, without the screams and those other sounds that frightened him so, he could come out. After a few days, what was lying on the floor would be gone. At times there would remain small reminders but mostly all that would be left was the floor.

His life would change the day he heard not one but two noises from the main room. He heard the same high-pitched scraping. As usual, the light would change but this time something was different. From the darkness, in the shaft, he could see white light. He has faint memories of that white light. Those noises come again. "Mommy! Mommy!"...over and over again. He tried to understand why he could hear both the "Mommy" sound and crying at the same time. He'd never heard them together before. The sounds that would usually come from the main room had always been separate. Two sounds, one source.

And the lights. Why was the white light on? The white light of the fluorescents had been turned off shortly after he was lowered into the mine. His eyes hurt as he got closer to the exit of the darkness. The pain was so intense that the other boys would see him sitting with his eyes covered, his body covered with the tattered remains of his clothes. He sat on his bottom across the room from them. As he sat there rubbing his eyes, the other boys made their way to where he was. The trio remained together and has survived, and the ritual of the main room repeated itself many, many times.

The trio has heard many sounds coming from the main room, but Terri has them puzzled and agitated. The same ritual occurred, the scraping sound, then the change in light from the main room. There was that sound again, but this time it was different. Her voice, when she shouted at Oldson, it wasn't what they were used to. The trio had gotten used to multiple voices coming from the main room, and even this time they could hear two.

However, before they came out from the darkness to inspect, they knew this time something was very different. Her voice was soft and gentle. Even, when she raised her voice and scared them away, it was strangely pleasing. They can't remember why, but she reminds them of something or someplace. What is it about this new thing, here in their world? This tall thing that has the long hair, so clean, and when she makes those noises, for some strange reason, they feel safe. The trio watches Terri and the boy for hours. Paying special attention to her skin—those coverings, what are they? Something is so familiar. All they can do is look at Terri and wonder.

U.S. Department of Justice
Federal Bureau of Investigation

CHAPTER FIFTY-SIX:
Keep This Off the Two-Way
Present Day

"How many are there?" Banks asks Cherkoff as he stares into the main room of the mine.

"We have seen at least five. They all stay close to the exits of those tunnels. Now what the hell are we going to do?" she replies as Banks and Torres stand silently beside her.

Watching as the survivors shield their eyes from the bright lights shining into the mine, Banks says, "We need to get these lights turned down or off."

Torres is about to use the com to alert the surface when Banks stops him. "No, for now, we need to keep this off the two-way. I need to call Quantico. I need you both to try and determine just how many survivors we're dealing with. Do the best you can. We will have a private team meeting in twenty. This has just become—"

Cherkoff cuts Banks off, "A nightmare?"

***

Banks returns to the command trailer and clears all other personnel from the room. He makes two calls to Quantico. His first is to the deputy director informing her of the alarming discovery the team has just made. "As unbelievable as it sounds, there are survivors. Two members of my team are attempting to determine just how many. They appear to be adults. I will keep you posted." The uncharacteristic shock in his supervisor's voice as he describes the scene to her is almost as disturbing as the images of the survivors' faces in the mine. His second call is to Sanders.

Sanders can hardly believe what he's hearing. If it weren't for the tone in his boss' voice, he would have not believed it. Cases involving long-term entrapment, although very rare, do exist, and the bureau has dealt with them in the past. However, neither Banks nor Sanders can recall anything of this scale. "Cherkoff and Torres are studying them now, and we're going to have a team briefing in ten. Find out whatever you can." Banks instructs Sanders to do some speedy research and mobilize whatever resources the bureau has at its disposal to help deal with what they have found.

Banks hangs up the phone and looks out the trailer window in the direction of the media center and contacts Jenkins. "I need you and Lee back at the command trailer. There has been a development."

"What was that all about?" Lee asks Jenkins.

"Didn't say. We're to leave Clive at the sheriff's trailer and come on in."

Banks remains alone in the trailer. Numerous scenarios that may pan out with this new discovery run through his mind. *Survivors, why? How?* His team was prepared to deal with the aftermath of a mass grave, but this. Never for a moment did the team expect to find survivors. That possibility was unthinkable. His original concern was the validity of the site. If it were not for the impassioned pleading of the sheriff, he would not have mobilized his team to this site. Who are these people? Where did they come from? How long have they been here? What do we do now? Banks quietly recites to himself the words from the small plaque on his desk back in Quantico: *In very dark places, we will at times see a moment of light...*Those words have always helped to focus his thoughts but today, for some reason, they mean much, much more.

U.S. Department of Justice
Federal Bureau of Investigation

CHAPTER FIFTY-SEVEN: Beyond the Glass
Present Day

"We are all here Sanders," Banks tells Sanders as their video conference with Quantico begins. Banks has asked the sheriff to join his team for this private meeting. Banks brings Jenkins, Lee, and the sheriff up to date with the latest details concerning the mine. "Yes, you heard me, survivors."

"How is that possible?" Lee asks.

"Uncertain, but it is apparently possible," replies Banks.

"Do we know how many, and what are they? Boys, girls, or are we talking men or women?" the sheriff questions Banks.

"So far, we counted at least ten young adults, both men and women. The lights are causing a real problem down there, so telling for sure what the hell is going on is tough. They are very timid, but they appear alright and very much alive," reports Cherkoff.

"Remember those Chilean miners? Recovered after just two months in the darkness, they all experienced excruciating pain even with the aid of the welder's glasses," Sanders interjects. "If they have been in total darkness for years, any amount of light would be a problem, especially those work lights. Using night vision or infrared is probably our best approach."

Everyone in the meeting senses the growing magnitude of what they have discovered. The team had expected to find remains. Remains alone would be hard enough to identify but now they are challenged with the daunting task of dealing with a group of survivors. Imprisoned here, taken from their families.

"Profiling this unsub still remains our top priority, now, more than ever," Banks says. "This unsub may provide us our only way of putting names to those faces. Repatriating these people with their families, important as it may seem, for now, it is not our role. I have instructed Sanders, and he has contacted several specialists to help with that end of the investigation. The physical evidence collected from both containers one and two are being processed either onsite here, or in the case of the notebooks, on their way to Quantico."

"Where do we start with all of this?" Jenkins asks as she shakes her head.

"Properly dating the site and the residents of the mine is step one. Performing an accurate head count of the survivors must also take place immediately." The team is in complete agreement as to the matter of the media. "For now, the knowledge of their existence remains with us, and does not leave this room," says Banks.

A deafening silence fills the room as his fellow agents and the sheriff try to process these new facts. "When we first came here, our concern was, what would the reaction the press and the public would have with the possibility of a mass grave site. Now, the how, how could this happen, answering that will lead us to our unsub. When I spoke with the deputy director she was in complete agreement with this assessment."

"We saw no evidence on the trail leading in and out of the site to give us any idea when this unsub was here last," Jenkins informs to the group.

"At this point, the only thing we do know for sure is he would have had access to a heavy-duty specially equipped four-wheel-drive truck. Even Clive said, that his truck would have a darn hard time negotiating that path," Lee says.

"Jenkins, you and Lee, top priority, we need to know when the unsub was here last," instructs Banks.

The sheriff's two-way radio beeps, "Sheriff, we have something up here…you need to see this," reports a deputy.

U.S. Department of Justice
Federal Bureau of Investigation

CHAPTER FIFTY-EIGHT: How
Present Day

Banks' team and the sheriff arrive where the deputy has been working with one of the forensic techs. The tech has been examining the large rock the unsub used to block the drop shaft. Their attention has been on several large gouges worn into a rock. "Those aren't natural, and they look like they are from some kind of push bar, on a truck perhaps." The forensics tech carefully documents the impressions on the rock. He takes photographs and removes several samples for analysis. He has also discovered a set of rails that the large rock rests on. "These rails extend past the rock, and you can see, here, where the ground around the bottom of the rock has also been worn. If you want, we can use one of our field trucks and try to move this out of the way."

"You have both done excellent work here, but for now just, leave the rock as it is. Make sure Sanders gets copies of all this right away. It looks like you both could use a break." Both men agree and make their way back to the command area.

Banks must arrange for some specialized equipment and get it set up as soon as possible. The team will use the bureau's night vision and passive infrared imaging systems to view and document the survivors inside the mine.

***

Why do you just sit there? This is all for you, don't you see that? Don't you realize? It is safe in here. And now, so are you. But still, you will not move. Your tears have calmed but still, you do not move. Where you were you had only chaos. Just a number, an appointment on someone's check list, but here, you have a home. I can see you breathe. I can hear you cry. Everything you need is right there. Why don't you just try?

So gently did you land down there, not like those others; my heart is still heavy. It was so difficult to see. Those sounds I would hear. Their eyes as their bodies just lay there as you do now. I watched, recorded, and learned, so you would not have to.

The lights are on. You're safe in there. Holde ham sikkert, skjul indtil mørke, Oldson thinks as he watches the little girl take a labored, final breath.

U.S. Department of Justice
Federal Bureau of Investigation

CHAPTER FIFTY-NINE: Her New Home
November 1963

"Fifteen, sixteen, seventeen. Okay, it's just a big room, the size of her high school football field. These lights, how long have they been on for? Oh Teddy, I know, I don't know either. What time is it? What day?" Terri's voice a little louder than she had expected as it echoes slightly in the main room.

When the lights have been on, she has taken the time to inspect the entire main room. "I can barely see down this one." Terri says. The light from the main room illuminates just the entrance of the tunnels. When the lights are on, most of the rats disappear deep into the tunnels, leaving only a few—the boldest, oblivious to even her loudest, "Get! Shoo!"

Teddy remains by her side, holding her hand as she walks the room. Dressed only in her top and skirt, Terri is amazed at how comfortable the air temperature is, even the humidity is very similar to her bathroom at home after a shower. She feels no chill. *Is it still November?* Terri shakes her head slightly, unable to answer her own question. When the lights are off, the sharp darkness slowly fades to a cool grey, twilight. Surprisingly, her eyes are becoming more-and-more comfortable when the lights are off than when they are on.

Her other companions also have shown more and more interest. And appear more comfortable with her presence. The three little boys, led by the tallest, have become more daring as Terri becomes calmer in her new surroundings. Terri sees the trio as they slowly exit one of the tunnels. The black boy is always first to enter the room. Terri and Teddy stand their ground. Her height towers over all the boys so she decides to kneel. Terri reaches her left arm out extending her hand to the leader.

"It's okay, my name is Terri…what's yours? This is Teddy." She points to her companion as she introduces him to the others. "How long have you been here? Where are you all from?" She asks questions that she knows they probably cannot answer, at least for now. The sound of her voice, she sees their reactions, and in a curious way it calms her as well. The leader looks at her arm, then her hand. How clean she is, the color of her skin and how different her fingers look. He slowly reaches his hand out to touch her skin. His touch resembles that of someone testing the water to see if it is too hot. No sooner does his finger touch her skin than he draws it back. A second try lasts a little longer, then a third, until finally curiosity conquers fear and he holds her fingers.

"My name is Terri," she says as she points to her chest with her one free hand. Terri slowly sits on the ground as all the other boys surround her. She can see the fascination in their eyes as they look her over, up, and down, staring at her long blonde hair as it cascades over her chest and down her back. The shape of her body, her breasts, hips—all seem so foreign to the boys. "You haven't seen your mothers in a very long time, have you?" Each boy has very little clothing on, just rags. Nothing on their feet, which makes Terri realize her shoes are gone as well. "What are your names? Your names...what did your mamma call you?" Each time she says names, she points to each boy. Then she repeats, "My name is Terri," pointing to her chest once again. The boys fixate just on the sound of her voice as she speaks but do not answer. "You must have names." Her tone changes, almost pleading with the boys to answer. Without noticing, she has started to caress the little black boy's hand. As the soft feeling of her touch warms his hand, he starts to pull away, but then remains, holding her hand and listening to her voice.

"It's okay, I'm Terri and we will find away and get out of here!" Her eyes look around the room as they all sit together on the floor. She can only estimate the height of the mouth of the shaft from the floor. *There is no way.* She thinks to herself. Even if she could get up to it, the sides look smooth. As she sits with the boys, Terri starts to put together in her mind what has happened and what's going on. Are these his only other victims? What is that sound, off in the distance—the sound is faint, but familiar. Water, as it trickles through the underground passageways. The quality of the air has surprised her as well. Not just the temperature and the humidity but the smell is not what she would expect.

Terri feels a gentle breeze but where and how? *If there is a breeze, there must be an exit. Why haven't these boys found it?* Thinking as fast as she can and with no way of knowing how much longer the lights will remain on, her thoughts continue to race. *He must still be here…but where?*

Terri wants to search the mine further. She motions to the little boys that she wants to look around. "Let's look around a bit while we can, while the lights are still on."

U.S. Department of Justice
Federal Bureau of Investigation

CHAPTER SIXTY: Exploring November 1963

As she stands the boys watch her closely. She follows the direction of the breeze. The breeze appears to flow into one of the tunnels. She stands at the entrance; the light illuminates only the first ten or so feet, but as she enters the tunnel the black boy pushes his way in front of her.

Standing his ground, he guards the entrance. His tiny form defiantly blocks Terri's path. He broadens his shoulders as wide as he can make them, shakes his head at her, and pulls at her arm motioning her to stay out. He makes no sound, but his orders scream like a drill sergeant's.

"Okay, okay, not this one, I understand," Terri says, and as she does, a faint but pungent smell wafts from deep within the tunnel. *But why?* "Oh shit!" Terri says quietly, as she gets an answer to one of her earlier questions. The light shines just far enough into the shaft and exposes several leg bones lying on the ground. The two other little boys don't come near the entrance to this tunnel; they remain together several feet away.

Did she really see that? She knows that somehow, she must see what's in there. But for now, she will have to wait. The little boy used all his power to hold her back and for now she must obey. Not wanting to upset their new friendship, Terri follows as the little black boy leads her to one of the other tunnels. The boys scurry when they walk, keeping most of their weight on the tips of their toes. They only use the soles of their feet when they stand still. Terri wonders if they're trying to look taller. The boys lead her to the tunnel where the sound of water is strongest. The light shines deepest into this tunnel. Terri can see the floor of the tunnel drop off into the darkness.

The three little boys scamper in without hesitation and Terri tries to keep up with them. Teddy's grip grows strong, holding onto her hand as she walks into the darkness. She feels his pulse quicken as the tunnel gets dark. "Slow down! I can't see where you are…where are you?" It's so dark, but the other three boys navigate it as if it were lit. The black boy makes his way back to Terri; she suddenly feels his little hand reach up to hers. Grasping at her hand in the dark, he tugs and pulls her, motioning her deeper into the tunnel. "Teddy hold my hand, okay? It's alright you're safe," she quietly says as they follow the boys into the darkness.

As the group walks down the tunnel, there are tiny droplets of light reflecting, sparkling in the walls. *How can this be? Am I imagining this?* The air is getting a bit cooler and the ground feels as though she is walking down a hill. The sound of the water is very clear now and if she concentrates and tries to focus, she can make out the surface of the stream. *Is it ten…no, fifteen feet away?* The boys stop, and each finds his usual spot on the floor below to sit. Terri and Teddy do the same. Terri looks back in the direction they came from and tries to remember, *how many steps, how long did that take? Did we turn? Oh God, how can I do this?* Everything is so dark. Then she remembers the faces of those little boys sitting right with her—*They did it, Terri. So can you.*

She feels her hand move, startling her, as one of the boys takes her hand and places it on a smooth rock. The rock has a glassy surface, and she hears the little boy's hand tap the stone. He pats it several times and tugs at her hand. "Sit here?" Terri asks as she sits down. His tapping stops. Sitting in the dark, Terri squints and rubs her eyes as she adjusts to this new place. Looking up she notices a myriad of tiny cracks and fissures in the ceiling of the tunnel. Speckles of light dance all around her, as she sits with the little boys. Terri cannot help but think of her own little brother and where he is right now. Is he safe? The feeling of the little boy's hand is so rough and calloused. She covers her eyes for a moment, and then laughs quietly to herself. *Why are you covering your eyes?* How can such a dark place be filled with so much detail? Everything in this place is magnified. The sounds, the smells, the feeling of it all screams in Terri's mind louder than her own fears as she slowly gets accustomed to her new home.

U.S. Department of Justice
Federal Bureau of Investigation

CHAPTER SIXTY-ONE: Water, Food, Shelter
November 1963

In the distance is the sound of the rats as they scurry about. There are so many, the sound of their feet beating together and reminds her of the marching bands in the parades back home. Their sound draws closer, then dissipates as the black boy stamps his feet on the ground. He rapidly pounds his feet into the ground and hits the rock; the rats flee.

Her thoughts of Josh, her family, and even Oldson are slowly fading. They're being replaced with the sound of her own voice reminding herself, *My name is Terri*. She has no idea how long she has been with these boys in this tunnel. Time has suddenly become a visual thing as they sit in the darkness. Only her stomach can serve as a reminder that it has been quite a while. Teddy sits tightly beside her, clinging to her skirt like a security-blanket. Her eyes are becoming adjusted to the level of light and she can make out the edge of the stream. The stream runs across the bottom of the shaft they are sitting in. Terri crawls across the floor on her hands and knees and reaches the edge of the stream.

The water is cool and tastes clean. Terri can't remember when she has ever tasted water so clean. She sees the reflections, the tiny spots of light flickering all around her, however, she can't see clear enough to tell what they are or if they are even real. Their image reminds her of a time lying on her back in the field at night with Josh, holding hands and looking up at the stars. *Josh what happened to you?...I love you.* She cups several handfuls of the cool, clear water, drinking each one after the next and with Teddy close by her side, she places her cupped hand to his mouth and he drinks. "It's okay, it's alright. Doesn't this taste good?" Her voice is very calm, and Teddy eagerly drinks the water. Terri knows that Teddy will be getting hungry soon, as she feels her own stomach growl.

When she speaks, the sound of her voice echoes in the tunnel and she can only guess as to the size of this part of the tunnel. Terri stands and places her hands on the wall. Her fingers lightly scan the rock and feel its rough face. She realizes the shiny flecks are some type of mineral reflecting what little light is in the tunnel. The little boys sit closer and closer to her. The smallest has even gently poked and touched Terri and her clothes. As she moves about the tunnel, she tries to map in her mind this new home, its size, what the floor might look like. She can only think and imagine and draw its picture in her mind. The sound of one of the boys as he walks away from the group has Terri concerned. *Where are you going? Which one?* She scans the room for the heads of the remaining boys.

The leader has left the tunnel. The sound of his feet disappears into the main room. He has no sooner gone than he has returned with something in his hands. He stands in the center of the group and proudly places his prize on the floor at Terri's feet. He motions to the other boys who each grab at the dead rat, each swiftly tearing a piece off. Terri can only hold her hand to her mouth as she tries not to gag. She watches as the boys eat the warm, freshly killed rat, chewing at the legs like you would a chicken leg. The leader takes a small rock and carves at the side of the rat, shearing a piece of muscle, and offers it to Terri.

Teddy is very curious and too young to understand why Terri is hesitating so. The others are eating, why isn't she? The leader offers the piece to Teddy. He holds the warm piece of meat between his tiny fingers. Instinctively holding it to his nose, Teddy gives it a sniff and then raises it to his mouth. *Did he really eat that? Oh God,* Terri says to herself. She feels the growing hunger in her own belly. The leader shears another piece off and shows Terri how he places it in his mouth and chews it up. He makes sure that she can see what he is doing, and this demonstration, obviously for her benefit, has its impact, and Terri accepts his gift. She places the warm meat in her mouth, trying not to smell it as it passes under her nose. She swallows the piece of meat whole.

She sees in the leader's eyes that he is perplexed, why didn't she chew her food? He continues to carve up this tiny bounty, handing each their portion. He uses the rock to carve the rat, and passes the warm organs to the others, keeping the heart for himself. Watching this tiny person take such good care for her and the others has Terri in awe. *If I only knew your names.* Terri is tempted to name them like she did with Teddy. However, she knows she must not if there is ever a chance for the boys to remember their own names, but why won't they speak?

As the group finishes, the easy routine of the leader killing and serving up their meal both comforts and concerns Terri. *How long before this is all normal…for me?* As she rests, Teddy cuddles up beside her and they fall asleep in the tunnel with the other boys, their hunger satisfied, for now.

U.S. Department of Justice
Federal Bureau of Investigation

CHAPTER SIXTY-TWO: A Third Container
Present Day

"Agent Banks, we have found another container." Reports one of the techs who is working with the ground penetrating radar. "The unit appears to have machinery and other large items in it and there's a tunnel that connects this unit directly to the surface."

"Excellent. Jenkins, you and Lee head up there right now. One of the engineers will meet both of you," Banks instructs. As soon as he has the pair dispatched, he receives a call from Sanders.

"Boss, the two specialists have just landed in Kalispell, they should be onsite by dusk. I have spent the past four hours trying to figure out these notebooks. This guy is good. I mean scary, twisted, brilliant good. He combines coding, ciphers, and pictography in his work. On the surface, his notes just look like gibberish. The rambelings of a crazy-person, until you consider them all together. His code evolves through every notepad, picture and drawing. He will refer to an article in one of the newspapers, then a sentence or even an entire chapter from a previous notepad. I can see what he's writing, the pattern but without the key, it's all meaningless. To understand what this guy is doing, imagine you're falling into a kaleidoscope, the lens is turning, and the shapes and colors in front of you are constantly changing."

"So, the key would be how fast you turn the lens?" asks Banks.

"Bingo! And without knowing the cadence used to turn it, some of the shapes will form, but not everyone and not in the exact way or order. This is the brilliant part though. Without his key, you can decode some of what he writes, but not everything. Just pieces of his story, or work but without the correct context it's...all meaningless."

Banks hears the frustration in Sanders' voice. The smartest kid in the room saying he's stumped but is still not giving up on solving the puzzles entrusted to him. "Martin, if anyone can figure this out, you can. These survivors all have names, families to be notified, this unsub stole their lives. They need you. Cherkoff and Torres are working in Container Two, and the techs have just located a third container. It appears to be where the generator and the rest of the infrastructure for the mine are housed. Maybe there are more notebooks there as well."

***

With the aid of the passive infrared in combination with the night-vision lenses, Cherkoff and Torres have been studying the victims inside the mine for the past hour. So far, they have seen twenty-five different faces men and women, even several prepubescent boys and girls. Now that the lights have been turned off, the victims have slowly started to go about their daily routine.

"Looking at them like this, I feel like we're…"

"Spying on them?" Torres says. The agents continue to document and photograph each new face that they see. Cherkoff looks back at the chair sitting in the middle of the container.

"With all these survivors, there must have been…" Cherkoff stops for a moment.

"I know. At least as many that didn't make it."

"So, he sits down there, and what, waits for them to die?" Cherkoff talks as she walks to the chair. "And then what, he sketches the whole process? Why did these people survive? How, why are they still here? Those sketches were very detailed and graphic. He specifically focused on the level of decomp. It just doesn't make sense."

Torres says, "Then why the dried potatoes and rice? Why feed them?"

Cherkoff points to the bottom of the shaft leading to the ceiling of the main room. "There is no visible access into the mine from the container. I suppose he could have dropped the bags into the mine through that shaft." Cherkoff rubs her eyes for a moment, while she thinks. "He took the time to draw it. So, did he need them to last longer? It just doesn't make sense. All the sketches, especially the time-lapsed sketches, are so detailed, why would he be feeding them if he wanted them to die? None of his drawings have any indication that the victims were starving. What the hell are we missing here?"

"Cherkoff, what if we're looking at this the wrong way? He named those two drawings, what were they?"

"After four weeks, and one to—"

"Yes, and one to twenty-one days—what if they were achievements, not failures? He was documenting the failures. He wants them to survive down there! We need to talk to the rest of the team."

Torres and Cherkoff head back to the surface to update Banks and the rest of the team.

U.S. Department of Justice
Federal Bureau of Investigation

CHAPTER SIXTY-THREE:
Drawings and Notebooks
Present Day

Agent Banks has been reviewing the findings of the forensics team. The litany of fingerprints lifted from various surfaces from the containers all belong to one person. Prints that do not hit any database: the Combinded DNA Index System (CODIS), Automated Fingerprint Identification System (AFIS), and all government or public employee records also come up blank. "Go ahead Sanders, what's up?"

Sanders attempts to calm his own voice as he begins to speak, "This guy is good, but he's also arrogant as hell. He's feeding them. Extremely well—I mean, athletes would be so lucky to have this diet, rich in proteins and stacked with power carbs. When this guy has a breakthrough, he wants everyone to know about it. I didn't believe what I was reading at first, but sometimes you just have to get up and clear your head a bit. His notebook, *Dietary Supplements of Primates and Other Hominids*, is their menu. It just looked like more of the same confused code, but then I started to see a different pattern, a very simple code hidden within all the rest."

Sanders continues to describe how the unsub disguised his feeding formula within his notes. Sanders explains to Banks in detail the feeding regiment that the unsub would give his victims when they arrived at the mine. "Remember how I told you that everything this guy records relates to everything. The sketches, the newspapers, everything, it's all connected. While I was trying to decode the dietary book, I came across something. As I got familiar with the code he used, I discovered references to a group of sketches. Each of these sketches has an ID mark, and when you look at the sketches on their own, they're benign in comparison to the rest. I'm sending you a copy of these four drawings to your tablet right now."

Sanders waits for Banks to let him know that he has the file. During this time, Cherkoff and Torres have entered the command trailer and are standing with Banks.

"He's feeding them!" Cherkoff announces to Banks who reacts only by nodding as the four images start to display on his tablet. He motions to the pair to listen to Sanders.

Sanders says, "You can see these drawings show the inside of the first container. There are several small markings on each sketch. I couldn't understand what they were until I decoded the nutritional book. They're registration marks. He refers to them in his book and explains how the pieces are to be put together."

As Sanders explains his findings, the images on the display line up and form a very clear picture. "There she is. Whoever she is," Sanders says.

The team members look at a detailed drawing of a teenage girl, dressed only in a light top and flowered skirt. He drew the details of each petal of each flower and the frayed ends of her bindings. The shades of color in her cheek shaded so carefully in pencil, the intricate detail of the wrinkles in her neck as her head is tilted back. She is sitting on top of the workbench, hog-tied. Her mouth is open, and a large feeding tube is down her throat.

"Out of all his drawings, she's the only post-pubescent subject, and this is the only sketch composed this way," Sanders explains.

"Is she his first victim?" Torres asks.

"We counted at least twenty-five survivors, men and women, even a few kids, there are probably more but we can't tell. They're mostly young adults. How do you manage to abduct that many people? That many children, and we're only seeing the survivors. God knows how many were actually put in there." Cherkoff continues, "He has no preference to sex of his victims and now this…a teenager as well. This guy is just all over the place."

U.S. Department of Justice
Federal Bureau of Investigation

CHAPTER SIXTY-FOUR:
Girl in Flowered Skirt
Present Day

This unsub seems to fall nowhere in the team's current list of stranger abductors, a list that contains pedophiles, sex-trade-profiteers, serial killers, and childless psychotics. At this time, they cannot determine whether the victims have been sexually assaulted. They strongly doubt that this was the case. With the absence of any photographic evidence to that effect, the possibility of the unsub having profited in any way also seems very remote. Without knowing the exact identity of their unsub, they also cannot rule out the possibility that he is a childless psychotic, who abducts their victims to fill a void. They tend to be individuals who are not able to have children of their own or have lost a child and seek out another to fill that void.

***

"So, he takes them, brings them here, and feeds them. We all know most children are killed by their abductors within the first twenty-four hours. Not here." Banks continues, "If he is only abducting young children, what triggered this dramatic age change? Sanders is there any way you can determine when her picture was sketched?"

With the image of the shaft that the unsub used to lower his victims into the mine going through her mind, Cherkoff says, "They are trapped down there. The lights, the window, his chair—it's a fish tank. I'm not trying to be cruel but think about it. Is his bringing them here the extent of his contact with them?"

The girl in the flowered skirt, as the team has decided to call her, is the only subject in all his sketches composed this way, and she is also the only teen. Jane Doe is a term used to identify a corpse, so for now, she will be referred to as the girl in the flowered skirt. "He left no clues when this was drawn. There's nothing to indicate any timeline between this and his other sketches; the only items in the main picture are the girl and the feeding tube. The four individual sketches also have no unique items or markings. There is one thing though—the dietary book mentions this picture several times. He wanted it to be found. He wanted her to be found. I can't explain why, but I'm sure of it."

Banks and the other agents the agents all agree that this teenage girl is very special. The unsub took the time to draw her image in a cryptic fashion while at the same time leaving enough clues so that her image would be found.

"His sketches, the two that he named, *After Four Weeks* and *Four at Twenty-one Days*, what if his motivation for drawing these is to record the progress, not illustrate their deaths?" As Cherkoff poses this to the group, their meeting is interrupted with the arrival of two specialists. Deanna Cornell and Cho Lau are colleagues from the University of Oklahoma's Anthropology Department. During their flight, they reviewed the files that Sanders provided.

Deanna's expertise is in the areas of enculturation and sociocultural development. She has written numerous papers including an extensive study on the critical period hypothesis, the period in a child's life when language and social interaction skills develop. Cho is a lifelong friend of Sanders and his knowledge and background in literary and artistic analysis will no doubt be put to the test as the investigation progresses. Banks and the agents exchange greetings with the pair and the discussion is resumed.

"If I remember those sketches, the facial images were erased," Torres says. In Quantico, Sanders checks both sketches confirming what Torres said. He informs the team that facial marks were erased. The unsub removed the nose, eyes, and brow line from the sketches as the body decayed.

Cho has been studying the images that Sanders provided. "Those images are gruesome but in no way are they perverted or grotesque. Don't get me wrong—they are very explicit in their detail. The detail is this artist's true subject in the composition, which is not lewd in any way." He draws the agent's attention to specific parts of the sketch *after four weeks*. "Here, the child's image is in the foreground, but it's not the focus of the artist's composition as it progresses. As the series of pictures progress, the surroundings, and the artist's surroundings get more and more detailed. He highlights the cigarette ashes that have fallen on his arm and the small pieces of fungi growing on the ground around the child. In fact, as decay takes place, he has sheltered the child from seeing what is going on…he removed their faces, turning them away."

U.S. Department of Justice
Federal Bureau of Investigation

CHAPTER SIXTY-FIVE: The Infrastructure
Present Day

Cho shows the group faint impressions where the artist lightly drew the facial features on the second and third sketches. "At first glance, it looks like he erased the eyes, and the noses from the second and third, but he took the time to turn their faces away. Not with pencil, he just etched it."

Cherkoff suggests, "Could we be dealing with a guardian protector? Think about it for a moment." Banks nods, and the group hears Sanders typing away feverishly over the speaker.

"From what I understand aren't guardian protectors mainly family members?" Torres asks.

"Most cases involving guardian protectors involve some level of familiarity between the unsub and their victim. There have, however, been extreme cases where victims were abducted at random," Sanders says.

"You tend to guard what you know, what you care about," adds Cherkoff, her tone growing somber as she speaks.

Torres says, "Why, what's the problem?"

Banks and his fellow agents stand silent for a few moments as they come to terms with what may be the only logical answer and explains the presence of the survivors. Agents Lee and Jenkins have just returned from their inspection of Container Three. They are quickly brought up to speed with the latest details and theories the group has shared.

"That makes sense; he has an elaborate electrical system, complete with analoge-timers, relays, and other controls installed in the third container," Lee says. "It's set up to power the entire complex. The generator has been converted to use natural gas as a fuel source, and it too is on a timer. The engineers have told me it should turn on in another twelve hours or so and run for a few hours, then shut off. The relays control other timers, and the lighting schedule begins again, but at random. No pattern. We did find serial numbers on the generator and a few other items in there. Sanders, you should have them now. We also found a rope that has been set up as a hoist. It has a seat and it looks like the unsub could have used it to lower the victims into the mine, down the shaft."

"There wasn't any indication of when our unsub was here last, except that the supplies in that container have a fairly heavy layer of dust on them," Jenkins says. "Best guess, he hasn't been here in months. The generator has a very large cooling fan; it gets quite breezy in there, yet dust has settled on other items, including several bootprints on the container floor."

"The newspapers we found date from 1961 to 1983," Torres says. "If they refer to his abductions, this makes our unsub in his late sixties, seventies? What are the chances he is even still alive?"

Banks asks Sanders to look through the newspapers that were recovered. Sanders says, "Okay, we have twenty-seven papers that Cherkoff and Torres recovered from the first container. They range from the *Tampa Sun* in the south to the Edmonton edition of the *Globe and Mail* in the north."

"What about the West Coast?" Cherkoff asks.

"In the west we have the *Seattle Times* and as far east as the *Buffalo News*. The bulk of the papers are from the Midwest. There's no pattern, but he does reference several of these papers throughout his notes, when I can understand them, of course."

Torres and Cherkoff were only able to identify twenty-five individuals currently in the mine, despite finding twenty-seven newspapers.

"These papers were all very well wrapped, protected," Torres says.

"Absolutely, the unsub used high-quality sheet protectors, like you would find in the archive department of a newspaper," Sanders says.

The team decides that this unsub's most likely victims would be young, ages five to ten years old. The existence of survivors indicates that this unsub's motivation isn't sadistic or malevolent. However, at this time, they cannot verify that theory. Banks instructs Sanders to compile a list of open cases involving missing children. He is to search in each state or province where the newspapers were published, then correlate the search with each paper's date. Until the team can safely gain access to the interior of the mine and the victims, they will have to rely on proven procedures employed in other cases. He teams Cherkoff and Torres with the specialists, charging them with the daunting task of identifying and documenting each of the survivors.

U.S. Department of Justice
Federal Bureau of Investigation

CHAPTER SIXTY-SIX: The Profile
Present Day

Ready to present their profile to the sheriff and his team, Banks, has asked Cherkoff to address the meeting. "At this time, we would like to bring everyone up to speed. Sheriff, we cannot express how grateful our team has been for the support your people have provided. Our team in Quantico, working closely with us here, has just released specific details pertaining to this case to the media. We have released this information hoping that the unsub will be listening. This unsub, who we believe is still alive, is what we have come to know as a guardian protector. He is highly intelligent, university-educated, and very successful. He probably has a family and is well respected in his community. He is extremely comfortable around children and can easily adapt to any situation. He has been able to fine tune his capture techniques over many years." Her statement to the group details how the unsub would have been able to blend into his surroundings, locate and capture his victim, then disappear, undetected, in only a few moments.

Cherkoff steps back and lets Banks address the meeting. "Guardian protectors are by nature very organized and focused. They refer to their victims as rescues and frequently will interject themselves into the course of the investigation. Their fear of capture is overridden by their need to protect their victims from a world or environment that they deem harmful or unsafe. He is not from *this area*. This area is merely his dumping ground, but he is extremely familiar and comfortable with this place." Banks' comment prompts stern looks from several of the deputies. He continues, "This location simply had what he needed; the resources, and especially the privacy. He could access the site and could come and go unnoticed. His victims, we believe, at the time of their abduction, were between the ages of three and four. They were most likely abducted from orphanages from many states and provinces."

While he talks, the rest of his team watches the expressions on the faces of the sheriff's men as they digest what they're hearing. Sanders has provided them with a list of potential victims, all of whom had been reported missing between 1960 and 1970. The list is overwhelming, and Banks makes sure not to divulge what they believe could be the total number of victims. "This type of predator, from what we know, will have had minimal physical contact with the victims." As he finishes speaking, Banks tells the group that they have considered many different scenarios and profiles as they reviewed this case.

"Our unsub traveled extensively throughout the US and Canada over the past. His ability to blend in is probably his greatest weapon, and I have no doubt that he was seen numerous times, both in and around Evergreen. You all know someone, an old friend, a relative who has seen this man," Banks reports. He then instructs the sheriff's team to canvas every store owner, resident, anyone who may have had contact with this man. He could be anyone; their only solid lead being that he drove a red 1959 Ford F-250, with "that lovely leather bench seat" as Charlie had described. The thought that their small community, once known as one of the country's most popular camping and hunting spots, may now have the dubious distinction of being the location of one of the nation's deadliest child abduction cases, has all the staff members unnerved.

U.S. Department of Justice
Federal Bureau of Investigation

CHAPTER SIXTY-SEVEN:
Trucks and Newspapers
Present Day

Banks has just met with the three members of the media he chose to relay certain information to the public. He has given each of them a small list of names. The list was compiled by Sanders and is accompanied by several pictures of various styles of F-250 trucks available to the public in 1959, and a color copy of the map detailing various locations across the US and Canada. Images of the red pins that Sanders placed on the original map mark the cities associated the newspapers that were found in the mine. There is also a typed press release. "Your viewers need this information, and we need you to deliver the message…as written. Thank you."

In the conference room, the speaker phone is turned on while Sanders talks to Banks, Torres, and Cherkoff. "The Michigan Company Amco Commercial Leasing provided financing for anything. You want to buy machinery, real property—they provided capital and financing from 1941 until the company was sold in 1990. I won't go into the all the details, but I searched their client list and available records of mortgages and lien registrations. It turns out that a series of Ford pickup trucks were leased to a company based in Marquette, Michigan, called Ely & Co." He goes on to tell the team that the trucks were eventually sold off, most ended up in various junkyards. Two remain in service and are owned by antique car hobbyists. Ely & Co., he also informs the team, serviced many of the areas where the unsub collected newspapers from during the target time. The company operated out of Marquette until 1988, when the business closed. The sons of the company's founder still resides in Marquette with their families and the Detroit field office has dispatched officers to interview them.

As requested, the three major networks broadcast the information provided by the team. "In a very interesting twist in the story our Ashley Blair has been following from outside Evergreen, authorities have just released these pictures." The video cuts to Ashley reporting, "Agents investigating the illegal dumping operation have told me that they believe this site has been operating for some time from this location. New evidence has just been transferred from this site and taken for further evaluation." The video cuts to an aerial image of the crime scene. "And authorities on site have released to CBS a copy of this prerecorded statement from Supervisory Special Agent Christopher Banks."

The network cuts to the video of Banks.

Banks is shown standing in a conference room in front of a large color map of the US and Canada.

Pinned to the names of cities are flags. Twenty-seven large red flags highlight the locations of the newspapers. A well-orchestrated and edited video focuses on both the image of Banks speaking and the map. The video lasts just under sixty seconds. As Banks finishes speaking, the video fades to a picture of a red 1959 Ford F-250 four-by-four truck, then back to the reporter. "Agent Banks has told CBS that the extent of the items brought into this location is, in his words, astonishing and that he believes this highly organized operation has gone undetected here for over forty years."

The anchor asks Ashley, "How was the site discovered? Do we know that at least?"

Ashley answers, "Surveyors, working for Deep Image, made the initial discovery."

"Well Ashley, this all sounds fascinating and rather disturbing that all this has gone on for so long. Now in other news…"

U.S. Department of Justice
Federal Bureau of Investigation

CHAPTER SIXTY-EIGHT:
More and More at Home
1964

The lights in the mine have come and gone so many times she can't remember. *Was that ten, fifty, one-hundred?* Terri asks herself. There's no way for her to know how many days, hours it has been. She can only imagine. *Is he here? Is he watching, what the hell is going on?* Without answers, she can only guess and try to keep the others safe. When the lights come on, the illumination causes their eyes to burn and inflicts a searing pain. If they are caught in the main room when the lights come on, all they can do is cover their faces and scurry into the safety of the shaft. There are times when the lights just come on all at once, then other times when they start as a low, red glow and slowly become brighter. Terri keeps the children deep in the shaft, away from the light, safe.

From her perch deep in the shaft, she sees that the lights have gone off once again. Even though everyone is eager to head into the main room and forage, their eyes still need a little more time. "I know, but we must wait…it will be safe…just a little longer. He might still be there. You're safe with me," Terri quietly speaks as she holds Teddy's hand. When the lights are on, she always remains in the shaft with the boys. She positions herself in front of them and blocks the shaft with her body to protect them. She's never quite sure why she does this—is it intentional, maternal, or just a reflex? There's never any sound; he doesn't come in, and he just brings more children.

Teddy is a shy little boy and so very tiny. *How old are you, sweetie?* Terri contemplates. He holds close to Terri and frequently looks at her; "Mamma Terri?" he says in his soft voice. It is the only thing he ever says. The others have slowly started to speak as well; the black boy first to speak, saying just, "Terri," as he touched her hand.

U.S. Department of Justice
Federal Bureau of Investigation

CHAPTER SIXTY-NINE: Adam
1964

When the lights come on this time, Terri knows that something was different. She hears a noise like nails on a chalkboard, then thud, thud, thud, as several heavy bags fall to the ground from above. One final tiny thud sounds, then another child crying out echoes and echoes. The loud scraping tears through the air as the rock is replaced.

Terri tells the others to stay where they are, as she creeps up the shaft. Terri keeps her distance, so as not to be seen, but positions herself in a way that she can see the new child. "Shhhh, it's ok sweetie…I'm Terri and you're not alone. I will come for you the moment I can!" Hearing the child's cries and not being able to help rips at Terri's heart but she doesn't want Oldson to see her. If he is there, she won't come out until the lights go off, then she will rescue the child. As she speaks, the child's cries calm, just a bit. "Soon, sweetie, very soon, I'll be there."

With the lights off now, Terri walks to where the child sits. His cries are even louder now that the room is so dark. Terri hears the rats as they scramble everywhere, searching and feeding. As she reaches the little boy, she says, "I'm Terri you're safe now nothing will hurt you." She takes his hand and leads him into the shaft where the others are. The little boy's cries for his mother have subsided and Terri asks him, "What is your name?"

"Adam," he says, and his voice cracks a bit as he sniffles, trying to be brave, not to cry.

Terri gently holds his hand and looks him over. *What did he do to you? Did he hurt you?* Terri wonders as she feels his arms and his back. She looks for any sign that the boy might be hurt; thankfully, she finds nothing. "No one will hurt you here. We are all friends. I know it's dark and things are so strange but you're safe, I promise! How old are you? Where are you from, where do you live?" Terri tries to take his mind off his surroundings and learn as much as she can.

The memories, those horrific first few hours in the mine with Teddy by her side, come back to her as she speaks with little Adam. How she felt, as she got used to the darkness, and what he must be feeling right now. "Wow, you're four…when is your birthday?" The more she talks, the calmer he gets. Even Teddy and the others join in with "Hi!" and "She's Terri!" They are simple words, but in this dark world, it's comforting to know that he isn't alone. "Where's hoster house?" Terri asks Adam.

"News York," replies Adam

"That's where you lived…or…oh foster house, did you mean a foster home?" Terri asks.

"Yep, hoster home."

251

In the darkness, she sees his little head nod as he says, "hoster home." She introduces Adam to the other boys. "We are all kind of playing hide-and-seek right now. You must stay right here with us, okay? Understand?" Terri asks, and Adam agrees. "We are all friends, and no one will let anything bad happen to you."

"She's Terri!" The little black boy instructs, then adds, "Dis is new hoster home." Terri can't believe what she has just heard him say. The only way he would understand what a foster home meant would be if he had also been in one. This little boy, who still hasn't told her his name, can remember this, but why?

"You know, you know what a foster home is? How?" Terri asks. His only response is one sharp nod of his head. He turns his back to her and the others, then he says, "Bad place...place." And for the first time, Terri hears sadness in his voice. This strong little boy, who was the first to reach out to her, now sits by himself, holding his arms around his chest. Terri moves to his side and places her arms around him. He buries his face into her chest and breaks down into tears. She feels his little body tremble as he cries.

"You're not there anymore, you're here with me...it's okay." She continues to stroke his hair and hold him tightly, calming him down. *What had happened to this boy to make him only cry at the memory of his foster home and not this place?* This first sign of sadness Terri has seen in him troubles her. Her thoughts turn to her own little brother: *Is he safe? Where is he?* These thoughts weigh on her mind, but she knows she must be strong. She has no choice; Terri must be strong, strong for everyone.

The heavy bags that were dropped into the mine and their contents will be quickly dispatched by the rats unless the group can retrieve them. This is the first time since Terri has been here that Oldson has deposited bags, but the other boys understand what is waiting in the main room. They each motion and insist that they need to go. She follows as the trio scrambles into the main room, chasing away the rats, tossing small rocks into the air and at the ground. The bags have already been torn apart, but as they grope around the floor in the darkness they can find the good ones.

"Take now," a tiny voice shouts.

Another young voice breaks in. He is holding a corner of another bag. "Take dis, Terri, take dis." The boys and Terri scavenge all that they can carry and retreat into their home.

Terri finally realizes what is happening and grabs everything she can. Her size and strength allow the group to take so much more than they would have been able to in the past. Her height alone has opened new areas within the mine for the group to forage for food. Areas that once were inaccessible now provide places for storage.

U.S. Department of Justice
Federal Bureau of Investigation

CHAPTER SEVENTY: Ely & Co.
1964

"That ready yet?" A foreman's voice barks as two men finish loading a flatbed. One man is operating the forklift, while the other stands on the trailer. They all work for Ely & Co., based in Marquette, Michigan. Trailer 212 is being loaded with generators, lumber, and various other construction-related items, including several heavy large wooden crates. All the items are destined for different locations in the Northwest. Ely & Co. has been transporting equipment for the construction and mining industry for half a decade now. The company employs over fifty workers, and the freight in the yard must be transferred to trailers so the drivers can get on their way.

Trailer 212 is scheduled to leave the yard by ten o'clock. With only three hours to get the work done, the crew will have little time to spare. The driver will have one stop to make after he leaves the yard, which will be in St. Paul, Minnesota to pick up the remainder of his load. Kenny has told his dispatcher that he should be at the Marquette yard by ten o'clock and ready to roll. He has been driving for Ely for the past two years since coming home from Vietnam. Most of his trips last a couple of weeks as he crisscrosses his way through the various states on his route.

The load is secured, strapped, and chained down, and a heavy black vinyl tarp covers it. There is enough room on the end of the trailer for the small machine he's picking up in St. Paul. Kenny should be there by the end of the day, just in time to meet the piece of machinery coming in from Winnipeg, Manitoba. The driver for Cattlemen Trucking based in Virden, Manitoba left Winnipeg the day before and will deliver one small generator to a warehouse in St. Paul, where Kenny can pick it up. The generator is then to be delivered to a company in Boise, Idaho.

"I know...got it... I'll be in Bismarck in two days, as long as that damn Canadian driver gets the genny to St. Paul on time. I better not have to sit around and wait for him, like the last one!" His frustration is normal under the circumstances. He doesn't get paid to wait around and on trips like this when another truck's schedule can interfere with his, the pressure is on. Ely & Co. frequently works with other truckers, transferring freight as needed when schedules and routes conflict. "The customer pays all our bills, and your damn paycheck!" owner Ely Watkins often says. Ely is a third-generation trucker and has run a very tight and profitable shop in Marquette. Their clients also include many firms that decommission old factories, power plants, and mine sites.

U.S. Department of Justice
Federal Bureau of Investigation

CHAPTER SEVENTY-ONE: Receiving
1964

"Yes, we got that one here. It came in early today. You got a truck?" Oldson hears the shipper's voice as he arrives at Twin Cities Warehousing. He is there to pick up a wooden crate dropped off by his supplier in Winnipeg. The shipper brings the crate to the dock, and the two men slide it into the back of his pickup. The man signs the shipping receipt, carefully places a black tarp over the box, and drives off. Once on the highway, Oldson glances back at the tarp and calmly says, "You'll be home soon."

The wooden crate, with its worn edges from the numerous forklifts and freight handlers that have worked with it, appears rather nondescript. The word *Fragile* is in black paint on all sides. Stamped below is *Use No Hooks* to insure no sharp instruments are used to transfer the crate. What better way to bring such cargo across the border? Just another pump or box of supplies as listed on the bill of lading. Weighted just right, and constructed with the best soundproof materials, almost anything could be placed in here undetected.

Oldson has used this method several times. "Do you have room for a small piece of freight?" he would ask. What trucker could resist a cash-paying customer? "Just this box, I need it to go to…" and that would be that. A few short days later, he would arrive to claim his goods.

Oldson understands the chance of a trailer full of goods getting inspected as it crossed the international border, especially at one of several smaller commercial crossing locations between Canada and the US, is much lower than his pickup being inspected. He would always follow his freight to make sure all went well. If the load was inspected, the trucker would have some explaining to do, both to his dispatch and no doubt the authorities. Fortunately, this never happened.

There was one time, however, when his cargo was almost discovered. One of the trucks charged with carrying one of his special packages was involved in an accident. The truck collided, head on, with a tanker truck carrying four thousand gallons of gasoline. Both trucks caught fire on a snow-covered highway in Northern Wisconsin. Neither driver survived this horrific accident. By the time the authorities arrived on scene, both trucks had been burned beyond recognition. The cargo was a complete loss. All Oldson could do was slowly drive past the wreckage and continue his journey. When he arrived in Minot, North Dakota a day later, he made a point to purchase a copy of the *Minot Daily News*.

U.S. Department of Justice
Federal Bureau of Investigation

CHAPTER SEVENTY-TWO: Shipping 1964

When Oldson used the services of a trucker to transport his merchandise, the trips were generally short. Oldson would prep his merchandise in the usual fashion. He would insert a feeding tube and administer the correct amount of food and water. There was even an occasion when Oldson estimated a longer travel time. To ensure everything went well, he put a couple of boxes of cookies and water in the crate with the merchandise. The wooden crates that he used, which appeared quite normal on the outside, would be constructed in a way to eliminate any sounds coming from within the box.

The insulation he used to soundproof the box also proved quite helpful in keeping his merchandise at a regulated temperature during transit. Inside the crate, he would strategically place several bags of dried potatoes, rice, and seeds needed at his site. The bags added another layer of insulation, both against noise and any movement, and provided protection to the delicate cargo hidden inside. If the crate was ever opened by an official, at the border perhaps, they would have to move all those big bags to get to the heart of the matter. Safeguards like this were never put to the test, and his shipments were rarely delayed in transit.

Oldson would always arrive shortly after his package was delivered. When it was safe, he would open the crate to inspect the contents and if, for whatever reason, the merchandise in the crate required anything, he would provide it then and there. Oldson understood that in the early years, finding his victims and capturing them was not the problem. The time it would take to bring them to their new home—now that was time he could better spend doing other tasks, rescuing more for example; so how could he solve this problem? That is when he developed the delivery system, which worked better than even he could have ever imagined. It was cost-effective and expeditious. The only factor limiting the logistics of his plan was the supply, but Oldson knew the best places to solve this issue.

There are so many, sad, scared, and alone. Every town or city has the spot where he could find what he was looking for. That someone special, left alone, ignored, sad, or even in danger. Time is always on his side and by the time the victim is noticed missing and the authorities notified, Oldson and his merchandise are gone. The process is working.

U.S. Department of Justice
Federal Bureau of Investigation

CHAPTER SEVENTY-THREE: 1964

Carefully, Oldson writes in his notebook. The fluorescent lights are now on as he observes the main room of the mine. He has been eager to see the progress since his last visit. He scans the room; the sacks lay on the floor in the center. Patiently he sits and waits. The lights in the main room have switched on. The relays have slowly brought the intensity of the lights up to full wattage. The thick, one-way glass keeps everyone, everyone safe. Oldson opens a fresh page and begins to sketch.

The faces slowly emerge from the darkness in the shaft. Led by Terri, one by one, the four small children and Terri group around this sixth small person. A tiny little girl, a Cree Indian, her face, her color, quite different from theirs, and they poke at her and touch her clothes. Terri, who is sitting nearby, is more intent on feasting on a freshly killed rat and a handful of the lovely sweet fungi that for, some reason, only grows on the table in the office. It is such a treat. "And you shall be eight?" Oldson's eyes widen as he looks at Terri, who has turned just enough for Oldson to notice her belly.

The black boy reaches out and takes the little girl's hand and leads her into the shaft as the other boys gather bits and pieces of dried potatoes the rats missed. The little girl's cries subside as she joins the group. Not a sound or word is spoken by anyone while they are in the main room. Terri motions to the others to take the new girl into the shaft, safe from harm. Terri tells the children: "Make no sound, don't speak. We only talk here, in our home." Their home is the safety of the tunnel, out of sight.

She has been here now for four months; now very pregnant Terri continues to feed. Soon after being placed in the mine, Terri noticed her appetite increase and had problems keeping food down at certain times of the day. When she missed her period, she knew what was happening. *Josh*…she thought to herself. His name and face have all but faded from her memory. Her survival, and now also her unborn child, are her only thoughts.

Oldson can only look on, pleased at what he sees—no deaths, everyone is still here, safe and happy; it is working…finally. He sketches only the surroundings today.

***

"Thanks, man, have a great day. Nice to see stuff happen the way it's supposed to for a change!" Kenny cheers, as he ties down the last couple of straps on his tarp. The generator was at Twin Cities Warehousing when he arrived. After a quick call into his dispatch,

Kenny heads west. His first delivery is in Bismarck, North Dakota, then on to Boise, Idaho to deliver the generator. With only three deliveries, he should reach his last stop in Spokane by the end of the week.

U.S. Department of Justice
Federal Bureau of Investigation

CHAPTER SEVENTY-FOUR: Logistics
Present Day

In the command trailer, Banks has been discussing the logistics of what the unsub has accomplished with the sheriff and his fellow agents, Jenkins and Lee. The terrain surrounding the mine is very rough, and there's no evidence of an airstrip. Driving into the site is the most logical choice that remains. The sheriff explains as he points to the map of the area surrounding Evergreen, "US highways 93 and 2 have been around for years. Tourists, truckers you name it, from the east and west you have highway 2 and if you're coming from the north or south you're gonna use 93. These are the only roads in or out of here. No big interstates, just the old scenic route."

"He drove these roads," Jenkins says. "If you're driving, you sure as hell are going to need gas. We should get Sanders to look for any service stations that have operated around this area over the past twenty years."

"No need for that," the sheriff says. "I can save you the time—Charlie Watkins. He ran a group of stations on both 93 and 2."

Everyone in and around Evergreen knows Charlie. His stations have been supplying gas to the residents and tourists for over forty years. Charlie sold his stations off several years ago, but he made many good friends throughout the time. Charlie now lives in Kalispell with his wife and a couple of dogs, Darlin' and Hank. Banks dispatches Jenkins and Lee and the sheriff agrees to escort the agents.

U.S. Department of Justice
Federal Bureau of Investigation

CHAPTER SEVENTY-FIVE: Do We Enter?
Present Day

Cherkoff and Torres have been working with Deanna and Cho for the past couple of hours. The specialists have been observing the victims and cataloguing details about each individual. Sitting and watching the victims go about their daily routine, but not being able to enter the mine and free them, is very difficult, but for the time, necessary. The team made the decision only to observe those in the mine for now, as they didn't know how the victims would react to an outsider. The team has no way of knowing how many survivors remain inside. Their field of vision is limited to the main room and the immediate entrance points of three shafts.

The technicians working with the generator and electrical system have deciphered the lighting schedule. The timers used to regulate the amount of light have been programmed to allow for less and less available light. Moreover, the entire complex has been in the dark for weeks. According to their best estimate, the lights are due to come back on; they're just not sure when. They could, if the team wants, easily bypass the timers and turn all the lights on. Banks decides to let the system, schedule play out as planned and not to interfere.

A solution to their problem will be arriving in the morning. The team will prepare to insert a remote-controlled vehicle, like the type used by the bomb squad. The RCV is equipped with several cameras, passive infrared as well several high-definition lenses. The RCV also has a bank of LEDs and the level of light can be adjusted similar to a dimmer switch. The RCV will be able to penetrate the shafts of the mine and allow the team to find any victims who have not come out into the main room. It will also provide the opportunity to discover anything else that is hidden out of sight.

"Look at this one. Oh my, look at how he is showing the little boy how to hold the rock." Deanna draws both agents' attention to the tall figure in front of them. The team has named him Hunter. He is by far the most efficient hunter of the entire colony and works with at least two other men. They corralled a small group of rats and, using either rocks or a prized leg bone, quickly dispatched their prey. Although a proficient hunter, he is not the alpha male. Alpha is a black male who they guess is in his late forties. He stands just over six feet tall but has as slight curve in his spine.

Alpha was the first one of the colony to look directly at the container window. He also has been seen breaking up small scuffles among the younger males. Several females vie for his attention. They bring him handfuls of the tiny buttercup fungi that only grows in one small area of the main room. Respected by most of the residents they have seen so far, Alpha would appear to be the leader, at least for now.

The residents have adapted remarkably well to the harsh environment in which they have been forced to live in for many years. "It is absolutely remarkable," Cho says. "Their overall health appears to be excellent. Sure, they have the odd scar here and there, but all things considered…" They continue to list the identification markings of each victim.

U.S. Department of Justice
Federal Bureau of Investigation

CHAPTER SEVENTY-SIX: Alpha
Present Day

The fluorescent lights have started to come on, the timing device on the generator working as planned. "We found supplies of fluorescent grow tubes in the third container. The techs have told me that they are all very high-end—excellent-quality, full-spectrum lights," Torres explains to Deanna and Cho.

"Mr. Sanders said that the unsub had provided them with a special diet," Deanna says. The victims have obviously benefited from his research into supplements. No doubt it came at a heavy cost though." Torres asks her to explain. "Judging by their average age and appearance, most are middle aged. Man started out living in caves, fending and feeding himself and his family. Most caves and even mines will have subterranean streams and rivers. In this region, they would be fed by glacial runoff. A mine this deep into a mountain's core should have a comfortable ambient temperature. There are many vineyards in the Sonoma Valley that use the surrounding mountains as their cellars. Humidity and temperatures running at a constant sixty-nine degrees and fifty-five percent relative humidity—this all sounds nice, but what were the conditions like when Alpha was first introduced into the mine?

"Who came out of the darkness when they heard his cries, did anyone, and when?" Deanna asks continuing, "As the hours passed, were these lights on or was he immersed in total darkness? Somehow, this little boy survived and grew up to be the alpha male. How did he manage, this is…it's simply amazing! He is amazing. Look at him, my God, all these years in there!"

The team can only imagine what it was like when Alpha sat in the dark. He would have eventually needed water, but they can see no signs of water in the main chamber and with the shafts unlit, would thirst alone be enough to drive a young child deep into the unknown dark world and seek a distant water source? The experts are both appalled and fascinated with these possibilities. Alone and scared, he could only cry out for help; a help that he could only hope would come.

Amid the harshness of this environment, the team also witnesses tender moments between one of the victims, an Asian female who stands about four feet tall, and a baby. They have named her Momma Grace, and she is caring for a tiny baby boy, nestled tight in her arms as he suckles. Grace came out of the third shaft, carrying her baby. She walks around the main room, going into the old office and snacking on the fungi growing in there. Walking slowly to the room with Momma Grace is Little Sam. He is a small boy, probably five with a horrible scar that transects his forehead. The team can only guess at what happened to him and are equally puzzled at how he could have survived such an injury.

"A laceration that produced a scar that large, I doubt he got stiches," Deanna says dryly. "A community of this size has taken decades to develop and at a very high cost. We are looking at a very mature ecosystem and balanced enough to support all their lives. The victims need the rats; the rats rely on the victims and so on. However, to get here, what was the cost?"

Deanna explains, "With survivors we are aware of, the numbers of those who didn't make it could be staggering. We could be looking at a ratio possibly as high as five or even six to one. Their survival rate increased as your unsub's ability to provide increased."

The possibility of their unsub having abducted one hundred or more young children and bringing them to this place is hard for any of them to fathom. However, the evidence he left behind, the survivors, cannot be ignored.

U.S. Department of Justice
Federal Bureau of Investigation

CHAPTER SEVENTY-SEVEN: Charlie Watkins
Present Day

When the trio arrives at his ranch, Charlie greets them and invites them into his home. "Charlie, these are the federal agents that I told you about. They are investigating—"

Jenkins stops the sheriff mid-sentence, "We understand you operated five gas stations around the Evergreen area?"

Charlie describes his stations proudly. "I began to work for the Union 76 Company, just pumping gas at the station in Whitefish. It started out as a summer job. Earning a little extra spending money but when things got real tight, there wasn't a lot of work around here for my daddy, so I had to quit school to help the family. Eventually, Mr. Parsons, the man who owned the station, retired and I was able to buy it from him. By 1976, I had five stations: Whitefish, Eureka, and Polson, all on 93, and Libby, out west on 2, and Cut Bank, out near Shelby on 2." He points as he lists each station's direction. "My stations were famous for my little handpainted signs posted along the highways warning travelers not to run out of gas. 'It's a long walk back' and 'Don't forget the tires.' Best darn five bucks' worth of paint I ever bought."

"Mr. Watkins," Jenkins says.

"Darlin, it's Charlie, everyone calls me Charlie!"

"Charlie, we are looking for a person, a man, who would have made frequent trips in and out of the Evergreen area over the past thirty years. He would have travelled alone, in some make of four-wheel drive pickup or similar heavy-duty truck." As Jenkins explains, the room echoes with Charlie's laughter.

"Darlin, that sounds like most every vehicle you would have seen on the roads back then…even now. These weren't city roads back then. Traffic was mostly truckers, campers, and hunters. We had no Walmart back then. If you were driving through here, you were either on your way to Canada or going camping in Flathead." Flathead is one of the area's many national forests. There are also several Indian Reserves. Glacier National Park flanks the area, and the Rocky Mountain Range transects it. That means tourists flock seasonally to the area. Access to most of the spots requires a heavy-duty car or truck.

"Families would come in here from all over during the summer, still do! Hunters, hell, when the season opens I would need a second and even a third drop from my fuel supplier just to keep open." Charlie clears his throat. "Some days only a handful would come by; others it was nonstop."

Jenkins says, "The man we are looking for would not stand out. In fact, he could be your uncle Bob—"

Charlie cuts in, "I had an uncle Bob... passed away in 1989, God rest him! Sorry. What were you saying, darlin?"

"His truck would have been immaculate," Jenkins says. "He would be well dressed and groomed but he would not stand out. Even though we believe he is not from this area, he would look like he belonged here." As Jenkins describes the unsub, Charlie raises up a bit as he begins to remember someone fitting the description.

"That was Hank," Charlie says. Jenkins and Lee are intrigued as Charlie mentions a name.

The sheriff pulls Lee aside and quietly explains, "They're all Hank, the men, and the ladies were Darlin." Lee shakes his head at Jenkins as they continue to listen to Charlie.

"There was something, something about that fellow. Let me think...drove a Ford '59, a F-250, one of them brand new four-by-four models. I can still see the bench seat. It sure was a beauty. Always kept it shiny and had his gear already in the back. He was a hunter; I always asked him if he was going for deer or elk."

Jenkins asks Charlie to describe as much detail as he can about the truck. "Are you sure of the year?" She gets a stern and firm yes from Charlie, and she understands not to make that mistake again.

"Charlie, you mentioned his gear in the back?" Lee asks.

"Yes, like most everyone around here, his gun rack was in the cab, but he had his storage box under his tarp, in the box of his truck. Nice and organized, he had the straps for the tarp always placed just so. Heck, most of the truckers running flatbed loads would have been proud if they could have tied down a tarp that well," Charlie says.

"I don't understand, tied down that well?" Lee asks.

"Oh, it's a trucker thing, I guess. Flatbed loads that need a tarp, well, the tarp gets held to the trailer by straps or bungee cords. The rookies can put the tarp on, but it won't be straight or even at the sides. And they never get the straps all pointing the same way. I remember seeing him first up in Eureka in the late fifties. He just got the truck. What a beauty. Leather seats, you know, that smell…oh my! Still can make my eyes water just thinking about 'em. Seat belts! Yes, seat belts, not every car had them, let alone every truck, but his did. Three! Always right there, draped across the bench nice and neat."

As Lee continues to speak with Charlie, Jenkins excuses herself and steps out on to the front porch to call Banks and Sanders. "Hi, we have something here; he drove a '59 red Ford F-250 four-wheel drive with lovely bench seats and three seat belts."

The level of detail that Jenkins has told both of her colleagues about the vehicle has them somewhat stunned.

"Are you sure, a '59 F-250?" Banks asks skeptically.

"Mr. Watkins is quite the character, but his details about this truck are vivid, right down to the seat belts. He even mentioned that the back of the truck was always covered with a black tarp, well organized, nice and neat."

Sanders searches all available DMV records and contacts an acquaintance of his who once worked at the Ford Motor Co. With the details Charlie provided, this is the first major break the team has had since their arrival.

U.S. Department of Justice
Federal Bureau of Investigation

CHAPTER SEVENTY-EIGHT: Little Josh
June 1964

The other children haven't seen Terri for most of the day. She left the group the day before as they all slept. She has remained in the deepest shaft alone, sitting in the stream, the warm water caressing her legs. The cramps she feels are like none she has ever felt before. The pain is intense but for some reason she is not afraid. Something very natural about this whole process is overwhelming. With each cramp, she feels the urge to push and bear down. It's time, she realizes, her baby is about to be born.

She feels its tiny head as it turns and begins to exit the safety of her body. Squatting in the warm water and with a final push, she feels the tiny legs, then it's over. "Huu phew, oh God," Terri says quietly, her legs and hands trembling as she reaches down with both hands, cradling her baby boy. Her stomach heaves as her breathing calms. As soon as his little body hit the warm water, he started to cry. Terri takes a few moments to clear his eyes and mouth, gently rinsing him in the water. In the darkness, she feels the placenta still attached to her baby and hanging from inside her. Terri finds a sharp rock. She grabs the end of the cord as it hangs between her legs, pinching it as tight as she can. With a swift stroke she cuts the cord below her hand and with the other hand, she ties a knot in each end.

With no formal training in this and never witnessing a child being born, Terri can only wonder where this skill has come from. Suddenly she feels an intense cramp as the after birth is delivered. She remains in the darkness relaxing with her baby boy cradled tight against her breasts. His tiny hands hold her breasts; he searches for a nipple.

They sit together, mother with her new baby boy, as Terri speaks, "I'm your mommy, and my name is Terri. Hello, Little Josh. I've been waiting to meet you for so long." She gently kisses her son's forehead. She is about to stand up and leave the shaft when a horrible feeling fills her mid-section. More cramps, but these are much more intense than before. Her forehead fills with sweat as Terri doubles over in pain. Her screams echo throughout the mine. Everyone hears her and the others in the mine can only look in the direction of this noise and wonder.

The little black boy stands and heads in the direction of Terri's voice. Even in the darkness of the mine, his pace is rapid as he runs to where the sound came from. Terri hears his footsteps as he starts down the shaft. "Stay away! Go! Go! Get out now!" He stops dead in his tracks and kneels holding the ground with his little hands. "Go…away. Go back." He remembers the last time she said this—the first time he ever saw her and Teddy. But this time is so different. All he can do is honor her command and he retreats to the shaft with the others.

The pains in her stomach are getting faster and faster. Terri feel something, *another* she thinks to herself? She barely has time to contemplate the thought of giving birth again and it is over. Out of her body and lying in her hands is a second, a girl, but this time things are very different. There is no sound and no warmth when she touches her baby. Just stillness and cold. Terri desperately attempts to revive her baby but no matter what she does, she can feel no life.

She sits there with both of her babies for as long as she can. Terri returns to the group the next day with her son. In the mining area, at the deepest part of the second shaft, Terri lays her little girl, placing her gently under a few rocks.

The others are very curious at what this new thing is. It is so tiny, somewhat familiar and yet so foreign; everyone wants to look at it. Where did she find it? They have never seen anything like this, anywhere. Can you eat it? Is she going to eat it? Something told them that this was special. The way Terri holds it, placing it to her chest. Teddy is first one she let touch her baby, followed by the black boy, then the rest. The only thing they know for sure is that it is hers, and hers to deal with.

Teddy brings Terri handfuls of snails and fungi as she rests for many days. He's quick to realize she needs his help. Her attention is focused on this new thing; it makes noises and squirms around a bit but always on her belly. Terri speaks so softly when she looks at it or touches it. The best Teddy can figure is that it was sick, and hopefully it gets better fast, so Terri can get back to being Terri. *She really needs to come help us,* Teddy thinks.

U.S. Department of Justice
Federal Bureau of Investigation

CHAPTER SEVENTY-NINE: 1959 Ford F250
Present Day

In their morning briefing, Sanders has been updating the team with the results from his queries. "In the US alone, a child is reported missing every forty seconds of every day. That translates into over eight hundred thousand reports per year; with a possible one hundred fifty thousand cases still open. Eliminating abductions and disputes over custody and in the regions covered by the newspapers that we found, the number is still way too high. What keeps an open case from becoming a cold case?" Sanders poses the question to the team. "Don't worry, you don't have to answer that—it's pressure, pressure from the parents. So, if we are dealing with a possible number of abductions topping out at say, one hundred, and over a timeframe based on the newspapers we collected, how does someone make that many kids just disappear?"

Cherkoff holds her hand to her mouth as she shakes her head, "Oh God, you're not serious?"

Sanders continues, "Orphanages and foster homes eliminate the desperate next-of-kin calling and hounding the authorities for help. They can just disappear into the dark. I ran our data looking only for children between the ages of three and six reported missing from group homes, foster homes, and orphanages, nationwide, between 1960 and 1985. Even the most overworked social worker would have made a valiant effort to recover a lost child. Unfortunately, there's a keyword, overworked. Without blood relatives' pleadings, cases easily ran cold."

"That's still very disturbing, all those. At least the list is manageable," Lee says.

"I also eliminated runaways from the list. I know we can't officially rule them out, but I wanted to see what happened to the list if we removed this factor," Sanders says.

Banks reviews the condensed version of the list. With open cases stretching from Florida to New York, and Virginia to Washington, he requests that Sanders pulls the cases that have evidence or photos in the case files. The initial reports from the officer will need to be reviewed—contact names, addresses, and any other pertinent information. Sanders will need to determine if the persons who filed the reports are still alive. "Sanders get whatever files you can. Start with those. We are sending you updated pictures of the residents we have catalogued so far. Compare what we have with what you find from the files. Our victims came from somewhere."

Sanders is about to end his portion of the teleconference when he realizes he has forgotten something. "Ford: fix or repair daily."

"Excuse me?" Banks inquires.

"Sorry, cheeky acronym for Ford products, but as luck would have it, even the famous '59 F-250 needed constant attention. There were thousands manufactured during that model year but less than one hundred were equipped with seat belts and only twenty left the factory with a full complement of three and they were all—you guessed it—red. Special order, apparently. Amco Commercial Leasing. I won't bore you with all the details. They provided capital and financing from 1941 until the company was sold in 1990. Amco underwrote the leases for several of these F-250s to a Marquette, Michigan company, Ely & Co."

Sanders continues to explain, "It would appear this was a fleet purchase. All trucks were returned to Amco for disposal at the end of the lease's term. However, as luck would have it, I managed to cross-check a couple of databases and found that Ely & Co. operated in several areas where the unsub had collected newspapers from. The company closed in 1988; however, the founder's sons still reside in Marquette with their families. I have already contacted the field office in Detroit and they have dispatched two agents to interview both men."

"Sanders, as usual, you are amazing, thank you," Banks says.

***

"We've needed that baby for days! Let's get you unloaded," shouts a foreman working at a construction site in Boise, Idaho as Kenny's truck pulls in. His trip from Bismarck is going as planned, and the construction crew off loads the cargo. The foreman signs for the delivery. With his freight delivered, and the paperwork done, Kenny navigates his truck back to the highway. He should reach his final delivery in Spokane early the next day, completing another uneventful four-day trip.

U.S. Department of Justice
Federal Bureau of Investigation

CHAPTER EIGHTY: Have You Seen Her? Present Day

"Thank you very much, Frank. We have an update on that developing story outside Evergreen. We turn things over to Ashley Blair," the evening anchor for CBS says as the video breaks to the feed.

"Thanks, Frank. Federal agents investigating this illegal dump operation have released this statement along with this picture. The statement includes details with regards to this person of interest, as they have called her. Her picture was broadcast this morning in a nationwide request by the FBI. They believe she may have vital information with regards to this investigation."

The network cuts to a prerecorded message from Quantico. The voice-only recording of Banks is played while the sketch of *Girl in Flowered Skirt* is displayed. The sketch has been altered and only displays the girl's face.

"Agents, working in cooperation with the local sheriff and state police, have uncovered what appears to be a very sophisticated operation with ties to several states and even a couple of Canadian provinces. We are requesting that if you know this woman's whereabouts, do not approach her. Instead, call our tip line. That number is on your screen. Thank you."

The recording of Banks concludes, and Ashley sums up the statement for the anchor and her viewers. "This is Ashley Blair reporting for CBS."

***

"Now why would a pretty little thing like that get messed up in something like that?" is heard from across the table at the Walcott 80 Truck Stop. Opened in 1964, it is the largest truck stop in the world and has been serving all-day breakfasts to thousands of visitors since then. Situated in Walcott, Iowa, on Interstate 80, it has remained under the same ownership for many years. Drivers from all states and countries visit Walcott along their way. One driver, sitting at a table across from the buffet, asks the question to an older gentleman standing beside him. The pair watches the newscast playing on the TV. The sketch and Banks' words capture their attention. "Shame…just a shame what they're doing these days. It sure looks like she's going to have the whole damn country looking for her now." The man chuckles as he gets up from his table and walks to the cashier to pay his bill. The older man just stands and quietly listens to the broadcast.

***

"She is someone's daughter or sister. This sketch might as well be a photograph. It's so damn clear.

Sanders stay on top of the tip line. Let me know if anything credible comes in," Banks say.

"No problem, mon capitaine! As it happens, I am in the process of sending Jenkins and Lee a text with some names to follow up on, people who worked in this mine. Go figure, several still live in Evergreen. They should have them…now." Sanders says as the sound of his fingers tapping away on his keyboard echoes in the background.

U.S. Department of Justice
Federal Bureau of Investigation

CHAPTER EIGHTY-ONE: Lee's Dilemma
Present Day

Jenkins and Lee receive a text from Sanders in Quantico with updates on several new leads. They include the names of three people who still live in Evergreen and had family members who worked at the mine; included in the list, Mr. Lloyd Grady. Jenkins arranges a time for Lee and her to speak with him. The drive from the mine into Evergreen is just over an hour. Since arriving in Montana, the team has been working on very little sleep, operating mainly on adrenaline.

"How are you holding up?" Lee asks as he drives.

Jenkins tries to crack her neck, squeezing the left side of her neck as she stretches. "Day three and, where are we? No closer, more questions than answers, and I just can't—sorry just way to tired I guess, that's how I'm holding up, and you?" She casts a sarcastic grin in his direction.

Lee is the most recent addition to the team and was recruited directly by the FBI shortly after 9/11. During his years working in the NYPD Special Victims Unit, Lee has seen his share of depravity. "It's horrible to think, but there were so many cases, hell, I can remember one. Can't forget it. A call came into us from the two-seven, twelve-year-old girl is missing; she didn't come home after school. Her mom was a single parent, so she's at work, and the deal she had with her kid was a quick text when she got home from school each day. A simple, *mom home ok*, so Mom thinks everything is fine. Her shift ends at five thirty and a thirty-minute commute, then Mom gets home."

"Her daughter wasn't there?"

"No, first thing Mom does is call all of her friends. She's pissed thinking that her daughter has fooled her and is out with her friends. Two more hours pass before it starts to sink in."

"What happened?"

"We found the girl three days later. She was naked and had been raped numerous times. He dumped her body beside the Cross-Bronx Expressway, not even two miles from her home. About two weeks after the body was found, her mother jumped in front of a subway train."

"The text message, the unsub sent it?"

"Yes, she was abducted during lunch and with kids cutting class and teachers too busy to keep track of everyone, she just got missed."

"And the unsub?"

"Still at large, a couple of weeks after her mother committed suicide, the towers got hit and then, well you know the rest." Lee pauses as he looks at the mountains in the distance. "We have found these victims, survivors, how do we repatriate them? Can we, and hell for that matter, should we? If Sanders is right, and they were abducted from foster care or orphanages, what are we going to do with them they've got no one? Just this place and each other. For all we know, this place is the only place they know. This is their home. If we rescue them, we might as well be abducting them all over again. What the hell are we going to do with them?"

U.S. Department of Justice
Federal Bureau of Investigation

CHAPTER EIGHTY-TWO: Lloyd Grady
Present Day

They arrive at Mr. Grady's home. Seventy-eight-year-old Lloyd Grady welcomes the two agents to his house and directs them to his living room.

"My name is Sandra Jenkins and I am the Behavioral Analysis unit of the FBI. This is my colleague, Thomas Lee. We would like to ask you a few questions about the Prevail Stewart Mine. We understand that your grandfather worked there?"

"Granddad worked for several mines back in his day. He mined these mountains for over forty years he worked at Prevail and a couple others. You see, when the ore ran out or the mine got shut down for whatever reason, the men would get shuffled around, looking for a place to work. He'd do just about anything, anything to keep his family fed."

Mr. Grady shows the agents several old photos of his grandfather. "This was one of granddad's favorite shots of the mine, that's him right there with a couple of his chums. That poor fellow right there, he died three days after this picture was taken. Wall caved in on him crushed him. They were always worried about cave-ins, lots of blue gas down there you know.

Granddad figured that they must have hit a pocket of gas. Bam! And the poor fellow was gone. Young lady, I might be up there in the years, but I have always been a good reader of people. When you live out here and all alone like I do, the TV tends to be your best friend. And I watch the news, and I've been watching. The old roads into that site have been gone for years. Part of the plan when it was closed, things just weren't worth mining. Ain't an easy place to bring in anything, let alone make this a damn dump operation."

Lloyd's astute observations and comments surprise both agents.

Lee looks in Jenkins' direction as the agents decide who will field this question. Lee says, "Mr. Grady, you've hit the proverbial nail on the head. Our team has been asking that very question time and time again since our arrival. That location, as you know, is so very remote and that's why we need to enlist help from people such as yourself. Cases like this, the devil is in the details."

"Back in the day, people, businesses were always just tossing trash here and there. Some pretty bad stuff too; I can still remember that TV commercial with the Indian and his tears looking at all the pollution. This is a big state, and we have so many hidden places to do stuff like this, why there? It used to take us two, three hours to get into town from the mine. We would only leave the site on the weekend, or at the end of our rotations. Heck if you've been there, you've seen the countless other spots along the way...why did they pick that site? I guess if you're bringing real dangerous stuff and need a place no one would ever find it, there you go. There's a lot of easier places to dump things around here, that's all I can say."

Mr. Grady shakes their hands as the agents conclude their interview and motion to get up.

U.S. Department of Justice
Federal Bureau of Investigation

CHAPTER EIGHTY-THREE: Eco-Town
Present Day

"This unsub is an extremely organized white male. He is very well educated and most likely financially very well positioned," Cherkoff tells the members of the sheriff's team. Banks and the others listen and observe the faces of the numerous deputies present. "He is a preferential abductor—"

"But you said there are both men and women alive down there," remarks a deputy.

"Yes, there are survivors of both sexes. He does not have a sexual preference for his victims, but he abducts victims he believes are discards, wards of the state, for example. He has been successful at this for at least thirty years."

"This unsub picked this location for a very specific reason—it is self-sufficient and far enough away, yet still accessible," Banks adds.

Cho and Deanna have just returned to the command trailer with Cherkoff and Torres. On the table in front of agent Banks is a large map that the techs have been putting together. The map has been created from the survey of the crime scene and our techs have used data from the ground radar scans as well as from information that George and Carlo collected. Deep Image provided the team access to all the company's survey data.

"What's this?" Deanna asks as she holds up one of the advertising brochures for Eco-Town. She takes a few moments to realize the contents of the package. "This is beautiful." Deanna hands the brochure to Cho. "And they're only 2.5 million, sign me up!"

Cho glances over her shoulder at the brochure.

"Can I see that?" he asks and walks over to the board where the team has displayed copies of the unsub's sketches. Cho tacks the brochure to the center of the board, displaying the conceptual plan of Eco-Town. He stands back from the board. "The artist that drew this—also drew these." Cho points to the brochure, then the sketches.

Banks and the other agents focus intently as Cho explains his findings, "Our handwriting and signatures are as personal and unique as our fingerprints. Especially our paintings. You can hide your feelings in your mind and watch what you say but what you draw or write…no." Cho shows the agents the identifying features and trademarks that the artist used in his creations. "There is no doubt in my mind only one person did these. Just as a bomb-maker has a signature your pen, pencil, or brush strokes are unique."

Immediately Banks contacts Sanders, "Pull up the information you have on the company that hired these surveyors."

"Done, what's up?"

"Where are they located?"

"Hartford, the owner's name is Otto Kinderson; he is seventy-nine years old. What am I looking for?"

"We need the contact information for the artist who drew the concept sketch for Eco-Town; Cho believes it's the same person who drew these sketches. As soon as you have them—"

Sanders cut Banks off, "I'll have it to you in five!"

U.S. Department of Justice
Federal Bureau of Investigation

CHAPTER EIGHTY-FOUR:
Details and Paperwork
Present Day

"Our Ashley Blair has been following a story out of Evergreen. Here she is with more details on this incredible illegal dumping operation. Ashley, what can you tell us? From what we heard, there are even possible ties to the Middle East?"

The video switches to Ashley, broadcasting live from the Federal Building in Chicago.

"Well, not exactly, Dan. My contact at the FBI reported to me earlier today that their task force is currently working with DHS agents and are tracing the origin of three shipping containers. The containers were discovered during their investigation."

The video of Ashley cuts and a recorded statement from Banks is played. The video shows the side view of each of the containers. The image has been enhanced to remove any evidence of their burial and all identifying marks are censored. "Our agents, in conjunction with the field office of the Department of Homeland Security, are working to identify the person or persons involved with the transportation of these containers. At this time, I cannot go into more detail as to the contents, but I can say that items have been removed and are currently undergoing evaluation."

***

"That's the last one for today. Your doctor said he would come by later this morning." Mr. Kinderson's executive assistant has been faithfully bringing in papers and files for him to sign since his arrival at the hospital. Mr. Kinderson is breathing with the aid of an oxygen machine and is in the final stages of lung cancer. The bulk of today's business consists of lease contracts and drafts of purposed tenders due to be announced shortly. Tanya is careful to ensure that the most important documents are taken care of first, leaving drafts or items lower on the priority list to the end of their meeting.

"Sir, you need to get your rest…oh and that package was sent via FedEx yesterday." She packs up the files and is about to turn off the TV in his room when he shakes his head.

"News? You should be at least watching something more entertaining!" Her boss insists that the news be left on. With that, Tanya says goodbye and leaves the room.

Kinderson switches the TV back to CBS from another news channel and gives his morphine drip a slight squeeze administering a small dose to calm his pain. Closing his eyes his mind drifts, *just a few more days, just a few.*

U.S. Department of Justice
Federal Bureau of Investigation

CHAPTER EIGHTY-FIVE: A Special Gift
1976

Remember tickets for the Bi-centennial Fair and Barbeque scheduled for this weekend are available here at the station and at various locations across town. Oldson exits US Highway 93 and turns onto the frontage road that heads into the mountains. He turns off his radio as the announcer's voice fades. He's had little free time, and it's been almost two months since his last visit. He was more than pleased to see how all the residents of the mine were progressing, especially Terri's son.

At twelve years of age, he is the first resident to only know this place. Since his birth, several other children have been born and each has taken to their home, safe with their birth parents close by. For whatever reason, the parents keep the little ones deep within the mine until they are almost one year old. As he drives to the site, Oldson remembers his feeling at the first site of Terri's son. The little boy came into the main room, crawling beside Terri as she foraged for food, surrounded closely by the others, especially the black boy and the little boy he placed in the mine with Terri. Oldson was strangely satisfied at how dutiful the little boy was to both Terri and her son. Her son is the spitting image of Josh.

The ease at which the offspring of the mine's residents adapted to the environment he created for them has been more than Oldson could have hoped for. The little ones all interact so well. Their parents each take turns watching over them on the various outings into the main room. Terri is always very close by; she is always helping the other young mothers, helping and teaching them how to care for their babies. Oldson knew she had this special quality. She just needed a safe place to call home.

Oldson vividly remembers the day when Josh had explained how Terri had raised her younger brother only to have the state step in and take him away after her father was arrested. At that time, Oldson knew what had to be done. And after leaving Terri and Teddy in the mine, Oldson would not stop until he was able to reunite Terri with her younger brother, Robbie.

During December 1963, Oldson located the foster home where Robbie lived. In a strange twist of fate, Oldson's business schedule included several stops in North Dakota that month. As fate would have it, his and Robbie's paths would cross just in time for Oldson to give Terri a very memorable Christmas gift.

U.S. Department of Justice
Federal Bureau of Investigation

CHAPTER EIGHTY-SIX: First Contact
Present Day

Cherkoff and Torres are working with Deanna and Cho continuing their efforts to identify the total number of survivors and locate any possible remains. They're using one of the bureau's bomb disposal robots. The RCV, as the team calls it, is equipped with directional cameras and LED lights. It's being lowered into the mine's main room. The RCV is a self-contained unit, but the team has attached a tether that will allow for retrieval.

"Okay, lower it slowly," Torres instructs the operator.

The technician operating the remote camera explains, "We've got two 4K Ultra HD video cameras and thermal imaging scanners. This thing makes quite a bit of noise, the tracks and all. We have plenty of onboard lights, so it really doesn't matter what the conditions are down there, we can handle it." He will keep all the lights off until the residents have had a chance to inspect it. Once they are comfortable with it, then the tech will proceed to move the RCV into tunnel two. With the RCV safely on the floor of the main room, the tech turns on the infrared and the thermal scanner. Within a few moments, several images are seen approaching the RCV. As foreign to the residents as a UFO would be to the agents, the victims poke and prod at the RCV. They turn it over and try to pull pieces off it, but to no avail.

"It's not a threat, and it obviously is not a food source," Deanna says. "When it's turned on and starts to move, that will be when they may consider it a threat."

***

The team has adhered to their earlier plan, keeping the mine illuminated. The unsub's generator had recently turned on, and shortly after, the relays tripped, bringing on the lights. Banks decided to override the timers and keep the lights on. Only a small portion of the tunnels receives any illumination due to the mine's topography.

The RCV remains off until the residents appear comfortable with this strange thing and Torres instructs the tech to turn it on. The unit, which stands just less than three feet tall, has triangular shaped tracks on both sides. The tracks are designed so that when the unit tips, it can self-right. The team decides that the unit's lights will be turned on and the video camera will be used, rather than the infrared. "I have no way of telling where the walls are unless the lights are on. The infrared will only register heat sources," the tech explains as he hits the switch. Immediately, the victims still in the main room scatter in various directions.

Alpha, along with Joker, can be seen reaching for whatever they can find to use as weapons. As the tech starts the RCV, Alpha charges the little machine; something flashes past the camera as Alpha strikes the top of the machine. On the monitor, the team realizes what they are seeing. Alpha has hit the RCV with a human leg bone he was using as a club. The tech focuses one of the cameras on the ground surrounding the RCV, where shattered bone fragments lay. They also see Alpha reluctantly retreat, seeking shelter in one of the tunnels.

With the main room clear, the tech directs the RCV to the entrance of tunnel one. "Can you adjust those lights, change their color?" Deanna asks the tech, who in turn adjusts the tint of the LED lights. "That's much better. Warmer colors will cause the least stress." As the RCV enters the mouth of the first tunnel, the team receives their first glimpse beyond confines of the main room.

The victims have worn a path in the soft ground. The walls of the tunnel reflect where pieces of quartz and other reflective minerals are present. The tunnel descends gradually. The RCV continues deeper into the tunnel. The cameras so far cannot detect any movements. The thermal scans do not reveal the presence of any heat source, except for several rats scurrying past. Near the entrance of the shaft, a variety of vegetation is growing.

"They sure have enough mushrooms and whatever the hell that is," Cherkoff remarks to the group. The ability of the various species of plants and fungi to adapt to this environment impresses all the team members watching the monitors.

With the RCV now more than one hundred feet into the tunnel, a tiny figure appears coming over the crest in the floor. Winnie is one of the youngest girls that the team has observed in the main room. She is slowly walking toward the RCV.

"Stop it right here, let's see what she does," Deanna says. Winnie's gait is clumsy; she falls as most toddlers do. Her age is estimated to be three or four. One of the males of the colony, possibly her father, rushes into view. It's Joker, the community's prankster, as his name implies. The team has seen him before, in the main room guarding Winnie and bringing her small pieces of fungi. He always makes sure that she only returns to tunnel one. True to form, Joker heads to where Winnie is and takes her away from the RCV. The pair disappears out of sight, deeper into the tunnel.

The RCV is now almost three hundred feet into this tunnel. The team notices that there are more and more footprints and evidence of traffic. "It looks like we're probably coming to the end of the tunnel." The tech confirms this with the drawings that the radar images had earlier provided them. With just enough light to see where the unit needs to be directed, the camera shows what once must have been the mining room at the end of the tunnel. The shaft opens into a very large room.

The tech refocuses the light, changing it from a spot to a flood. The single flood illuminates the entire room and the team sees where most of the survivors spend their time. They quickly realize why this is.

"Oh my God!" Cherkoff exclaims.

U.S. Department of Justice
Federal Bureau of Investigation

CHAPTER EIGHTY-SEVEN: The Room
Present Day

In the room, the team sees the gentle stream that carves its way through the mountain. The survivors huddle together near the stream's edge. Deanna instructs the tech to record the images of all the new faces they are seeing. The tech keeps the RCV far enough away from the survivors so as not to alarm them. "Good, they're calming down. There are so many of them. What's the temperature here?" Deanna asks.

"Sixty-nine degrees, fifty-five percent relative humidity, and see this..." the tech points to a gauge on the screen, "...a slight breeze. The slope of the tunnel is acting like the flue of a chimney. The air quality down here is better than any major city. Pollen count is nil."

"I don't see Alpha, where is he? Turn the RCV around and head back to the main room." As Deanna speaks, the tech maneuvers the RCV around. Using the bidirectional tracks, he turns the unit around.

"Before you—wait, hang on. Can you turn these lights off please? I want to see just how dark it is here. What is it like for them?" Deanna requests.

The tech turns the RCV so that it is positioned facing back to the main room, then he switches the LEDs off. Almost immediately, the tunnel fades to black. Within a few moments, faint specks of light sparkle. "It's the quartz fragments in the walls," the tech explains. "They will luminesce even in very minimal light. If you're down here long enough, your eyes will adjust, and you would be amazed at what you can see."

The team is hoping that not only will the RCV give them the answers to the total number of survivors but also answer a curiosity. Since they have been observing the survivors, the team has noticed that shaft two, for some reason, is off limits to everyone except the survivor they named Oscar; he is somewhat of a loner and not very clean. He spends most of his time standing guard in front of shaft two. He only ventures into the main room when no one else is around and if someone else does happen to enter the room when he is out, Oscar will always withdraw back into the depths of shaft two.

As the RCV enters back into the main room, Alpha can be seen walking around the perimeter. His attention is focused on the RCV. Several of the other males are standing nearby as they try to figure out what this strange new thing is. When the RCV moves, the group of men retreats immediately.

Deanna has theorized that the residents living in this artificial world have managed to succeed for many reasons. The strongest, no doubt, survived. This is not just determined by physical strength, but they would also have the necessary mental powers and inherent will to live. "This environment is in no way ideal," Deanna says. "However, it is extremely human-friendly with warmth, abundant food sources, and access to drinking water. As a species, we are physically ill-equipped for survival. Our offspring require years of comfort, support, and nurturing. When we are born, we are defenseless and even when grown have limited resources with which to defend ourselves. In this environment, however, the residents are immediately top dog. Once they got over the fear factor, the darkness, they let their number one survival tool take over. Their brains."

The tech operating the RCV rotates the camera around. For the first time, the team can see into the first shaft. The shaft's floor is as smooth as the main room's. Abundant supplies of fungi and lichens are visible. "Everywhere you look, there appears to be some variety of button mushroom and those are puff balls. But that species is imported." The tech focuses the camera on one large mass of mushrooms.

The RCV moves toward the entrance to the second shaft as the team watches the reaction of Alpha and the other males standing in the distance. Alpha, moving with purpose, is gradually getting closer to the RCV.

U.S. Department of Justice
Federal Bureau of Investigation

CHAPTER EIGHTY-EIGHT: Josh Bolton
Present Day

"We just received a call about the woman wanted in connection to the Evergreen case." An agent assigned to the tip line provides Sanders with the caller's contact information and a transcript of the call. After reading the details of the ten-minute conversation, Sanders immediately contacts the command center in Evergreen.

Agent Banks answers Sanders' call. "Sir, I have a couple of updates." Banks informs Sanders that he is on speaker phone as Sanders continues, "So far, the tip line has received numerous calls, possible sightings, names...what can I say, the geese are flying and, well, sorry, I digress. We received a call last night. For some reason, the call was not directed to me until just now. The call came from Holman State Prison outside Atmore, Alabama. The caller is an inmate named Josh Bolton who said he recognized the sketch of the girl."

Banks then asks Sanders what he knows about the caller and if he verified his story. Sanders tells the team that he listened to the tape, and what caught his attention was when the caller said that "she isn't from Evergreen and her name is Terri. The caller also gave her home address, 145 Terrace Drive, Beulah, North Dakota, and her full name is Terri Heaton."

Sanders explains that the caller was convicted and sentenced to death for a murder he committed in 1963. "He was sentenced to death for killing a college girl in Birmingham. His sentence was eventually commuted to life without parole. The case the prosecutor had against him was highly circumstantial. They found him half dead in an empty railcar, with blood on his shirt, and they also found a pair of woman's panties in his pocket. Their investigation led to two murders where the victims' panties were taken. He had absolutely no idea where he was and could recall nothing at the time. Unable to adequately aid in his own defense, he was tried and convicted. Sad thing though, with the evidence they had against him. If this case were under investigation today, he probably wouldn't have even been charged, let alone convicted."

"What do we know about this girl?" Banks asks Sanders.

Sanders sends Banks a picture of the girl from her high school yearbook. "As they say a picture is worth a thousand words. It's definitely her. Our *Girl in Flowered Skirt* is Miss Terri Elizabeth Heaton. Born October 7, 1944 and lived in Beulah, North Dakota. She has one younger brother. He was placed in foster care after the father was arrested. Her mother has several convictions for prostitution and died in 1964 of an overdose. With her father in prison and her younger brother…oh crap…"

"What's the matter?" Banks asks.

"Her younger brother was four when he was placed in foster care," Sanders states as he continues to gather information on Terri's brother. "Oh Jesus, he was reported missing in early December of '63; he was last seen during an outing at a local playground. His case is still open. There were just a couple of leads, no real suspects. The case remains open."

"What else did the caller tell you about the girl?" Banks inquires.

"They were both nineteen when he and Terri were hitchhiking across the country. That was the last time he saw her, in late November 1963. When he was found in Alabama, he couldn't recall anything and the deputy's report states that when he made his phone call home, his father hung up on him. I'm getting all of the evidence from the original case expressed to here."

Sanders also informs Banks that since his incarceration, Josh has taken a correspondence course studying law. He passed the bar and has represented himself several times, winning an appeal and stay-of-execution, which lead to his sentence being commuted to life without parole. He currently has a motion before the court to reopen his case and have it retried. Banks decides that his story is worth a follow-up and sends Jenkins and Lee to Alabama.

U.S. Department of Justice
Federal Bureau of Investigation

CHAPTER EIGHTY-NINE: Misha
Present Day

As the tech continues to operate the RCV, it slowly makes its way to the entrance of the second shaft. Alpha has gathered enough courage to come a bit closer to this strange thing. Without warning, Oscar darts out from the depths of the shaft and blocks the way. When the team was deciding on a name for him, they almost chose Caucasian male with short temper. Oscar has defended this tunnel from the approach of every resident. They can at this time only guess at his age, but he is at least forty, as his body is slowly getting covered with white hairs. With both of his arms stretched out and his chest as wide as he can make it, his form dwarfs the RCV and causes even Alpha to back away from the shaft. The tech immediately stops the advance of the RCV. The camera's field of vision into the tunnel is blocked by Oscar but the team can see Alpha approaching the right side of the RCV.

"Don't move the unit; just turn the camera so we can see Alpha." Deanna asks the tech who rotates one of the video cameras. "Oh God!" A startling image comes into focus. Alpha is standing within reach of the RCV and is holding a human leg bone in the air.

His posture is more curious than aggressive; however, Oscar is standing firm, holding his ground. There is no doubt; Oscar will not allow the RCV to proceed any further into the shaft.

Suddenly both Alpha and Oscar's attention is distracted by a sound coming into the main room. The team members also hear the faint sound as it slowly gets louder. "Turn the camera, where is she?" Deanna says. The video camera on the RCV turns and they see the face of one of the young female survivors. The team has named her Misha, an Asian girl in her late teens. As her image comes into full view on the monitor, they realize that something is terribly wrong. Misha whimpers and cries as she tries to walk across the floor of the main room. Deanna and Cherkoff saw Misha earlier as she entered one of the other tunnels. She was quite pregnant. "Her legs are covered in blood! Where is her baby?"

"It looks like she hasn't dealt with the placenta properly," Cherkoff says as Torres motions to one of the techs to go find Banks and bring him here immediately.

"She's lost a lot of blood, way too much, look at her. Her eyes are sunken and my God, she's so pale," Deanna says. Misha takes one more step and then grabs her stomach, collapsing onto floor. As her body hits the ground, Oscar comes into view of the camera. He cautiously side-steps his way past the RCV, not turning his back to it, and with his head tilted down, he sits on the ground beside Misha. His large, weathered hands push at Misha's side, but she does not respond. Oscar leans over her, reaching under her back with his hands, and gently picks her up. He carries her back into tunnel two.

The tech attempts to follow his path with the camera as Oscar and Misha disappear into the depths of the tunnel. "Follow him!" Cherkoff orders the tech to power up the RCV. Before the tech can get the unit moving, Alpha rushes past it and stands guard, blocking the tunnel. "Damn it! We have to get in there now. There's no way she will survive," shouts Deanna as Banks comes into the room.

"It's the pregnant girl, Misha," Cherkoff explains to Banks. "She is in really bad shape; she's losing a lot of blood."

U.S. Department of Justice
Federal Bureau of Investigation

CHAPTER NINETY: Dazed and Confused
Present Day

While onboard the jet, Sanders updates Jenkins and Lee with more about Josh. "You have to understand the culture back then. This poor dumb kid was found all scratched up. And stoned out of his mind. His shirt covered in blood, which I might add, matched the blood type of the girl from Birmingham; however, it also matched his. They are both O-positive. Yes, I can hear the groans in the background as O-positive is the common of all the blood types. Bolton had no clue where he was. He was carrying a good supply of marijuana in his pockets, had an aroma of other drugs on him as well. It looks like he has spent the past forty-five years locked up based on a bag of weed and a ton of circumstantial evidence. Well at least he isn't African American, you know what I mean, sorry."

Jenkins says, "We can connect the dots."

After he finishes with Jenkins and Lee, Sanders sorts through the items that have just arrived from Birmingham in a musty, brown banker's box with BH-63-13 stamped in black on the end. Inside the box he finds evidence bags, still sealed, that contain various items, including the shirt Josh had been wearing.

Sanders catalogues the items and requests they be taken to the lab for analysis.

Upon arriving in Birmingham, Jenkins and Lee meet with Assistant District Attorney (ADA) Marie-Anne Stolz, who informs them that Josh did have a substantial amount of marijuana on his person at the time of his arrest. There was a witness who placed a man fitting Josh's description with the girl the night she was murdered. Unfortunately, the prosecutor from the case recently passed away but the sheriff and deputy are still alive. She also explains that Bolton remained on death row for many years until he exhausted all possible avenues for appeal. Eventually, he was awarded clemency and his sentence reduced to life without the chance of parole. That appeal was based on certain doubts surrounding his guilt.

"One thing that does indeed stand out is that at no time did the accused ever admit to killing the girl. In fact, he offered very little. He was unable to provide the prosecutor or his defense lawyer with any information that could have helped him prove his innocence."

The transcripts for the trial show that Josh was unable to answer key questions posed to him by the prosecutor.

"It makes you wonder how many other accused went through this," Lee comments to Jenkins after they leave the ADA's office. "You know, there's a good chance this guy is innocent. Sanders said the DNA results from the shirt should be back later today." The pair would prefer to know the results before their interview with Josh. They have Josh's DNA on file, which had been collected several years ago. With the nature of the crime he was sentenced for, he was placed on the National Sex Offender Registry and listed as a violent offender. Once at the prison, they're greeted by the assistant warden, who escorts them to a room where Josh is waiting.

"What can you tell us about this inmate?" Jenkins asks as they walk to the interview room.

U.S. Department of Justice
Federal Bureau of Investigation

CHAPTER NINETY-ONE: Holman Penitentiary
Present Day

"His file is very clean, been in a few scuffles, a few extra charges in-house for a couple of fights. He spent some time in solitary but overall, for someone in here as long as he has been, just another lifer."

They enter the interview room and sit down across the table from Josh. At sixty-six years of age, Josh has known Holman Penitentiary as home since the facility opened in 1969. He was transferred here the year it opened. With his short grey hair, he has the appearance of a retired businessman, except for the bright-orange prison jumpsuit. He's no longer the disheveled drifter as seen in his mug shot.

Jenkins and Lee introduce themselves to Josh. They had decided earlier that Jenkins would take the lead in the interview. "Terri, you call her, what can you tell us about her? When did you last see her? Where was that?"

Josh asks, "The news said she had been seen in Evergreen, Montana and was wanted because of some kind of illegal dumping operation?" His confusion stems around the picture. "If she's wanted now, why do you have such an old picture?"

His posture becomes very rigid and both agents sense his concern for Terri. Jenkins offers Josh a glass of water as she explains, "We cannot get into many details right now, but we can assure you, she isn't wanted or involved with a smuggling operation. We have been trying to locate her."

Josh says, "That's Terri! We were like nineteen years old, man, and that was a long, long time a go!" Josh lifts the glass of water to his mouth, taking a sip. Tiny waves ripple across the top of the water as his hands shake. Jenkins looks at his eyes as they well up with tears.

Jenkins slides a box of tissues across the table. Josh's left hand cups his mouth as he begins to speak, his voice is very shaky, "She was my girlfriend." Both agents appear surprised with this information as Josh continues to speak, "Look, I know this sounds strange but until I saw her picture on the news, I had just about forgotten about Terri and me. Getting older, I guess. Seeing her picture was like turning on a spotlight in my brain! Since then I've been getting bits, chops of memories flashing through my mind, of her with me. Man, how do you forget someone like that and…a whole year of your life, everything."

The agents can feel his anguish as they listen to him desperately recall these lost memories.

"She and I were hitchhiking across the country, on our way to California. She had friends there and we were going to stay with them. I remember getting a ride from a trucker and, okay, never mind…we had to help him unload, way up north."

"Do you have any memory of where that might have been?" Jenkins asks.

"That trucker was going somewhere up north in Montana, can't remember where, and we agreed to help him unload things when he got to his destination. Terri sat right there." He gestures indicating that Terri was seated behind him. "I remember he had one of those sleeper trucks, and she rode in the back as he drove."

With each word, the events of their trip slowly come back to him. He tells the agents she had worn the skirt, the one from the sketch, and a nice top, and when it got cool, she would put on a light green sweater overtop." For a moment, Josh bows his head to the table, clutching the picture of Terri in his hands. When he lifts his head back up from the table, a flow of tears stream from his eyes.

Jenkins manages to get Josh to focus past the picture of Terri for the moment. "The two of you got a ride from a trucker. Can you remember anything about him?" Josh recalls a generic description of the trucker who gave them a ride. Jenkins then asks what Josh could remember after they were dropped off in Montana. "We worked all day with this guy, had a load, those burlap bags for onions and potatoes. We helped him unload at some feed mill way up north. Yes, and he had to go on to Canada after, so he dropped us off on the highway—"

"You say he dropped you off?" Jenkins asks. Both agents try not to alarm Josh. "He just dropped you off, or both?"

"Both, I mean Terri, I'm sorry, I can't. It was Highway 93, somewhere near Highway 93," Josh replies.

U.S. Department of Justice
Federal Bureau of Investigation

CHAPTER Ninety-Two: Oldson
Present Day

"Somewhere near Highway 93, can you remember anything about it, smells, other roads, signs, anything?" Jenkins asks.

"I remember camping with Terri, near a lake. Real private. I remember that!" No matter how hard Josh tries to connect his memories, his next solid memories are from Birmingham and the railcar. "I remember that goddamn prosecutor laughing at me when he asked me 'Who's the President?' and I answered wrong. Where was I when Kennedy got shot? You tell me! Imagine that I didn't even know our president had been shot."

Lee passes Jenkins a file folder.

She opens the file and removes the uncensored sketch of *Girl in Flowered Skirt*. "Camping, you were with Terri, and the truck driver, or just Terri?" Jenkins asks, as she waits for his answer, she watches as his eyes wonder, looking first at her, then glancing to the file and what she's holding in her hand.

Josh shakes his head. "Maybe just her. Camping, yes, we were camping."

Lee motions Jenkins to reveal the sketch.

Jenkins then places the sketch face up in front of Josh. "Did he do this? Did the driver do this to Terri?"

Jenkins slowly slides the sketch across the table placing it directly in front of Josh. Josh's eyes widen in horror as he stares at the sketch. Leaning back from the table for a moment, he combs his hands through his hair pulling them by the roots. His face turns ghostly white and beads of perspiration form on his forehead.

The sketch of Terri—the bindings, her skirt, the position of her body raw and graphic—Josh reaches slowly for the sketch holding it by the edges with just the tips of his fingers. His body slumps into his chair as he brings it closer to his face.

Jenkins and Lee both remain focused on Josh's reaction, watching for any tell, any sign. Their collective training is in the highest of gear at this moment. His pulse, the dilatation of his pupils, eye movement, his reaction to this grotesque image of someone who had, at one time, meant the world to him. Posed in this manner and now in his hands. Josh sits like a statue, holding Terri in his hands. Two small tears fall from the corner of his left eye. His only reaction.

"Oldson! Ole-se...how did he say it...yes, Olesun! No, no the trucker dropped us on the side of 93. He gave us, he gave us a bag of weed and a couple of bucks. We unloaded his truck for him. Yes, he was heading somewhere else, not California. He dropped us off, but like not there."

Jenkins tries to get Josh to expand, "What do you mean by *but not there?*"

"Not where we met this guy." Josh lowers the sketch down so both agents can see Terri's face. "We camped near 93 after the trucker but we met this other freak. We got picked up by this big guy in a pickup truck."

"The pickup truck, can you remember *anything*, anything about it?" Jenkins asks.

"The smell," Josh takes a deep breath through his nose, "leather. The interior of his truck man, it was spotless, leather bench seat, that smell."

"Keep going Josh," instructs Jenkins.

"It was red. A red pickup, and Oldson was the guy's name." Josh pauses for a moment, his brow furls slightly, then his face flushes with rage as more memories come to the surface. "He killed her and that little boy—he fucking killed them both!"

Jenkins pauses for a moment as both she and Lee try to digest Josh's revelation. Josh notices their confusion and focuses his thoughts attempting to remember more. "There was a box, a wooden crate in the back of his truck, in the bed. He had it covered with a black tarp." Josh stops talking as his eyes widen in fear. Jenkins notices his body language change dramatically. Josh composes himself and continues to describe the events, "He had a red truck! I made her lift her skirt up, so he would stop, oh my God, I got her killed!" he screams.

Jenkins reaches her right hand across the table, and gently places her hand on Josh's, attempting to calm him down.

"You're doing great Josh. Just take it easy, you're doing great," Jenkins says. "We don't know what happened then, that's why we're all here now. Try to focus and talk to me." Her voice is very calm, and Josh relaxes enough to continue.

"We saw his truck coming down the hill, and Terri lifted up her skirt and showed a lot of leg. He pulled over and we got in. It was a real nice red truck, and…" Josh pauses for a moment while he pieces his shattered memories together. "Leather! I remember the smell of leather…it had a big bench seat, a beautiful leather bench seat!"

As Josh describes the truck, Jenkins takes a picture of the F-250 from her file and hands it to Josh.

"That's it, that's the truck but wait…" Josh scans the photograph, paying particular attention to the front of the truck. "His had something, a different front-end. The bumper was bigger, way bigger."

"What else can you remember about his truck?" Jenkins asks. While Jenkins continues her interview with Josh, Lee excuses himself and exits the room. From the privacy of the hallway, Lee places a call into Quantico.

"Sanders, I have a name I need you to research, anything you can find. Oldson but it is pronounced Olesun. And look for any records; he may have owned a red F-250," Lee says.

While Lee talks, Sanders begins to run his search, asking, "Oldson, pronounced Olesun. First name or last?"

"Unclear right now, just run it."

U.S. Department of Justice
Federal Bureau of Investigation

CHAPTER NINETY-THREE: Find Misha
Present Day

Banks and the team members gather around the monitors watching the RCV as they attempt to gain access to the second tunnel. "Can you try to move the RCV slowly past him?" Banks asks the tech.

Alpha is standing steadfast, looking straight at the RCV. His posture is quite different than before. With Oscar not at his post, it is his turn to guard this tunnel…but why? The RCV starts to move toward Alpha. There is no fear or confusion in his eyes this time, only contempt, for this strange thing that will not obey. "Keep going," instructs Banks as the tech changes the angle of the lights, hoping that this will give Alpha cause to move. As the main lights of the RCV rotate to focus higher on the tunnel walls, Alpha leans his body back just a bit but refuses to give up any ground.

"Slowly, just keep it moving," Banks instructs the tech.

"She could be dead already," Deanna pleads with Banks.

"If we can't get past, him," Banks points to Alpha, "with the RCV, chances are he wouldn't let any of my agents past either. This is the best option we have right now. We will get to her with the RCV and assess the situation then," Banks explains to Deanna, sharing her concerns for Misha. The tech has managed to bring the RCV within inches of Alpha, who stands his ground.

Banks and the other agents know that the RCV is extremely durable, almost indestructible. With only his hands and any possible items he could use as a weapon, Alpha would not be able to inflict any serious damage to the unit. Banks' concern is more for Alpha, who is showing obvious signs of stress. "My priority here is everyone's safety. Misha's, my agents', all the victims'. There is too much at risk here for us to just blindly break into this place. I must limit the potential for casualties; we will find her.

"He's moving out of the way," Cherkoff says.

The unit continues into the tunnel. Alpha reluctantly gives way.

"This is probably the first thing he has encountered that he is actually afraid of," Cho says. "Think about it, the environment is harsh, but these victims are the top of the food chain."

U.S. Department of Justice
Federal Bureau of Investigation

CHAPTER NINETY-FOUR: Who Is She?
Present Day

The RCV reaches a point where the team can hear movement and sounds from what must be the end of the tunnel. The tech has changed the color of the lights to flood the area with a warm amber tone. The infrared camera is the first to pick up the images from deep in the tunnel. "Okay, there are three figures, that one, that must be her there. The one lying on the ground." The tech points to the figure on the monitor. One of the other figures turns in the RCV's direction.

Oscar stands directly in front of the RCV, the light allowing the team to see other figures behind him. Misha, her baby, and an older woman huddle protected by Oscar. Misha is on her side, barely conscious.

"Who is that?" a tech asks.

Deanna tells the team that this resident has not been seen until now. The woman beside Misha has long white hair and appears to be the oldest resident. Cherkoff, Torres, and Banks can only sit and look at her image. From the monitor, the team also sees eight small mounds of rocks. The mounds do not look natural and are not being used for sitting. Although curious, the rock mounds are not what grabs the team's attention. Oscar, and how protective he is of these two women and the little baby resting with them, has Deanna amazed.

The team has the tech stop the RCV. The familiar dirty face of Oscar is displayed as he slowly walks into the light. He has a very puzzled look is on his face. Is it because this is the first-time light has ever been this far into the shaft? His expression is one of curiosity rather than fear as he approaches the RCV.

Oscar touches the body of the RCV and leaves a handprint on the lens of one of the cameras. Several large brown rats also scurry past the RCV and out of sight. The walls of the tunnel are littered with fungi and marks can be seen where a rock has been used to dig for something. Oscar comes out from behind the RCV. The unit is just over four hundred feet into the longest tunnel in the mine. The tech moves the RCV a little farther, attempting to get a better view of the people behind Oscar. "Stop it when the main camera has a field of vision," Banks says.

The RCV continues for another twenty feet and the digital camera transmits the full image back to the team. Misha is on the ground, surrounded by Oscar and another female.

"Is this her?" Cherkoff asks Banks.

The second female is Caucasian and appears to be at least fifty, perhaps older. Her attention is focused on Misha.

"Stop it, stop it right here. We need a picture of the older woman," Banks says. She is by far the oldest survivor that the team has identified so far.

"What is she doing?" The tech captures several facial images of the older woman who is facing Misha, blocking the team's view.

The tech directs the team's attention to one of the monitors. "Misha's core temperature is no worse than the rest, her thermal image is excellent, considering." Now that the team can see her, it appears she's okay, for now. The older woman moves enough to give the team a view of her face. Her hands are covered with Misha's blood. A small pile of mossy-like fungi, also damp with blood, lies on the ground. The older woman raises a cupped hand to Misha, but the team cannot tell exactly what is in her hand.

U.S. Department of Justice
Federal Bureau of Investigation

CHAPTER NINETY-FIVE: Leather Bench Seat
Present Day

Josh continues his description of the driver's pickup. "We were real hungry, Terri and me. Pretty tired too and when we got in his truck, I remember talking to him while she slept. What did he call it? Yes, 'the best burgers on the highway.' He took us to a diner and that's when he played that goddamn game."

"What was the game Josh, what can you remember?" asks Jenkins.

"See we had our dinner, no I think it was breakfast. When the waitress brought the bill, Oldson played this little game at the end of our meal. There was a big black tarp over something in his truck's bed. And if I guessed what was under it…" Josh suddenly becomes very still. Jenkins senses something is wrong. The tone of Josh's voice changes dramatically as he continues to speak, "…he had big bags of feed, rice and potatoes all piled around it."

"Around it?" inquires Jenkins as Lee returns into the interview room.

"The crate, the wooden crate…there was a boy, a little boy in there too. Rats…" Josh shakes his head.

"I understand, it's okay if you can't remember everything, you're doing—" Jenkins is cut off by Josh mid-sentence.

"No, I don't mean it that way, I mean rats! Goddamn live rats, they were in the fucking crate too, with the little boy. He caught me sneaking a peek under the tarp. When we were camping, it was late that night. That's when he did it; it must have been. I was out, out cold and…damn it Josh, remember, remember." Josh slams his hand down onto the table. "I woke up and there they were, dozens crawling and clawing at me and the little boy. I couldn't do anything, nothing, just curl up and try to keep them off me and him." As Josh speaks, Jenkins hands Lee a page with some notes she has just written. Lee in turn texts Sanders that Josh was in Montana when the murders he was convicted for took place.

"Josh, excuse us for just a moment, please." Jenkins and Lee step into the hallway, dialing Banks as they walk. "Hey, Bolton isn't a killer. He's one of the unsub's survivors. Lee just sent Sanders an update and he's calling him now. We have to get this man out of here and up to the site as soon as possible." Banks listens, not questioning as Jenkins continues, "He has been trapped in the system just like that bastard's other victims have been trapped in there. Sanders is going to try to get him released into our custody. No doubt it will take a while, but we need to get him out of here right now."

"I'll call the deputy director and see if she can speed the process up," Banks says.

Sanders calls them both a moment later.

"Just a little over, maybe very over-caffeinated here—maps, missing children data, correlate those with that, ahh, you're a hedge! Where is…sorry guys, listen." Banks and Jenkins can tell that Sanders is trying to keep things together and that he's been working thirty-six hours straight. "No hits on Oldson or Olesun, just definitions and word origins but nothing else. However, I did happen to find Ely Watkins. He was born in Marquette, Michigan in 1916, father of two sons and proud grandfather of five, died in 1989. Not our man, so why the hell am I telling you all this?"

Sanders informs the pair that Ely's company leased ten Ford F-250s from Amco Commercial Leasing. Three of the trucks were sub-leased to employees and one, a red F-250, was delivered as a gift to a customer from a trucking company that worked as a subcontractor on many projects; a Canadian firm based in Virden, Manitoba. "You guessed it. A beautiful leather bench seat, full complement of three seat belts and get this: a bush guard." Sanders explains that he has been able to provide the complete history of the truck based on the vehicle identification number, (VIN). The truck had been transferred to a Canadian resident in 1959. "Now, I don't think you want me to get the records myself," referring to his wonderful computer abilities. He tells Banks that the RCMP is currently searching vehicle records for the truck's history as well as the ownership status of Cattlemen Trucking.

U.S. Department of Justice
Federal Bureau of Investigation

CHAPTER NINETY-SIX: Collateral
Present Day

"I'm confused, Josh and Terri were nineteen in 1963," Jenkins says. "These weren't little kids, and if the unsub started his collection in the late fifties, then she wasn't his first. Why her? And why spare him? This is a huge deviation from the profile, risk a potential witness? It doesn't make sense."

"He was just collateral. He needed her, and Josh wasn't a target, just an obstruction," Sanders says as he reviews several files both on his desk and on his various monitors. "Remember what Ms. Cornell said about his earliest victims: 'There will have been many failures.' What if he added an adult into the group? Someone to help, comfort, and raise the children. We know she had a younger brother who she raised pretty much by herself. He needed her."

"What younger brother?" Jenkins asks.

Banks provides an update for Jenkins and Lee. "We believe the unsub managed to find and abduct Terri's little brother as well. Robbie Heaton was reported missing in December 1963. There were many searches, but no evidence, witnesses, nothing. The case still remains open."

Sanders supplies them with the rest of the details, copies of Terri and her brother's birth records, and the open case file pertaining to his disappearance. "This bastard took her little brother too?" Jenkins' pen digs into the pad she is writing on.

"It would appear that way," Sanders says. "And Josh was simply in the way. He needed to be dealt with and fitting the profile, our unsub would first have to disable him to get to her, then dump him somewhere. He's a guardian protector, not a killer. Jenkins, when you talk to Josh again, ask him if the unsub was aware of her younger brother. Most likely, he was. The deaths of his early victims would affect a guardian protector terribly—it's the ultimate failure. With her in his world, he could focus on perfecting his ecosystem, and not constantly restocking the pond."

"Hang on a moment." Banks looks down at his tablet as a text comes in from Sanders. The text reads, *the facial image comparisons from the images captured in the tunnel are positive for Terri Heaton.* Banks quickly replies to Sanders text, instructing him to send Jenkins and Lee the images.

"Jenkins, while Cherkoff and Torres were working with Deanna, they have managed to identify one of the victims, still alive in the mine. You need to look at your tablets. She is still alive, still here." As Banks speaks, Jenkins and Lee open the files, Sanders has presented them with the digital images the RCV produced, along with an animated series of images, showing the girl in the flowered skirt's face age. Although disturbing, it is a perfect match.

335

Jenkins and Lee walk back to the interview room. "Who gets to tell him the news?" asks Lee, shaking his head. "Your girlfriend was abducted in 1963, oh and by the way, you've spent the last four decades locked up for a crime you didn't commit. And now for the bad news."

U.S. Department of Justice
Federal Bureau of Investigation

CHAPTER NINETY-SEVEN: Stolen
Present Day

Jenkins and Lee now must to speak to this innocent man who is still in custody. How he will take the news opens an entirely different set of issues. "Josh…Mr. Bolton." *Mr. Bolton* is a title Josh has only been called during trials and his appeals. Jenkins says, "Our colleague in Quantico has been working on several aspects of your case since you contacted our tip line. Since you were obviously not in Alabama during the dates that the two girls were murdered, we are going to have you released into our custody, immediately."

A look of tremendous relief and terror washes over his face as Josh listens to Jenkins. Getting his formal release and the murder charges overturned will take some time, but at least Josh will have some degree of freedom. Freedom from Holman Penitentiary. Freedom to leave this place, his home, after all these years.

"Thank you, my God, thank you!" Josh shakes hands with both Jenkins and Lee.

"You're welcome, there's more though…" Jenkins' voice softens as she places the picture of Terri, taken earlier in the mine. Sanders has blocked out the background; just Terri's face is visible. Jenkins also places the age-enhanced animation of *Girl in Flowered Skirt* in front of Josh. "Terri is still alive. Did the man, Oldson, did he know about her younger brother? The man that took you to the diner. What else can you tell us about him?"

"Robbie! Oh my God, yes, during the drive to the diner. While she was asleep, I told him, I told him about both of our families. Why? Did I cause all this? Is this, this all my fault. But I heard those gunshots! She's alive? Where? I want to see her. Right now, I have to see her right now!"

Jenkins assures Josh there was nothing that he could have done, "Josh, listen to me..." Jenkins speaks as Josh sobs, "You survived—do not blame yourself. We will take you to see Terri. We will help you get through this; I will help you."

"Ole-sun, his name was Ole-sun! He made this big deal about it. I called him Old-son and he couldn't stand it. He said it over-and-over again, 'Olesun, Olesun that's how you say it.' He took us somewhere. He was heading to Idaho, Idaho Falls, and after we stopped at the diner, we drove until it was getting dark. He took us to a place he said he had camped at before and it had a lake. Shit, he even caught us dinner and cooked up a hell of a meal. He caught three fish and cooked them up for us."

"Three fish?" abruptly inquires Lee as he scans through the digital files and pictures stored in his tablet. He finds one of the sketches from the unsub's notepads, the one of three fish lying on a rock.

338

"Yes, he caught fish for us, gutted them, and while he was cleaning them, he did this thing, this ritual. Some damn kind of ritual, I can't remember."

U.S. Department of Justice
Federal Bureau of Investigation

CHAPTER NINETY-EIGHT: Imprisoned
Present Day

In the command trailer, Banks, Cherkoff, and Torres have been discussing all their findings, as well as what information the team in Alabama has uncovered.

"What would be worse, being trapped in there," Cherkoff says, "or finding yourself accused of a crime with no way to defend yourself? And then you find out you inadvertently gave the unsub another victim."

"Our unsub created two equally brutal hells," Torres says. "Our victims trapped in there for all those years and that poor kid he just dumped in a boxcar. One thing I just can't understand: if he abducted Terri when she was nineteen, why haven't we heard anyone down there speak?"

Deanna offers an explanation based on her years as an enculturation specialist. "Quite frankly, they most likely don't speak, at least not a language we would recognize. Enculturation is the process we all go through, at a very early age. It's when we learn the specific requirements our culture places on us. It's what we must do to be part of any society, no matter the size. We talk because we need something. A person's language skills develop in accordance with how complex their surroundings are. If your world has infinite possibilities, your language will reflect this. Their world, everything they have known, except for that brief time before they were brought here, is within those walls.

"They have grown up feral. This is the only home they have ever known. The only home they remember. They speak, just not in ways that we relate to, at least not just yet. All cases of discovered feral children show the same characteristics—severe social skill issues, especially around language development. For many reasons, they fear saying the wrong thing, something that would provoke their attacker. They're afraid of being heard by their attacker, or if they were hiding, being found."

"So, the unsub brings a victim here, just to what, drop them in here and see what the hell happens?" Torres asks.

"This unsub has created this underground society. The residents would have to either adapt and adjust into this new world or die. As new additions were forced into this, it would not take long for them to become encultured. They would have to adapt or die. Getting accepted, whatever the cost, into the group was paramount to any new addition's survival, not just on a physical level but emotionally as well."

Fascinating and disturbing, Deanna's knowledge and experience with feral children has the team very concerned.

"Their deaths are a byproduct. Even in cases like Cindy, the Garage Girl, as some of the tabloids started to call her, she was kept fed, clothed and caged on a property in Florida." Deanna refers to the case of an eighteen-year-old girl who had been held captive for twelve years. "Her captor abducted her and kept her locked up in a shed he had constructed on his farm. The shed's floor was made from soundproof material, as were the walls. She had access to a toilet, TV, a chair, and a bed. This twelve-by-ten room was all she saw for many years. Her stay was not a solitary one, unfortunately. After her discovery, it was determined she had been repeatedly raped and had given birth to several children, all of whom were found with her in the shed.

"When children are born, they are born defenseless. Your unsub, having placed his victims in that mine, for whatever reason, would have seen many of his first victims perish. Most likely they died sitting exactly where they were lowered into the mine. As children, our needs are very simple. Feed me! I'm hungry! I'm scared! Where are Mommy and Daddy? I want a favorite toy, perhaps. You are three years old, say even four, and have just been stolen from the world you knew. It's all gone, and you have been brought here. Your fear will paralyze you, even past the pains of hunger. Dropped into the dark, the unknown, your mother and father gone. Your room, your toys, everything has now been replaced with rocks, dirt, fungi, and rats. After a few short terrifying days, alone, you die."

U.S. Department of Justice
Federal Bureau of Investigation

CHAPTER NINETY-NINE: Decomposing Boy
Present Day

Cho asks the team if he can see the sketches, specifically the one they have titled, *Decomposing Boy*.

"A guardian protector would be devastated if he saw his charges just perish," Cherkoff says as Cho examines the details hidden in the unsub's drawings.

"He was." Cho points to specific areas within the sketch as he explains his findings. "He drew, then erased, then sketched back in this boy's face several times, only to finally remove it. The pressure he exerted on his pencil varied each time."

"So, Terri is what, the matriarch?" Cherkoff asks the group.

"No, actually, she is even more than that, much more," Sanders says. "The unsub would have looked at her as the savior for his flock. When Josh inadvertently divulged the story about Terri's younger brother, her fate was, well, it was a done deal."

While the group speaks, Sanders has also connected with Jenkins and Lee via broadband. They are in the team's jet en route back to Evergreen with Josh. Josh is resting and not privy to their conversation. "I brought everyone together here for a reason, folks,"

Sanders says. "I have been going over the name Josh gave you. I found no one living or dead, in the US or even Canada. I ran dozens of variations of the name and nothing stood out. Not until I remembered the concept sketch of Eco-Town. Everything about this unsub he codes in the notes; he has created this world down there, and even his own language. I broke the name into syllables and that's when I found him! The owner of the Eco-Town development is Dutch. Mr. Otto Kinderson. So, I decided to translate Ole into Danish, then into Old Norse, and voila—it means descendant's ancestor. And sun in Old Norse is just that, the sun. Otto Kinderson."

"Yes, Sanders, we all know this." Everyone can sense a level of annoyance in Banks' voice.

"Sorry, everyone. Please, bear with me here. I did some digging and Kinderson's birth name was Atta, which means father, and when I brought up everything I could find on him, I discovered that he is the son of Danish Jews who came to the US after World War II. His mother worked with the Danish resistance in the Cipher Room. Kinderson never married but he did have a brother who died during the war. This bastard brought us here. He is the artist. The project manager just emailed me the details about the sketch. Look at the bottom right corner of this copy of the sketch." Sanders transmits a copy of the sketch the development company emailed him with the artist name signed at the bottom. "Codes and keys, that's what this guy is all about. Six letters, but with no context, they meant nothing. I'm sorry this took so long. It was right in front of my face the whole damn time."

"Where is Kinderson right now?" Banks asks.

"He's dying, final stages of lung cancer. He's in a hospital in Hartford, on a ventilator, and from what I understand, we don't have very much time. I arranged for a charter; it's waiting in Kalispell as we speak."

"You said he had a younger brother?" ask Cherkoff.

"Yes, from what little records I could find, his name was Jakob. Died at age four," replies Sanders.

"How old would Kinderson have been,"

"Eight," Sanders says.

Banks immediately dispatches Cherkoff and Torres to the airport and Sanders will follow up with them once they are onboard. He picks up his phone and speaks with Jenkins.

"How is he doing?"

Banks is referring to Josh, who is still a sleep on the plane.

"He is quite a remarkable guy," Jenkins says. "We hit him with a ton of stuff today. And to have it all come out like this, but you know he said something as we were leaving the prison that I'll never forget."

"What was that?"

"He shook the hand of one of the guards, and as we were heading out the last door, he paused for a moment, then he said, 'Fate is a very strange friend.' I asked him what he meant, and he added that it brought Terri into his life and the unsub into their lives. It's like we are on a bus on a highway—

345

sometimes we can choose our stops but sometimes they are chosen for us. Sure, he is angry and confused, but I honestly sensed an inner peace almost zen-like connection to things. Once his memories started to flow, it was more a relief than anything."

"Agent Banks." The sheriff enters the command trailer with a FedEx envelope in his hand.

"Jenkins hang on a moment," Banks says. "Yes, Sheriff, what can I do for you?"

"This package was just delivered to our office. It's for you." Banks takes the envelope from the sheriff. The package is addressed to "Agent C. Banks, Federal Bureau of Investigations, c/o Evergreen Sheriff's Dept." The sender's information reads "Atta Kinderson, Hartford, CT."

"The sheriff just handed me a FedEx envelope…from Kinderson." Banks reports to Jenkins.

U.S. Department of Justice
Federal Bureau of Investigation

CHAPTER ONE HUNDRED: Granddad
Present Day

Sanders has emailed both Cherkoff and Torres copies of all the information he has accumulated on Kinderson. He included a timeline covering the Eco-Town development project and all pertinent contracts with Deep Image that Kinderson was involved with prior to his illness and hospitalization. The contacts at Deep Image have told the FBI that they were given specific locations in which to conduct their surveys. From what they understand, Phase I of the development had been presold and the investors have been pressing their firm to find the necessary location.

Cherkoff reads from the files that Sanders has forwarded. "It says here that his mother was a German-born Jew, and his father, a Danish-born scientist and real estate investor who made his fortune during the depression. They lived in Copenhagen, and they immigrated to the States soon after the war. Atta spent most of his childhood in boarding schools, where he was tested and recognized as being an art prodigy. You guessed it, his specialty was pencil and ink sketches."

When they arrive at the hospital where Kinderson has been admitted, they proceed to the nurse's station. Cherkoff and Torres are directed down a corridor toward Kinderson's private room.

"He doesn't get too many visitors, just his assistant. She's in there now," the nurse explains.

"Thank you very much." Torres says. When they arrive at his room they are greeted by his executive assistant, Tanya LaPierre. She has been Kinderson's assistant for the past seven years. "I am SSA Lee and this is SSA Cherkoff. We need to speak to Mr. Kinderson."

"He's resting right now but he should be up shortly. His lunch will be up here soon. Is there anything I can help you with?" Tanya asks.

"Yes, we have a few questions about the Montana property his firm is in the process of developing," Cherkoff replies.

"Is there something wrong? This is the second time in as many days that I have been asked about Eco-Town. Just yesterday, I had to supply Deep Image with the original town drawings."

"What can you tell us about Eco-Town?" Cherkoff asks.

Tanya describes that the development was planned to break ground early next year. The homes were presold online, geared to the wealthy, eco-conscious homeowner. "Everyone has jumped on the green bandwagon. Phase I sold out just on the drawings—how could anyone resist? It all looks so beautiful. Mr. Kinderson did the sketches himself. He's very gifted and our builders promised they would deliver on time." As Tanya describes the details, the agents notice sadness in her tone. "It's unfortunate that Mr. Kinderson won't live long enough to see it come to fruition. 'The firm must go on after I am gone,' he always says, and he wanted to find just the right place. If the surveyors could only find us a suitable location…Mr. Kinderson knew that the Thrust Belt was the best place to look for a sustainable supply of natural gas. Even on some of his worst days, in between radiation treatments, he wanted updates from the field about their progress."

"The nurse said that you are his only visitor?" Cherkoff asks.

"He has no wife, no children. Which is sad, always looked, to me at least, that he would have made a wonderful father. I think he would have been a great granddad."

"That's nice," Cherkoff says. Her sarcasm is quite clear to Torres.

Tanya informs Cherkoff that during the past five years, right up until he got sick, most of Kinderson's days were spent away from the office. He would telecommute from where ever he was but, of course, he physically came in for board meetings and certain occasions for which his presence was required. His base was Connecticut, but he traveled extensively throughout the US and Canada.

"Oh yes, from what I understand, as the firm grew, the company was involved more and more in funding large projects. Mr. Kinderson was responsible for this growth."

Tanya explains to the agents that, as the firm grew, there was an inherent need to diversify, and several spin-off companies were formed. "There were either mergers or the firm would invest in an existing industry. In the late seventies, the firm first got involved in agriculture and animal feeds. In fact, we have several large farms around the nation. You've probably eaten our mushrooms." Tanya leads Cherkoff and Lee into the board room where there are scale models of Eco-Town and six, very high-tech hydroponics farms in various states are displayed.

Their talk with Tanya gets interrupted when Kinderson's nurse arrives. Cherkoff and Torres decide to leave him alone for the moment and tell Tanya that they will need to speak with him shortly. They walk down the hall to the waiting room.

"Granddad, if she only knew," Cherkoff says. "Jesus Christ. Access to all this, his companies, his company jet. If she only knew."

U.S. Department of Justice
Federal Bureau of Investigation

CHAPTER ONE HUNDRED ONE:
The Envelope
Present Day

With Jenkins still on the line, Banks takes the package from the sheriff. Pulling on the tab to open the envelope, he removes the contents: two letter-sized envelopes, one addressed to him, the other blank. He opens the envelope addressed to him and finds a handwritten letter.

Agent Banks,

Evergreen is such a lovely place. It is such a lovely community where everyone knows everyone; their pains, their joys, their laughs, and their cries. No doubt you already know this. I must commend you on your newscasts and your diligence. I don't think I could have asked for a team better suited to face this challenge. I do wish though, that my condition would have granted me the opportunity to deliver this message in person. I trust you will feel no disrespect, as none was intended.

How many years passed for those I brought to this place, hidden under that rock and cradled safe within that special mountain? Did their fathers cry out or did their mothers weep for them? The caregivers who would let them run around the malls, banks, and convenient stores, oblivious. Those little boys and girls who they would let roam free. All I had to do was ask and they would follow. Never a hand did I raise, just extend and ask. Oh, the looks that must have been on the caregivers' faces when they finally realized the children were gone. But where, how could this happen? It was only a moment and…They were running wild, without boundaries; all I did was give them a purpose, a place, and a reason for being. In fact, as I watched the aftermath of what I had set in motion, very little was ever written, especially for those who died. You see, when you take the faceless, the nameless, no one cares. No tears were shed for these children.

They were alone, searching for anything, something to hold on to, something to eat. When you have nothing, anything is better. In your world, shrines are built to honor cowards and traitors. War heroes, mindless puppets fighting for something, something their masters would dare not do, but they must. We build shires for them, yet the innocent die alone, hungry, and in vain.

Now, has your team opened the box? Has your team entered their world yet? Do you dare? Can you or will your system, the system that made them so expendable, nameless, and easy to take, will that very system now force you to remove them from this place, the only real home they have ever known? How difficult their transition was those many years ago. What will this new transition be? How will they be? How will their newfound community be? Who will they fear the most?

Terri and her boyfriend, Josh but by now you must already know this. In his darkest moment, when he reached out for help, all he would receive was the silence—a dial tone, then the judge's gavel. Where will the social justice be for these people? My children. They were mere discards, but I gave them a home. He gave me a gift that I regret I will never be able to repay. When he told me Terri's story and how she too suffered as I did so many dark years ago, fate brought our paths together.

I trust you will find, when you take your samples, that none suffered any harm by my hands. They were provided for and given the shelter that they never knew. Without a family of their own, they would wake within their new world and find their soulmates, their comrades. Terri, as lost and scared as they were when I found her, became a mother to them all. She nurtured and cared for them as much as she did for her own little boy. I suppose congratulations should go to the father; he knows who he is, or does he? I trust he is already there in Evergreen or will be soon. A reunion is in store. Do ask him for me about a curiosity I have carried all these years: could he feel, or did he sense, that a child of his was alive? Did he even care?

I must go now, as you know my time is less and less each day. Please direct the other envelope to the person or persons who have been working to decipher my notes. They will find in there all that they need. It is all there, no secrets, no need anymore. You will understand which information is important. You will find him. You will know what must be done. The cruelty of our world, the chaos of everything. Anger, intolerance, hatred and distrust. So bright the light that it blocks out the clarity. Their world, where they thrive, where they have survived. In darkness skin tones disappear. Hatred is replaced with kinship. A bond is formed. Grey replaces the light and darkness of our world.

Thank you again for your time and diligence.

Respectfully
Atta Kinderson Esq.

U.S. Department of Justice
Federal Bureau of Investigation

CHAPTER ONE HUNDRED TWO: Monsters
Present Day

Cherkoff and Torres finish their coffees and are getting ready to go back to Kinderson's room when Cherkoff notices a message waiting on her phone, a text from Banks that reads, *call me asap*.

"What's up?" Cherkoff ask as Banks answers her call. After a quick update on what they've found out so far, Banks tells her about the letter delivered to him while they were en route to Hartford. "He did what? Unbelievable! No, you're right it, fits the profile, yes, I know…I just got it. We'll call you after we talk with him. We were just on our way up there." Cherkoff hangs up and motions to Torres to stay here. "You're not going to believe this, Kinderson sent Banks this letter. Banks wants us to review this before we talk to him."

As they scrutinize Kinderson's letter Torres asks, "I know I'm the new guy on the block here, but have you ever seen anything like this…"

Cherkoff shakes her head. "Guardian protectors are very rare, but this guy is on steroids. They all have God complexes to some extreme. They believe their purpose is to look after their charges, at all costs. If you think your parents are over protective, forget it. The bottom line is they truly believe that they have done nothing wrong and will never show remorse. They only have contempt for whatever they have perceived to be the threats to their charges. They have taken care of, guarded, and will protect them at all costs."

"You had better do the talking," Torres says as they walk to Kinderson's room. Cherkoff nods as she opens the door. Tanya is sitting in a chair by Kinderson's bedside going over paperwork with him as the agents enter.

"Atta, these are the agents from the FBI that I told you about." Cherkoff notices that Tanya's voice is louder than when she was speaking to them earlier. His bed is elevated and Kinderson sits just below eye level with Cherkoff. Torres motions to Tanya to step out into the hallway. "I'll let you folks have some privacy," Tanya says.

Cherkoff waits until Tanya has left the room and the door is closed. "Good afternoon, Mr. Kinderson. I am SSA Cherkoff and this is SSA Torres. I need to inform you that we are currently investigating a series of crimes and that the questions I have to ask you pertain to these crimes." Cherkoff continues with her introduction and reads Kinderson his Miranda rights. "Do you understand these rights, sir?" Kinderson says he does, and Cherkoff removes a piece of paper from a folder. She places it on the tray table in front of Kinderson.

Kinderson glances over the document, which is a typed version of the Miranda rights, which he signs. Cherkoff is pleased, but in no way surprised, that this guardian protector did not ask for a lawyer.

"There you go, young lady. I trust you have spoken with Mr. Banks prior to your arrival?" Kinderson hands the page back to Cherkoff. "Now, you see, I am not the monster you have envisioned, am I?"

After numerous radiation treatments, the bulk of Kinderson's hair has fallen out and what is left is cut short and soft white in color. Based on his size relative to the hospital bed he is lying in, she can only guess his height to be around five feet six and his weight to be one hundred pounds or less. To describe him as frail would be an understatement.

Cherkoff pauses as she decides how to respond, "Looks can be deceiving." She reaches to her belt, removing her pair of handcuffs and proceeds to lock one loop onto Kinderson's right wrist, attaching the other end to the railing on his bed. Kinderson glances at his wrist, then attempts to make direct eye contact with Cherkoff. As the final click is heard, she sets the lock and continues the interview. "Mr. Kinderson I would—"

Kinderson cuts Cherkoff off, "Young lady, are these necessary? As you can see, I will not be going anywhere."

"That's not entirely correct, and yes, they are. The location outside Evergreen, can you tell us when you were last there?" Cherkoff maintains eye contact with Kinderson as she directs her question.

Kinderson attempts to take a deep breath, aided with the tiny oxygen tubes resting in his nostrils. "The beginning of this year…" he takes another breath, "…six months." Cherkoff waits until he finishes exhaling before responding.

"Before you met Terri and Josh, how many children did you rescue?" When she asks Kinderson this question, her tone is very dry.

Kinderson smiles as he looks at both Cherkoff and Torres, "As many as I could." His face brightens with pride as he answers.

"I can only imagine how difficult it must have been for just one person, not enough time and all. You could only save just so many, and all the ones that you were forced to leave behind…" Cherkoff confides.

Kinderson nods, acknowledging what she had just said. "You try to rescue them all but there are just so many, aren't there? Throw-aways!"

She adjusts her posture and leans into Kinderson. For the first time during their interview, Kinderson appears uncomfortable, his personal space invaded just enough.

Cherkoff opens her files and glances at the papers. "Watching so many die, while in your care, you needed something, no matter how hard you tried, it just wasn't working. How many were there before Terri?" Cherkoff is careful to keep an eye on Kinderson as she speaks. "Your first rescue, what was it, two, maybe three days before he died? And after all the trouble you went through. Finding that special place, preparing it, everything in its proper order, just one tiny problem. You watched him and what did he do, to repay your hard work? He just sat there, died, and rotted."

Torres stands silently in the background, as he listens to the harsh tone of each word Cherkoff says.

Cherkoff remains silent for several moments as she stares at Kinderson. Her look is of disgust, not at what he has done, but what his work failed to do. "You failed him, like you failed your brother."

Torres can barely hear Cherkoff's statement over the pounding of his own heartbeat. The room is dead silent.

U.S. Department of Justice
Federal Bureau of Investigation

CHAPTER ONE HUNDRED THREE: Victims
Present Day

"You probably changed everything, started to second guess yourself. To be forced to sit in that chair in that room and look through your window at them as they died one after another. Just rotting into the ground—even your sketches were wrong. You could do nothing, just watch. One thing I do know for sure, watching your first rescue die, you never drew him, never could, am I right?"

Kinderson does not speak but he does nod, just once.

Cherkoff has interrogated a wide variety of unsubs and from her experience, she understands that Kinderson has brought them all here. He has an agenda that must be addressed, and he is on limited time. "Ole-sun..." she makes sure to pronounce the name correctly, "... all that must have just made you sick. You do all that and give them that special place, but she changed everything, didn't she?"

"Yes, a bolt, a ray of light. You see, before Terri, they did not all die as you say." He pauses for a breath, "She met them, three of them, when I brought her, and the one I had already rescued before we met." His posture relaxes slightly. "And it was a cause for concern as the others disappeared. Watching them all, as you say, rot into the ground." A short gasp followed with a labored breath. Kinderson continues, "The place consumed their bodies and their energy was transferred into it. To create this, a base had to be developed. For it cannot be rushed; the process takes on its own form in its own time."

"Just answer the questions, no need to elaborate," instructs Torres.

While they still have time, while they still have Kinderson, Cherkoff must press for some vital information. Torres playing the bad cop politely makes sure that Kinderson will not pontificate.

"Yes, it all takes time," Cherkoff says. "We know that. Tell me this, how long did it take to set this up, to make things just right for Terri? You must have known that things were ready for her or why risk it?"

"Five years."

This is the only answer he will give her and nothing more. Cherkoff looks at her notes, reading to herself as she collects her thoughts. She has been interrogating him now for just under an hour. Sanders had explained to her earlier that with Kinderson's high IQ, and the fact he has gotten away with this crime undetected, he will still be in the driver's seat during her interrogation.

U.S. Department of Justice
Federal Bureau of Investigation

CHAPTER ONE HUNDRED FOUR: Hell
Present Day

Jenkins and Lee have just arrived at the command center, accompanied by Josh. They introduce him to Banks. Josh appears calm and Lee notices that his reaction to the site is more curious than fearful. Remarkable, considering the command area has the appearance of a military installation. Complete with checkpoints, the media center, and all the other mobile equipment in place, it is impressive and intimidating.

"I trust you all managed to get some rest on your flight in?" Banks asks his colleagues. They notice the hint of sarcasm in his voice. There's a multitude of empty coffee cups flanked by several Red Bulls littering the conference table.

When they spoke earlier, Banks and Jenkins debated whether to bring Josh up to speed while on the plane or to wait until his arrival at the site. They chose the latter. In their, opinion it was the lesser of the two evils.

After a long day being interviewed, Josh spent most of the flight resting. Sanders arranged for Josh to be released into their custody, and for the first time in more than forty years, Josh was not behind steel bars when he woke up.

Jenkins and Lee sit down at the conference table; Josh remains standing until Jenkins points to an empty chair. "Sorry, this is going to take a bit. I'm so used to being told what to do, when and where." Josh grins as he pulls the chair over to the table and sits down.

"That's perfectly alright. We all understand how difficult this must be," Banks says.

"Josh, the man that you call Oldson, he had been abducting children long before you and Terri met with him, and there is nothing, absolutely nothing, that you could have done to stop what happened." Banks pauses for a moment. "As agents Jenkins and Lee have told you, our job, in every case, is to develop a psychological profile of the unsub."

"You said he took other kids. How many are we talking about? Is he some kind of pedophile?" Josh asks.

"As we profiled this unsub, it became more and more apparent that he is what we call a guardian protector. His interests were in rescuing these boys and girls from a hostile world, a world where he believes they are cast-offs."

"Cast-offs, hell, you meet lots of them in prison," Josh says.

"I can imagine." Banks leans toward Josh. "Jenkins told me that you recalled memories of another child in the crate with you?"

"Yes, when I was in the box, when I first woke up. The floor of the box, you couldn't see, but it was bad.

Rats were the worst, all over you, sniffin' and biting at ya. He was so tiny, the poor little guy. I tried to keep the rats away from him, but he had me bound up. The ropes would tighten if I moved and choke me."

"So, you couldn't really see the boy at all then?" Banks asks.

Josh shakes his head. "I'm sorry, no…it was hard to breathe. There was something I…he had done. Damn it!" Josh struggles and grasps to recall these painful memories. "That damn box was so dark; he had piles of bags. Potato sacks, yes, I remember, and when Terri and I were camping that night with Oldson, I woke up. That game he had played at the diner was still on my mind. You know, what's under the tarp? I peeked under it, but something was wrong."

"What was wrong? The bags?" asks Banks.

"No, no, that's not what I meant. I got a good look at the bags and was getting ready to put the tarp back but that's when Terri surprised me. Nearly made me piss myself! We go back to our tent and were about to fall back to sleep when I heard it."

"You mean you heard him? Oldson?" Jenkins asks. She notices Josh's pulse quicken as she looks at the artery in his neck.

"No, it wasn't Oldson that I heard. That night, it got real windy, and I knew I tied that tarp back the same way. It was tight, but there it was. *Flap, flap*…it was makin' noise you see. I went back out to lash it back down, so he wouldn't know that I had been messing with it. I get out of the tent, sneak back to his truck and one corner of the tarp was loose. Next thing I can remember is being inside that damn box and the little boy. But how did, damn it, he must have been waiting for me. Oldson must have jumped me."

Josh looks to the agents hoping that they have the answers, answers to those moments in his life that Oldson stole.

Josh scans the command trailer, trying to settle his emotions. He focuses on the image he sees through one of the windows, the large white tent that covers the mouth of the excavation site. Several technicians wearing their white protective coveralls walk around with clipboards. After being confined in a prison for more than forty years, all he can remember from the drive into the command site was the beautiful scenery. For the first time, he realizes he is at a crime scene, *the* crime scene. "Josh, it's okay, you're here. You're safe," Jenkins says as Josh's face turns deathly pale.

"This is where...the gunshots, where I heard the shots? But you said he was a protector guard, what did you call him?" Josh's confusion is only adding to his frustration. "He shot them. I heard it. He took them both out one at a time, bang! When he took the little boy, I tried so hard to hold him. I wrapped myself around him but my hands, my hands they were behind my back too! Oh God, I couldn't save him or her!" Josh bows his head to the table. As Josh speaks, Banks looks to Jenkins, getting her attention he mouths the words, *does he know?* Jenkins nods.

Taking the lead, Jenkins speaks, looking directly at Josh, "Josh, he needed you to believe they were dead. Remember, we told you that Terri is alive."

"I'm confused, you caught the guy, right? Or, it's him…Oldson, right?"

"Our agents are questioning him as we speak." She glances at Banks and back to Josh.

"Then what did he do with her? How'd…" Josh glances back at the view through the window and the heavy machinery parked nearby. "What the hell is this place?"

U.S. Department of Justice
Federal Bureau of Investigation

CHAPTER ONE HUNDRED FIVE: Reunited
Present Day

"From what we understand, Oldson brought you, Terri, and the little boy here. And this is where you heard the gunshots. He kept his victims here." Jenkins' voice is very soft, trying to keep Josh as calm as possible. She pays close attention to his body language, checking for any tell. His pulse, complexion, anything.

"He kept them here? Way out here, where?" Josh says.

"This property houses an old mine, and he—"

"Buried them! But you said she's alive!"

"I know how hard this is to understand, but Oldson brought his victims to this place. He has provided for them over the years and from what we have seen so far, there are numerous survivors, including Terri." As Jenkins continues to talk, Banks hands several pictures that the team took of Terri in the mine to her. "Now these images are pretty graphic, are you going to be okay?" she asks.

"How bad could it be? She's alive you say, right?"

Jenkins places the photos down in front of Josh. Tears well in his eyes. Jenkins watches Josh pick up a picture of Terri looking straight into the camera.

"That's her…that's Terri." Jenkins and her colleagues sit silently as Josh holds Terri. Jenkins is focused on how still and calm Josh is. His ability to absorb and process what is happening is quite remarkable.

He has the eight-by-ten color photograph of his girlfriend here in his hands, and after being taken away from him in such a manner, all he wants at this moment is to look at her. Josh sits in the chair, tears in his eye but not falling and caresses her picture. He turns his head to Jenkins. Josh's voice cracks as he speaks, "This is her, Terri. I've missed her so much." Banks and Lee get up and leave Josh with Jenkins.

U.S. Department of Justice
Federal Bureau of Investigation

CHAPTER ONE HUNDRED SIX:
Dates, Names, Numbers
Present Day

"Any luck?" Banks asks Cherkoff. He has been receiving a flow of texts from Torres, with updates but has decided to speak with her directly.

"Not really, we just stepped out to let the nurse back in. I've been grilling Kinderson for an hour or so. Don't know how much more we're going to get. Not like we can threaten him with anything. I even thought about bringing his assistant in—"

"Yes, I got the text from Torres—the Granddad comment speaks volumes," Banks says. "Cherkoff, if you have to, use her, she'll get over it. Sanders has told me that he may only have a few days left. Keep at him—he stole countless lives and I'm not just talking about the ones here in the mine. Josh is onsite with us and he mentioned about hearing gunshots when he was captured. And Sanders also wanted me to tell you Kinderson's younger brother died at age four when he would have been eight. Squeeze this guy as hard as you can. You are the best interrogator this team has. I don't care what it takes. We need to know how many he took—dates, names, numbers."

"Copy that," Cherkoff signs off, her military voice rising to the surface. She looks at Torres and says, "If we threaten to bring his doting assistant back here and let her see him for who he really is…"

"Don't you think he would shut right down, lawyer up?" Torres asks.

"I don't think so, hell, he's dying. For all he knows he's gone tomorrow. That's why we're here. He wants to talk, we've just got to listen. She is so found of him and if he's aware of that; he won't be able to stop himself from protecting her. We've just got to listen." Her eyes open wide as she repeats herself as she remembers a passage from Kinderson's letter to Banks.

They walk back into Kinderson's room. Cherkoff picks up where they had left off and decides a little pontificating of her own might be in order. "Dying alone, to die alone and in vain, isn't that how you said it? The marvels of your work, all your effort to create for them, those cast out, and for what? To lie here and die, alone and in…"

Kinderson rises slightly in his bed, using the rails of his bed as support. He takes a very labored breath, "The innocent die alone and in vain. If you quote me, be precise, girl." Coughing more and more, he slumps back into his bed. His face looks greyer as he finishes his statement.

"Mr. Kinderson, without your help, your information, how are we to ever know just how many died? And the ones you saved, who are they? They came from somewhere and even if no one was looking out for them as you did, don't they deserve a chance to know the truth? Who they are? Where they were from? You are the only one who can help them." Her profound honesty and empathy is punctuated as she fills a cup of water and hands it to Kinderson, helping him clear his throat.

"It was five years, five very long years before Terri. How many did I rescue up to that point? As many as I could. I saw them every month, in every town, every park, even at a garage." Kinderson takes a small sip and catches his breath. "Boys and girls without someone to watch over them, alone until someone would help. What was I to do? Turn my back? Walk away? Not now, I'm busy! I'm busy!" Kinderson glances at Torres standing at the door, then to Cherkoff, and calmly says, "Forty-two, and you are correct young lady—I was only one, who could only do so much."

Deanna had explained that the early mortality rate would have been high but neither Cherkoff nor Torres had any idea that it would be this high. Cherkoff struggles to maintain her composure. "All that suffering, those children, all the preparations you made, but still, you couldn't save them.? Forty-two and you say only three were alive when you captured Terri?"

"Forty-two, the only consolation, they were not alone. They were with him always, and he was there safe with them. I was the one forced to bear witness. Forced to live it over…" Kinderson starts coughing, his cough becoming more congested. His pauses between speaking are becoming longer, and his voice at times barely audible. "Not just for what I had done but what I could not do. I was supposed to keep him safe. I failed him." His cough is so rough there is blood in his hand as he covers his mouth.

Cherkoff scans her notes. "You say there were forty-two. I need to know their names and where they were from."

"Your Mr. Sanders has everything he needs. They were from nowhere. I brought them to their home. Just for them. Safe, with him, and others to share their place. Others whose sacrifices helped make that place. Mr. Sanders will understand; he will figure it out."

U.S. Department of Justice
Federal Bureau of Investigation

CHAPTER ONE HUNDRED SEVEN:
She Is Going to Die
Present Day

"We have a major problem down there." Deanna expresses her concerns to Banks as she leads him to the mine's entrance. "It's Misha's baby. We are going to have to get in there. Now!"

Banks and Lee have been talking privately, while Jenkins continues to bring Josh up to speed. Banks and Lee follow Deanna into the mine, sensing the urgency in her tone. "Her little girl is having difficulty breathing. She's spit up several times during the past hour, mostly phlegm. Judging by her size, in comparison to Misha, I am pretty sure she's a preemie."

They reach the observation window in the second container and the tech lets Banks see the images on the monitor. Terri is working frantically over the tiny little girl, as Misha looks on. The tech points to Oscar. "That one has brought in several handfuls of the matt lichen. She's placed it over the baby, probably to help keep it warm." Everyone can see as Terri turns out of the camera's way, as Misha's baby's chest heaves with each breath.

"You say this has been going on for an hour? Is she getting worse?" Banks asks Deanna.

"Look at her! She needs to be in a hospital. She needs our help! If we don't do something soon, she may not have another hour and as you said, getting in there will take time."

The only access the team has into the mine will involve lowering someone down the same shaft the unsub used. "We could setup the A-frame and repel down the shaft," Lee suggests to Banks.

"Getting in there isn't going to be the issue," Cho says to both Lee and Banks, "We are dealing with a first contact situation, first contact with members of our own species. That's their domain, their territory, and they will defend it."

"And for all we know, the last person outside their world they had contact with was the unsub," Lee adds as he looks at the monitor. The team cannot just watch as the tiny baby girl suffers. Banks must decide which members of his team will be best suited for this mission. Misha's baby lies motionless on her chest.

"She is really struggling," Deanna watches carefully as the tiny girl's breathing slows. Each time she attempts to take a breath, her little chest heaves high, sinking down slowly.

U.S. Department of Justice
Federal Bureau of Investigation

CHAPTER ONE HUNDRED EIGHT: Rescue
Present Day

"Alright Lee, come with me. Get Jenkins from the trailer and have her meet us at the shaft," Banks says as they leave Deanna with the tech to continue to monitor the situation. Leading both Lee and Cho back to the surface, Banks asks Cho, "The dominant male's reaction is your greatest concern, correct?"

"Exactly, they have all been through so much, especially these past hours. They are just getting used to the RCV."

"How do you think he would react to a female, perhaps Jenkins?" Banks asks.

"That is probably the best solution, but there is no guarantee that he still won't become violent. We saw how he reacted to the RCV," says Cho.

Lee enters the command trailer. Still sitting with Josh, Jenkins has been explaining in as much detail what life must have been like for the survivors in the mine. "I still can't believe they could have lived in there for so long!" Shaking his head as he speaks, Josh is holding the most recent photograph of Terri.

"If it is of any comfort, the unsub made sure that they would have everything that they would need.

There were feeding tubes, probably used for an ultra-rich starter-meal. He provided scheduled food drops for everyone down there. He even paid special attention to developing lichens, mosses, and various other non-light-sensitive plants. He engineered meals for the rats so that their waste fertilized the plants. The lighting had an elaborate timing system as well. It provided enough UV and he even had a dietary plan laid out for them," Jenkins tells Josh. Jenkins looks at Lee, and asks, "What's going on?"

"Banks needs you up at the shaft. The little baby is in trouble." Lee escorts Jenkins and Josh to where Banks is waiting. Josh refused to wait in the trailer. Banks explains to Jenkins what the plan is. Both Lee and Jenkins are to be lowered into the mine. The techs have set up the A-frame over the shaft and the winch will lower them each to the floor below. The team plans the logistics with this operation. The rescue of the little girl is the ultimate purpose, Banks makes sure to point out. "We were never trained for something like this," he says. "Your safety is paramount; we'll be watching from the monitors. Keep in touch. Cho, any suggestions, anything you think might be of help?"

"Send Jenkins in first—the moment they hear the sound of the rock being moved, it's going to trigger memories. They are probably expecting another child to be delivered." Banks agrees with Cho's assessment. Cho looks at Jenkins. "You might as well be from another planet. Your clothes, gear, even Terri will have never seen anyone dressed like you. Don't make eye contact with Alpha, be submissive but don't hesitate when you move."

"My dad always said, 'have a purpose in your walk.'" Jenkins smiles as she responds.

Cho smiles back, then says, "Alpha's reaction to Lee—there's no telling how that will go. It could get very ugly, with no chance for Alpha to understand or come to terms with Jenkins' presence, then suddenly Lee's too. Make yourself as small as you can once you're on the floor."

"What if I go in there myself?" Jenkins says as the tech hands her a harness.

"Not a chance." Banks replies.

"Why not? You heard what he just said."

Banks shakes his head.

"I'll be fine. You know I'm right. This is the best way." Jenkins takes the hook at the end of the winch cable and attaches it to her safety harness.

"First sign of trouble and I'm sending Lee in."

Banks signals to the other tech to move the rock that covers the top of the shaft. Using a frontend loader, the heavy rock slides across the rails.

How many times did Kinderson do this? Jenkins thinks.

U.S. Department of Justice
Federal Bureau of Investigation

CHAPTER ONE HUNDRED NINE: Oscar
Present Day

"Now, it's about twenty feet down to the bottom, and they won't see you until you clear the bottom. Chances are, the sound of the rock being moved will have scared them all away. After you're down there, we're going to seal this back up with the rock." The tech points to where the shaft opens in the ceiling of the main room. "Cross your arms in front of your harness. Ready?"

Jenkins nods. She looks down for a moment at the mine's floor. The sunlight casts a small, square-shaped frame of light below. As Jenkins slowly gets lowered into the mine, the silhouette of her form is cast in a shadow on the floor. There's the sound of the winch cable and the darkness surrounding her as she is lowered into the narrow shaft. Jenkins tries to focus on her breathing. Tight and dark, the claustrophobic tightness of the shaft follows her. *What would this have been like for a child?* she thinks and steadies her breathing.

"Can you hear us?" Banks asks as Jenkins listens to his voice through the com. She looks up for a moment, thumbs up, as she sees the faces of the tech, Banks, and Lee grow smaller.

"Deanna, do you copy? Are you online?" Banks asks, and Deanna responds promptly acknowledging that she can hear what is going on.

"How is the baby doing?" Banks asks Deanna.

"She needs to get to her; her little chest is rising less and less. We might be too late," she replies.

As her feet lower past the opening in the ceiling, and she enters the main room, Jenkins scans the area for any of the survivors. She has repelled into hostile conditions before in the marines as well as with the bureau. However, she feels her pulse quicken as she reaches the floor. Pulling on the winch cable enough to remove the hook from her harness, she frees herself. "Okay, I'm down."

"Do you see anyone?" Banks asks Jenkins. The lights in the mine are on and illuminate only the main room.

Jenkins turns on her flashlight and shines it in the direction of the tunnel entrances. "Yes." She sees the faces of two of the older men. "Looks like Joker and Alpha. They're in the mouth of tunnel three. My flashlight beam is a little shaky."

Alpha stands in front as Joker tries to push his way past him to see what is going on.

"I'm going to make my way over to the second tunnel," Jenkins informs the team.

"Jenkins," Cho says, "don't ignore Alpha if he moves toward you. Stand your ground, don't make eye contact."

"Okay, thanks. Oh crap!" Jenkins yelps, her voice raised.

"What's the matter?" Banks asks.

"A couple of rats just ran out from behind me. Scared the crap out of me, you know how I hate rats!" She barely gets a chance to say this before Joker bounds from where he is standing and lunges for one of the rats. His actions are swift and with purpose, he grabs the rat and retreats to where he was standing, only to have Alpha grab it from his hands, tearing the rat in two. Both men quickly devour the rat as Jenkins stands and watches.

"Jenkins, the baby's breathing is shallow," Deanna reports.

"How many are in that tunnel?" Jenkins asks Banks.

"Just Oscar, two females and the baby. Oscar's nearest the baby and closest to the RCV," replies Banks.

"Jenkins, when you get in there, make sure you give Oscar the same respect as you would Alpha. No eye contact get the baby, and get out. No fast moves." A look of great concern comes over Cho's face as he speaks to Jenkins.

Off the com system, he says to Banks, "Oscar is far more unpredictable than Alpha. There is something about the second tunnel. For whatever reason, he's the only male we have ever seen go in there; it's his place."

Jenkins takes a deep breath as she figures out what is going to be her best approach. She starts to walk toward the mouth of tunnel two. Alpha drops what parts of the rat he hadn't yet eaten and walks to intercept Jenkins. Joker immediately scoops up the leftover rat parts licking up every little bit. Jenkins watches as Alpha has come even closer, almost blocking her path to the tunnel. Jenkins shines her light into the tunnel; the only thing she can see is just more tunnel, as far as the beam will reach. She is face to face with Alpha. A mere five feet apart.

Without thinking, she says, "It is okay. I'm here to help. I don't want to hurt you, it's alright." *What the hell are you doing?*

The sound of her voice travels like a shockwave throughout the mine, echoing, breaking the silence. She can see Joker moving rapidly in their direction. Alpha raise his chest and stands his ground. Jenkins cannot see what's happening in tunnel two, but she feels a change. There is a breeze and the sound of running. *How many is it, one or two?*

"Jenkins, Oscar's running, on his way to your location." The RCV tech shouts over the com. Oscar disappears as the camera stays focused on the baby.

"Jenkins, what's happening, you okay?" asks Banks.

Alpha remains motionless, standing just feet away from Jenkins as the sound of Oscar's feet get even closer. Jenkins stands back a bit. Taking a defensive posture, she raises her flashlight holding it in her right hand. She focuses the flashlight in the center of the tunnel, which drops into darkness as the ground slopes off. Alpha steps backward as Jenkins raise her flashlight.

Oscar's footfalls are getting heavier and closer as he quickly comes into her flashlight's beam. His pace quickens as he gets closer. From the corner of her eye, Jenkins notices Joker standing near Alpha but ready to flee. Alpha is unaware that he has ventured into tunnel two, directly between Jenkins and the fast-approaching Oscar. As Oscar reaches the mouth of the tunnel, all he can see is Alpha's silhouette cast by Jenkins flashlight.

How long have I been in here, five, ten minutes? Jenkins' heart races as she sees Oscar. A loud wail comes from Oscar's mouth shattering the silence, causing Alpha to turn around wildly. Oscar lunges at Alpha, body-slamming him out of the tunnel, hurling both of their bodies toward Jenkins. Their tumbling mass collides with Jenkins, sending her to the floor.

Jenkins' feet lift off the ground as she's knocked into the main room. Her flashlight launches from her hand tumbles and rolls toward tunnel three. Her head smacks the hard floor of the mine and the weight of the two men falling on top of her squeezes the wind from her lungs. The impact's sound is transmitted through the com.

"Jenkins! Are you okay? Did anyone see. Jenkins, do you copy?" Banks yells.

Oscar and Alpha are locked together as Jenkins sprawls and crawls her way out from under the pile. Trying to catch her breath, she reaches out in the direction of her flashlight, grasping with stretched fingers.

"Jenkins! Do you copy?" a pause, then Banks continues, "Lee, get ready to harness up."

U.S. Department of Justice
Federal Bureau of Investigation

CHAPTER ONE HUNDRED TEN: So Tiny
Present Day

"Jenkins, do you copy!" Banks urgently repeats an earlier call.

Joker, who arrived at the scene just in time to watch the tackle, chases after the tumbling flashlight as he would a meaty rat. He scoops the flashlight up and tears into tunnel three. Jenkins can only watch as both her light and Joker disappear into the tunnel. *Thank God you kept the lights on. Thank you, thank you.* She rolls to her knees, then to her feet.

"I'm okay, give me a second." Coughing and breathing fast, Jenkins slowly regains her footing.

"What happened?" asks Banks.

"I think my voice startled..." She pauses as Oscar turns his attention from Alpha to the sound of her voice. Trying to speak just loud enough to be heard over the com, she continues, "Oscar's pissed."

"Lee you're going in."

"No! It's okay, don't send him," Jenkins says in a forceful whisper. "I've got this." The more she talks, the pitch and timbre of her voice has calmed Oscar, for now.

"Jenkins, tunnel two is Oscar's domain, if you can get by him, I don't think you will have any issues from other males," Cho says. "His moods can swing wildly…"

"No shit," says Jenkins.

"We have never seen him aggressive toward females, just males near his tunnel," Cho adds.

Alpha remains standing, ignored by Oscar now right in front of Jenkins. She sizes up the situation: *I have got to get past you.* Quietly and looking directly at his eyes, she says, "I'm going in there." Without her flashlight, she is only able to see the tunnel's entrance. *Was it four hundred feet?*

"Four hundred what?" asks Banks.

"Thinking out loud, sorry. I lost my flashlight in the…" She cuts herself off, not wanting to escalate Banks's concern. "How far in the tunnel is the RCV and the baby?"

"Just over three hundred feet, but you should have light from the RCV halfway," the tech says.

"Copy." Jenkins starts to walk toward the entrance, repeating quietly but firm, "I'm going in there." Oscar's face widens, his brow and eyes stretch to their max. Jenkins holds both her hands low and in front of her, palms down. She steps to where Oscar is standing. She listens as both Oscar and her hear muffled echoes coming from deep inside the tunnel. His face changes as his eyes shift toward the sound. For the moment, she is not his concern. Jenkins continues into the tunnel, slowly passing Oscar. He takes a large deep breath through his nostrils as she walks by him. As

Jenkins tries to steady her own breathing, she repeats, "in...there."

The sound from deep within the darkness becomes much louder. Jenkins hears two separate cries. *Damn, it's dark, you can see me. I can only hear you.* She walks deeper into the darkness. Her best guess is Oscar is right in front of her, or is he beside her? Her arms and hands are outstretched, whether defensive or for balance, and her feet tentatively touch the ground before she transfers her weight from one to another.

"Jenkins, can you see the light from the RCV yet?" asks Banks.

"Not yet, just pitch black. Moving fast as I can, more like a shuffle-shuffle, am I going to fall on my ass, kind of walk. Oscar is, hell, he could be right in front of me with a gun pointed at my face and I wouldn't know. Everything is just sound in here. Intense, I can hear Oscar's breathing change as I speak. The cries from the tunnel got to him. It's getting lighter now. Must be getting close."

"Jenkins, listen, you don't have to respond," Cho says. "Misha, Oscar, you, everyone in that tunnel is there because of the baby's condition. Keep that in mind."

As she walks into the illumination cast from the RCV, Jenkins can finally see that Oscar is very upset. He has left her well behind and stands just past the RCV, between her and the others. Oscar stands very still, listening to the sound of her voice. He looks back in Terri's direction, then toward Jenkins. Her body so foreign, covered with her clothes, her belt, everything. He looks at Terri.

"I'm here to help," says Jenkins.

Terri and Misha have been too busy with the baby to even notice Jenkins. Suddenly Misha hears Jenkins' voice, causing her to sit straight up and look in Jenkins' direction. Terri also turns to see what Misha is looking at. Speaking quietly into the com, she says, "I'm here. I can't see the baby yet, oh God. It's tiny. I'm so close to them but I might as well be back in Quantico."

"Terri, are you okay?" Jenkins says. "I need to see the baby, I'm a police officer. Do you understand me? It is okay..." Jenkins lowers her body, crouching just a bit. Oscar looks back at Terri; his face is so very confused, his eyes dart between Jenkins and Terri searching for answers. With no advance on her position by Oscar, Jenkins takes this cue as an invitation to walk even closer, kneeling beside Terri and Misha. Oscar remains tense, standing by the RCV.

Jenkins slowly reaches out her right hand and touches the baby. "She is really cold, and her pulse is very fast," Jenkins tells the rest of the team. Misha's eyes widen and Terri stares at Jenkins but otherwise makes no sound or gesture. Jenkins can breach the distance and carefully take the baby from Terri. Jenkins is mindful of maintaining close eye contact with Misha and Terri while not provoking Oscar. "My God, she's tiny, maybe four pounds. I have no idea how much they understand me." Terri focuses on her voice, and Misha looks to Terry for answers. Jenkins speaks into the com trying to decide the best course of action. "She is very congested."

The little baby's cries are raspy. Jenkins notices Oscar's posture change as the tone of the baby's cry changes. "Congestion is very common with preemies," Deanna says. Jenkins removes her jacket and swaddles the baby. With her jacket off, the curves of her shirted silhouette now match her voice, and Oscar relaxes his stance.

As he watches Jenkins and Terri's reaction to this new face, Oscar moves closer to the group. The tone of the baby's cry has softened as the warmth from Jenkins' jacket sooths it. Oscar watches as Jenkins sways the baby slightly in her arms. Jenkins, oblivious to her own motherly actions, uses her fingertips to clean some phlegm from around the baby's nose and mouth. Oscar moves a little too close and Terri raises her head, "Teddy, no."

Terri shakes her head and her voice is heard loud and clear. By everyone.

U.S. Department of Justice
Federal Bureau of Investigation

CHAPTER ONE HUNDRED ELEVEN:
Her name is Terri
Present Day

"We all heard that, let's stay focused. Jenkins you're doing great," Banks says. The possibility of Jenkins being able to communicate with the survivors was only a thought, but now is a very possible option.

"How is the baby doing?" inquires Deanna.

"She's been coughing up a ton of phlegm. I'm been trying to keep her nose and mouth clear," replies Jenkins.

She tears a piece of her shirt off. Jenkins looks at Terri. "You called him Teddy, that's his name?" Jenkins points at Oscar.

"Her name Terri," Oscar says firmly.

Jenkins tries to keep calm and process everything as rapidly as possible. The baby starts to cough again but this time it is much worse. She spits up more phlegm. *How something so small can be coughing so much up?*

Without warning, the little baby is limp and silent. Jenkins' pulse races as she can feel the little girl's condition rapidly change from worse to grave. Instinctively, Terri understands the situation, and her eyes focus on Jenkins. Jenkins is all too aware the importance of these next moments. What if the baby dies in her arms? Does she rush for the exit? Should she alert Banks? With no time to debate options, her first-aid training kicks in. Jenkins opens her jacket to gain better access to the baby. The little girl's pulse is barely there, and her breathing has stopped.

The little girl's lips are more, grey than pink. Jenkins opens her tiny mouth, wiping out more mucus and gently turning the baby on her side, then she clears her air way. Jenkins places her mouth down to the baby and performs infant mouth-to-mouth nose respiration. She gently places her lips over the baby's mouth and nose. She exhales slowly and watches as the girl's chest rises. She repeats this several times, checking the baby's pulse.

After several rounds of this, her patient's pulse is much stronger, and both Jenkins and her patient are breathing easier. "She has so much congestion. She needs more than I can do for her," says Jenkins to both the team listening in and the concerned group with her.

"Baby sick, she sick bad," Terri's face saddens as she says these words.

"Jenkins, your call, what do you want us to do to help?" asks Banks.

"She can't stay like this, I barely got her going again. How much are you understanding me…"

"What?" Banks cuts in.

"No, I'm talking to her, do they understand what I'm saying?" replies Jenkins as she looks at Terri.

"Jenkins, Terri hasn't heard long sentences and complex phrases for a very long time," Cho says. "It's clear to her that you're not trying to hurt the baby. Keep doing what you're doing, be concise, short, to the point. She understands; she has heard those words."

"Copy that. Banks, we either need to bring medics in here or we have to figure a way to get the baby out. And honestly, I don't know what's going to be best. For now, get me some supplies."

"Jenkins, there is a female paramedic onsite now, what if we send her in?" asks Banks.

"Fantastic, we should be able to work that out down here." Jenkins smiles at her patient's family. Turning her attention back to Terri, Jenkins continues, "You called him Teddy?" She points at Oscar and Terri nods. "He came wit me." She struggles for a moment as she pronounces her words.

"With you, he came with you?"

"Yes, to help baby," replies Jenkins as she smiles at Teddy.

"No, when I came here," Terri says as she points to the ground.

In the commotion of everything, Jenkins has all but forgotten about both Lee and her encounter and lengthy conversations with Josh about his vivid memories. "When you were brought here, he was with you," says Jenkins.

"Teddy, yes."

"Do I tell her? Copy," queries Jenkins.

"About Josh?" responds Banks as he looks at the faces of his team and Josh, who are watching and listening together in the command trailer.

"It might help us extract them all from the mine," says Cho.

"All of them—the baby is the priority right now," adds Deanna.

Lee breaks in saying, "There's only so much this group will be able to handle. Their world is changing so fast, ever since we changed the unsub's lighting schedule."

"Let's not get ahead of ourselves, everyone," Banks says. "Stay focused Jenkins, Misha's baby is our priority. The paramedic is ready to come in on your call. As for Terri, let her know, copy."

"Copy that." She looks at Terri, Misha, then Teddy. The enormity of what Terri has been through since she saw Josh, would she even remember him? But then how could she forget? Josh's memories of her were vivid; surely, she will remember. The little girl coughs and squirms and her tiny hands try to push Jenkins' jacket open. Her cries are very different, and Jenkins quickly realizes she can no longer help her.

U.S. Department of Justice
Federal Bureau of Investigation

CHAPTER ONE HUNDRED TWELVE:
Who Are You?
Present Day

I can't understand what are you waiting for? Terri thinks. *It's obvious what she needs. This won't just fix itself. I can only assume you're slow or maybe confused like Josh used to get at times. Let her mommy have her. There now, that wasn't so hard was it?*

You helped her breathe but don't know about feeding? I feel sorry for you, not going to last very long in here. Just stay to yourself and out of my way and we'll help you; you'll make it, I promise.

Since first seeing Jenkins after Teddy showed up with her, Terri has been trying to figure out just who the hell this new addition is. They don't normally come in here so darn big, that's going to be a lot of food for that belly.

You still have all your clothes, he must have just snatched you, but we haven't heard that big rock move in so long and, well with the new baby I haven't been out to the main room in, how long has it been? That's funny how long? I just said that, how long? What is long anymore? Those bright letters on your chest, F B I, wow they are bright. They won't stay that way down here. Especially if some of the men see you.

I have enough on my hands with her and her new baby. So, someone else will have to teach you how and what to do here. When you speak, your words are so fast and so many. Slow down a bit can't you see there are important things to do.

"Teddy, food," Terri says.

Jenkins watches as Teddy stands up, quickly obeys Terri, and disappears into the darkness of the tunnel. "Terri do you remember…"

I remember everything. I take care of everything, everyone. You talk so much, why not just say what you want. "Remember?" Terri says.

"…when you first came here, with Teddy, do you remember Josh?" asks Jenkins. Misha, who has been nursing her baby, sit up as she hears the name. "Josh and you," Jenkins asks again.

Oh, you must have hit your head when he put you in here. Remember Josh? I had his babies. You were just holding his granddaughter. Do I remember Josh? "Yes, Josh." Terri says. *But what I would like to know is, how do you know Josh? You are way too young. I must be careful; you shouldn't know him.*

Jenkins hears Teddy's feet as he runs toward them bursting out of the darkness and into the light. He tosses two dead rats and a handful of fungi in front of Terri.

Terri looks up at Teddy. He sits beside her and rips the rats apart, handing one first to Terri then to Misha, who eagerly devour their meals. Jenkins tries to hold her own stomach down.

Give her some, I'm too busy eating this and if she's too slow, we must show her these things. Terri motions to Teddy who complies and puts a portion of the last rat in front of Jenkins.

"Oh God…"

Banks interrupts, "What is it?"

"Nothing, just a rat," replies Jenkins.

Of course, it's a rat. You'll get used to them. Yes, it takes time. "Warm meal," says Terri.

They have all finished their meals, with nothing left but the portion of rat still in front of Jenkins. The thought of even picking it up repulses her. Jenkins figures the only solution is to hand it to Misha. The new mother eagerly snatches it up and a few quick bites later, it is gone.

That was kind of you, but this place is about portions. Just enough for all, she had hers, now you have nothing. You'll learn.

"You remember Josh. Do you remember what happened to him?" Jenkins asks.

What happened to him? "He's gone," Terri says. *We looked, no, I looked. I didn't know until it was too late. He took Josh. Why are you asking this? Who are you? Bright letters.*

U.S. Department of Justice
Federal Bureau of Investigation

CHAPTER ONE HUNDRED THIRTEEN:
Bright Letters
Present Day

"Jenkins, what did Terri just say?" asks Banks.

"It sounded like bright letters. I don't know, I might be pushing this too hard, pushing her," replies Jenkins.

Josh is standing with the team in the command trailer, the monitors and speakers relaying the information from both the com and the RCV. "Your vests," he says.

"What's that Josh?" asks Lee.

"Bright letters, your tactical vest, FBI."

"Jenkins, she might be talking about the letters on your vest," Banks says. "The paramedic is ready to harness up, are you ready for her?"

"Not yet, the baby is doing a bit better, they've all just eaten. Fact is just as rapidly as things ramped up, they've calmed back down, for now. Just have her standby, copy," says Jenkins. Her attention back on Terri, Jenkins asks, "Bright letters?" Jenkins touches her vest.

"Bright."

"Terri, I'm Jenkins," touching her vest again, "I work with the FBI. I'm a police officer. Do you understand, a police officer?"

Jenkins studies Terri for any reaction, any indication that she understands anything that she has been saying. Terri looks only at her bright letters. "You said, 'he's gone,' Josh is gone?"

Misha's face flushes as Jenkins mentions Josh.

"Josh is gone, what does that mean?" repeats Jenkins. This time, Misha is very agitated and her eyes wide, looking desperately at Terri, then toward the tunnel and into the darkness. Jenkins also realizes that what she has said has Teddy upset. His respiration has increased and his cheeks flush.

"Josh not gone. Josh not gone," Teddy exclaims, his eyes widen and search as if he were looking for something as he repeats over-and-over again, "Josh not gone,"

Terri looks at him and says firmly and precisely, "Old Josh, Teddy, old Josh."

Teddy's face goes pale and he lowers his head. His sudden broken appearance a stark contrast to his animated mood seconds before. Jenkins remains silent and looks at Terri.

"Old Josh." Terri pauses and lowers her face, keeping her voice from echoing. "Old Josh dead." As quiet as she can speak, but still loud enough for Jenkins to understand her, Terri finishes, "Killed."

U.S. Department of Justice
Federal Bureau of Investigation

CHAPTER ONE HUNDRED FOURTEEN:
He's Here
Present Day

I'm not dead, Terri. I'm right here. Up here. Shit, I might as well be back in Alabama. But I'm right here. Let them help you—please, don't be scared. Fuck what am I saying, you're not scared of nothing. You stepped right in between your old man and Robbie, he split your head open so bad, and you didn't even flinch. You survived in there for all those years, I'm not dead, babe. I'm still here. Just try, Terri. Listen to Jenkins, let her help you. "I'm right here," Josh says.

Lee puts his hand on Josh's shoulder. With Misha's baby out of imminent danger for the moment, the team debates how they should proceed.

Banks' cell phone vibrates. He looks at the display. "I have to take this. Lee, you're in charge." Banks steps out of the trailer. Stepping down from the trailer he's greeted by one of the sheriff's deputies walking toward him. The deputy hands Banks a large envelope. Banks thanks the deputy and answers his cell privately.

"Jenkins, Terri said killed, right? We could barely hear her, copy," Lee says.

"Ten-four, copy," Jenkins says. "Josh killed?" asks Jenkins. Her voice carries, echoing slightly as each letter dissipates into the darkness. Terri waves her hands as if to shush the letters.

Looking directly into Jenkins' eyes, Terri says," Shh!"

Josh's eyes focus on the image of Terri's face on the monitor and he notices something familiar. "Keep it from the screws," he says.

"Josh?" asks Lee.

"The screws, the guards, prison guards. In the joint, when you don't want the screws to know what you're doing, you talk down to the ground. Jenkins didn't whisper, Terri did, then she got up in Jenkins face, why? What's the big secret?"

"Wait a minute, has Terri been in that tunnel with Misha since we lowered Jenkins in?" asks Sanders, who has been monitoring via broadband.

"Yes, Misha, Terri, and Osc, sorry Teddy, I guess we call him now," the tech answers.

"She thinks he's still there. Jenkins, Terri probably believes Oldson is there. How else could you have gotten in there? She's afraid. Josh's killer is right there, behind that window and he brought you there to die with the rest of them," says Sanders.

"That makes sense. How should I handle this?" Jenkins asks.

"Let her know we have found Oldson, and he's in custody. Just saying his name, will be proof enough," Sanders says.

Jenkins courses back through her recent memories of Lee and her speaking with Josh. Looking for the right bit of information, anything else that she knows, that only Josh or Terri would have been privy to during their time with Oldson. Terri must trust her so that she can help her. If Terri is fearful that Oldson is still here, the others would be as well, perhaps even more so.

"Jenkins, it's okay, you can do this." Lee's voice is calm and reassuring.

Jenkins looks down at the ground, and takes a shallow breath then makes eye contact with Terri. "Terri, Oldson gone." The words flow so smoothly off her tongue; it doesn't feel like she had even spoken. A name his young victims never heard. A name Terri remembers vividly.

Bright Letters, what did I just hear you say? Terri says to herself.

"Before you met Oldson, you and," Jenkins lowers her face and quietly says, "Josh," then returns to her previous tone, "you both were hiking to California." Jenkins says.

You shouldn't know, how could you know this? That was private. Just us no one else. We ran away. "We ran away, how you know?" Terri demands.

"Like I said earlier, I am a police officer." Jenkins points at her vest and her bright letters. "You understand?"

Terri nods.

Jenkins tries to decide the right way to phrase her next question. She knows what must be said, but how? Sorting the chaos of confused words in her mind into something that will inform, not harm. "Oldson took you. He brought you here. Oldson took Josh. We took Oldson," Jenkins says.

Terri stares into Jenkins' eyes surgically.

Jenkins slows down. "Oldson brought you here. He took Josh from you." Jenkins can see Terri's eyes dilate slightly as she said *took Josh*. Jenkins takes a pause and a breath. "We have Josh."

Josh and the team watch for Terri to react. Jenkins continues, "We have Josh. We found Josh. We found you." Jenkins points directly at Terri.

The only words Terri speaks, "Found Josh?"

"Yes, he's here."

U.S. Department of Justice
Federal Bureau of Investigation

CHAPTER ONE HUNDRED FIFTEEN:
Agent Banks
Present Day

"Agent Banks how are you and your team doing?" the bureau director asks.

"It's been a very busy few hours. Jenkins has managed to communicate with a small group of survivors. It has been just over an hour since Jenkins was able to stabilize the little girl. The paramedics—"

"I take that you've received the package I sent you."

"Yes, just a few moments ago. Are we sure about this? Has it been authenticated?" Banks asks.

"One hundred percent, he's struck again."

Banks turns slightly, looking at the A-frame erected over the mine's entry shaft. "What do you want me to do?"

"I'll notify the sheriff. I've just sent Sanders the file. Brief your team once you are in the air. We don't have much time."

With that said, the home screen on Banks' cell phone returns to a picture of his wife. Followed immediately with a text from Sanders, *???*

Banks texts his response, *Get Cherkoff and Torres in the air ASAP. I'll tell the others.* He hits send and pockets his phone. Agent Banks exhales heavy, his breath crystalizes in the cool air. Images quickly flash in his mind. This site, his team, this community, all the lives that Kinderson has touched. The image of Jenkins, and her face the first time he met her. The image of her coming out of the dark and into view of the RCV as she raced to get to that little girl. Watching and listening to Jenkins as she tried to bond with Terri. How was he going to tell her, especially now? He reaches for the handle, turning it, he opens the door to the trailer and steps in.

Lee is flanked by both Deanna and Josh, all three watching as Jenkins continues to speak with Terri, Teddy, and Misha. Agent Banks sees and hears the amazing progress Jenkins has made as Lee reaches to hand him the headset. Agent Banks waves Lee off. then motions Lee to mute the com and says, "We have, a problem."

"What's up," replies Lee.

"How's Jenkins doing down there?" Banks asks.

"She worked her magic, slowly walking Terri through some very rough memories. She just dropped the bombshell about our man here," replies Lee as he looks toward Josh. "So, what's the problem?"

"Let me have the headset," replies Agent Banks as Lee lifts it off his head and passes it to his boss. "Jenkins, do you copy?" Agent Banks' voice transmits over the com.

U.S. Department of Justice
Federal Bureau of Investigation

CHAPTER ONE HUNDRED SIXTEEN:
Sandra Jenkins
Present Day

How the hell could he be doing this? You have got to be kidding me. A cold shiver curses through her body as Jenkins listens to Banks' voice over the com. After all she has been through. And what they, have all been through. And now this.

I'm down here, I've touched them, they've touched me. Her mind races, as she holds Terri's hand. She took the news, *We have Josh, and he's here.* I wonder, how long has it been for her—how long since she cried for Josh? For anything? When was there time? Being down here. You must be down here to get it. Not up *there*, not just watching. Down here. This girl dropped in here, with that little boy. She, all of them, and what they have been through, even Josh locked away. Alone. You've just been watching, not in here. Jenkins smacks the side of the RCV in frustration.

In the trailer, the monitor blurs for a second as Agent Banks says, "Jenkins, we need to bring you back up here. Get you out of there. I understand your frustration, but we have to go. We developed a profile; the unsub is in custody—"

"You cold bastard," she says as she stares into the tunnel toward the darkness. "Banks, sorry that's wasn't meant—"

"For me. I know." Banks continues, "Sandra, you have done an amazing, no incredible, job, but we have to get you out of there. You have done your job. This is out of our hands now. We have to go, we have to go."

"Why now?" Jenkins demands.

"There has been another bombing. Zara just claimed responsibility. We're briefing on the plane in thirty," says Banks.

For the first time since entering the mine, the only sound she can hear is her own heartbeat.

***

The background whine of the jet engine provides the soundtrack to the view out her window. Her feet are up, and she reclines her leather chair. Looking out her window and down as the topography becomes smaller and smaller, Jenkins feels the shiver of cold sweat as the jet continues to climb. A few feet away, Sanders' voice comes over the speaker.

"We are in the process of returning Mr. Kinderson to Montana. The Montana field office dispatched a team to transfer Kinderson from Connecticut. Chances are you'll pass each other somewhere over Iowa. Sorry, rambling here," says Sanders.

Banks stands beside Jenkins, offering her a freshly poured cup of her favorite herbal tea. "Do you mind if I sit with you for a moment?"

"No, it's okay," replies Jenkins as Banks sits down in the lounge chair across from her. "I'm fine."

"No, you're not, none of us are. Not after this, not after having to leave like this. You and I have been together forever, and our team has just been drawn into something unimaginable. From the very moment that we discovered survivors, and the timeframe we were dealing with, this case was out of our hands. We developed a profile to allow for the capture and repatriation of—"

Jenkins cuts in, "Save me the sales pitch."

"It's not a pitch. It's important and needs to be said. Under normal circumstances, you would still be down there with them. Doing what you do best. Bonding with complete strangers, your empathy and people smarts have always been one of this team's greatest assets. We have been so busy these past seventy-two hours; there has been some information I have not been able to share with everyone. This unsub brought everyone here, including us. He's dying and hopefully the team assigned to transfer him will get as much information out of him while they can. We're not equipped to deal with these survivors. The director informed me, shortly after their discovery, that a special repatriation team would be formed and dispatched. They will work with Deanna and Cho. It is the best, no, the only solution for them, and the others who did not survive. They have spent a lifetime down

405

there and it may take a lifetime to figure out who they all are."

"You didn't see what I saw," replies Jenkins.

"I watched you."

"I don't mean the mine. When Lee and I met Josh at the prison, watching him, helping him recall with his memories and Terri's photos, all of them. And then when I was down there with her. I don't know." Jenkins sips her tea and wipes a droplet of moisture from her cheek. "I don't know, maybe I'm just tired. It's silly I just would have liked to see the two of their faces when they reunited. After all this, I feel ripped off. Stupid, right?"

Jenkins' attention is drawn to a small smudge of dirt on her vest. She brushes it off, slowly cleaning the letters on her vest. *They are awfully bright*, she thinks.

ZARA
(A PREVIEW)

CHAPTER ONE: Tier-Con Industries

"As you all can see, the images are pretty graphic. These are live. The media has converged on the site and the local authorities are doing their best to keep some sense of order. Rescue teams are trying to locate and recover any survivors," Sanders informs the team members as the briefing continues. "The blast happened just prior to shift change. About three hours ago."

"Maximizing potential victims, no doubt," replies Lee.

"From the aerial videos, it appears the detonation originated in the parking garage. The blast has leveled over eighty percent of the building. Urban search and rescue along with local fire and rescue have been onsite since the blast. The Department of Homeland Security sent a request to the director and with our team's recent history with Zara. This has become our priority-one case," Banks says.

"What was this building?" asks Cherkoff, her voice audible over the loud speaker in the plane. Cherkoff and Torres are en route after finalizing arrangements for Oldson's transfer back to Montana.

"Tier-Con Industries is the firm that owns and operates this building," Sanders says. "They provide business-to-business services. Everything from marketing to server farms and data management. This location, in Sumter, South Carolina is their latest facility. It just opened last month and housed both a call center and an integrated server farm. At the time of the blast, there were approximately four hundred employees and as many as fifty registered visitors logged in with security. The site is, as you can imagine is total chaos. The local authorities have several blocks evacuated and cordoned off. We have no idea at this time on numbers of victims, dead, injured, or otherwise. Zara released this written acknowledgement claiming full responsibility almost immediately following the explosion."

"During my meeting with the director, just before our dispatch to Evergreen, DHS had advised the bureau of an escalation in potential threats from Zara," Banks says. "They were also able to intercept transmissions pertaining to specific target locations. This facility was not on the list."

"Sanders, you said this site was a call center and server farm?" asks Jenkins.

"Yes, the first six floors housed the server farm and the top eight floors were clerical, open-concept-style call centers. They did everything from cold calls for rug cleaning to collections. Now, their server farm is where things get a little more interesting."

"Interesting how?" Jenkins asks.

"Well, first you have to realize a server farm is basically a data warehouse where you can store pretty much anything. You can park your website, use the farm for cloud storage, etc. We all know it's illegal to have certain images and articles stored electronically. If you check your tablets, I've just sent you Tier-Con's server farm brochure and website link. They have active data encrypting-archiving services listed as one of their best sellers."

"In English," Banks requests.

"Data-EAS, as it's termed, allows your data to be automatically translated and coded, then stored electronically on your allocated space in their server. This software allows only those with access to the translation codes to access the actual data."

"Any type of data?" Lee asks.

"Any," Sanders replies, and continues, "From what I've been able to get into so far, you could upload anything to one of their servers in this farm—hate literature, child pornography, anything. The only people who could access the information would be the owners of the data and those they have allowed access to it."

"For a fee no doubt," Jenkins replies.

"Unfortunately, I have no way of knowing what they had in this facility but from what I have seen in their advertisements for their other server farms, the sky is the limit."

"Cherkoff, you and Torres are going to be onsite first," Banks says. "I want you to speak with DHS Lead Agent Che Alvarez. She oversees the task force assigned to Zara. She and her team have been actively investigating any Zara-related incidents since they first came up on radar last year. This is by far their most deadly attack to date."

"This is a huge step up for these guys, until now, the worst that they've done was…" Torres pauses and flips through a notebook, "they torched a church, spray painted a mosque, and fire-bombed a couple of office buildings. Lots of property damage but very minimal injuries, and so far, no deaths."

"Well, they've just become big players in the terror game now. If it's attention they wanted, they're going to get it. We should be on the ground within the hour we'll keep in touch," Cherkoff says.

CHAPTER TWO: They Did This?

Cherkoff and Torres see the dark acrid cloud lingering over Broad Street as they drive toward the blast site. The main artery through Sumter, Broad Street has been closed in both directions and a two-mile perimeter is controlled by state and local police. Cherkoff and Torres badge their way past the roadblock and continue to the site. The media have been ushered back to the roadblock and both sides of Broad Street look more like parking lots for TV trucks than a city street.

Located between Columbia and Myrtle Beach, Sumter, South Carolina has a modest population just under fifty thousand and is enjoying a small economic boom. Several global firms have chosen to build and locate offices and warehouse facilities in Sumter. With its proximity to the numerous golf courses and the picturesque Atlantic coast only a short drive, *Call Sumter your new home* is plastered across billboards all over the region. Tier-Con, like many other firms, located their facility in the new business park located off Broad Street.

Local officials have evacuated an area one square mile from Tier-Con and have a temporary triage area set up in a Walmart parking lot. Torres parks their SUV as close to the site as they can. Fire trucks of all sizes and from dozens of counties have the entrance to the business park blocked. The only way to the site is by foot and the most direct route is through the Walmart that backs onto Tier-Con's property. The smoke billowing out from the remains blocks most of the view of what once was a ten-story building. Debris from the blast litters an area, several hundred feet in radius. Stepping out of the SUV, Cherkoff is immediately greeted by DHS Lead Agent Che Alvarez.

"Good afternoon, thank you both for getting here so fast," Che's voice is just loud enough to be heard over the chaos of sounds emanating from the remains of the building behind her. "We won't be able to access the site until we get the go-ahead from the fire department chiefs. My people are working the perimeter as we speak, getting as close as we can, but for now our focus is on rescue and recovery."

As they walk to the DHS command area, Cherkoff's eyes widen as two firefighters place another yellow vinyl body bag on the ground. "How many?" Cherkoff asks.

"Twenty-seven so far and the battalion chief said they haven't even entered the building yet," replies Alvarez.

"Jesus," Cherkoff replies as another two body bags are placed on the parking lot.

***

"I can't get over just how big a step up this is," Jenkins says. "The last confirmed Zara-related attack was the mosque in Newark, New Jersey. No injuries but the fire destroyed the building. Most of their activity has been in the upper East Coast. Sanders, do we have any information from DHS on the cell responsible for this attack?"

"You all have what I have, which isn't very much," replies Sanders.

"What's so special about this building?" Lee asks.

"Like any other unsub, we have to look for what caused such a radical acceleration in their activity. We are going to have to split our attention between the two operations contained in this building. Jenkins and Lee, when we arrive, I want you to work closely with Sanders and figure out what the hell they had stored in their servers. And Sanders, I need you to work double fast and find out everything you can about Zara. DHS is going to have their hands full on this one, so you are going to be—"

Sanders interrupts, "Got it boss. I'll have it to your tablets before you land."

Banks points to the video monitor showing live cable news coverage of the site. "This building was almost the size of the federal building in Oklahoma City and it's close to totally destroyed. I want to know what the delivery device was, how it got there, everything. Sanders, we need every piece of video surveillance you can find. In Oklahoma City, they used a truck. Assuming that's was how they did this, let's find it. And according to DHS, they have been monitoring increased Zara traffic, both on social media and web postings. Time is not on our side here."

ACKNOWLEDGEMENTS

I would like to take the time to thank my brother-in-law Kevin for his guidance, support and encouragement throughout the many edits and revisions that brought this story to life.
Claire and Chris from Eight Little Pages for their combined talents, that turned this jumble-of-text into an amazing work of art.

Joseph

Made in the USA
Columbia, SC
13 November 2018